Wooden Cow

T. Janakiraman (1921–82), affectionately known as Thi Jaa, is an iconic, widely read and revered Tamil writer, and one of the most influential figures of twentieth-century Tamil literature. A master of both the short story and the novel form, he won the Sahitya Akademi Award (1979) for his short story collection *Sakthi Vaithiyam*. *Mohamul*, *Amma Vandhal* and *Marappasu* are among his best known novels. Considered a modern classic, *Mohamul* was adapted for a film, and translated into Hindi by Bharatiya Jnanpith. Thi Jaa wrote, with P. G. Sunderarajan, the travelogue *Nadandhai Vaazhi Kaaveri*, tracing the historic journey of the river Kaveri; R. K. Narayan considered it one of the finest books in Tamil. It was translated into English as *Eternal Kaveri: The Story of a River* by K. Krishnamurthy (1993).

Lakshmi Kannan (born 1947) is a well-known contemporary bilingual writer and poet who writes in English and Tamil under the pen-name 'Kaaveri'. She has published twenty-seven books that include novels (*The Glass Bead Curtain*, 2016, reprint 2020), several collections of short fiction, poems, and translations. *Sipping the Jasmine Moon* (2019) is her fifth collection of poems. Her English translations of her own Tamil fiction include her novel *Going Home* (1999; *Aathukku Poganum*); *India Gate and Other Stories* (1993), *Nandanvan and Other Stories* (2011), and *Genesis: Select Stories* (2014). She received the 'Ilakkiya Chintanai Award' for Tamil short fiction, and the Katha Award for translation. She was a Charles Wallace Trust Writer in Residence at the University of Canterbury at Kent, UK (1994); a Fellow of the Indian Institute of Advanced Study, Shimla (1999); and a Sahitya Akademi Writer in Residence, Delhi (2009).

Anita Balakrishnan is a former professor and head, Department of English, Queen Mary's College, Chennai.

Wooden Cow

T. Janakiraman

Translated from the original Tamil by

Lakshmi Kannan

Orient BlackSwan

WOODEN COW

ORIENT BLACKSWAN PRIVATE LIMITED

Registered Office
3-6-752 Himayatnagar, Hyderabad 500 029, Telangana, India
e-mail: centraloffice@orientblackswan.com

Other Offices
Bengaluru, Chennai, Guwahati, Hyderabad, Kolkata,
Mumbai, New Delhi, Noida, Patna

Originally published in Tamil as *Marappasu*, first serialised in the monthly *Kanaiyazhi*, and later as a book by Meenakshi Putthakalayam (Madurai, 1975).

Wooden Cow first published by Sangam Books, Orient Longman Ltd. (Madras, 1979).
Second edition 2021
Reprinted 2021

ISBN 978-93-5442-014-6

038681

Typeset in
Cambria 11/13 *by*
Le Studio Graphique, Gurgaon 122 007

Printed in India at
Thomson Press, New Delhi 110 020

Published by
Orient Blackswan Private Limited
3-6-752 Himayatnagar, Hyderabad 500 029, Telangana, India
e-mail: info@orientblackswan.com

To the memory of Thi Jaa Sir and his wife Rajam

Contents

Acknowledgements

I am very grateful to Vidya Rao and Sudha Raghuraman, two renowned classical singers who helped me gloss the terms that are special for music and dance, and also for correcting a few errors in transliteration that occurred in the first edition of *Wooden Cow*. Thanks to Uma Shankari, the daughter and legal heir of the late T. Janakiraman, for readily giving us permission to revise my earlier 1979 translation of his Tamil novel, *Marappasu*. To Dr. Kalyana Raman, who lost no time in sending me the PDF of *Marappasu* from Chennai. To Dr. Sangeeta Kaul, the young Director of DELNET, Delhi, who encouraged me at every step of the way to take up this daunting work.

To my editor Moyna Mazumdar, who travelled along with me on our work for revising an old edition of a translation that I did nearly forty years back. I wrestled with a new kind of beast that is hard to describe and difficult to handle. It entailed managing the dance between the 'old' and the 'new', each fighting for its space. It is any day easier to translate a book starting from scratch. Moyna patiently worked with me through all the vexed moments when my role was rapidly turning into something like a negotiator between the 'old' edition and the 'new'. She worked diligently on each segment of a sentence to enhance readability for a contemporary audience, and also looked at the book in its entirety with a culture-sensitive understanding that greatly helped in preserving a Tamil flavour.

To Anita Balakrishnan, who agreed to spend her valuable time re-reading *Wooden Cow*—the first 1979 edition on Kindle, as well as this revised one—for her 'Introduction' to this second edition. The book is enriched by the way she has contextualised T. Janakiraman's works within his times, and his cultural roots, and by her sensitive understanding of the Tamil original *Marappasu*, a novel which was controversial in its times. Balakrishnan's 'Introduction' gives a valuable critical perspective that is important for contemporary readers and scholars of Janakiraman's works.

To the artist Pinaki De for the quietly elegant and evocative cover that speaks to the music within each one of us.

To my children Sridhar and Noopur, who gave me their unstinting support by taking on all my work during the severest phase of the Covid-19 pandemic and lockdown, and for settling me in the quiet space of my study to work on this revision. My gratitude to them is immense.

The Cadence of Life

Anita Balakrishnan

> Writing gives me much pleasure; it is a composite pleasure—like the pleasure of love: there is the thrill of expectation, the pain of disappointment, the joy of the union—but altogether it is a pleasure...And I write about matters I know. About the people I know and about the things I know. (Janakiraman, quoted in Zvelebil 1968)

T. Janakiraman, or Thi Jaa as he is popularly known, focused on a variety of themes mostly centred on the vicissitudes of family life in the small towns of Tamil Nadu in his writing. As he asserts, he writes about what he knows well, rarely venturing beyond themes taken from the seemingly placid everyday lives of middle-class families: the simple pleasures, the tragedies, the twists and turns in the relationships between men and women interlaced with the rhythms of Carnatic music. A calm and composed writer, Thi Jaa's true genius lay in his ability to transmute these mundane occurrences into fascinating narratives that explore the lives of his characters as shaped by their unusual choices and inner convictions.

T. Janakiraman was born on 18 June 1921 in Thevangudi, near Thanjavur. He began his career as a schoolteacher before joining All India Radio (AIR). He worked for AIR initially in Madras and later in New Delhi. After retirement he relocated with his family to Chennai, where he passed away at the age of 61 after a brief illness. The quality of his voluminous and wide-ranging oeuvre that includes twelve novels, numerous short stories, novellas, plays and several travelogues ensures that he occupies a preeminent position in modern Tamil literature. He won the Sahitya Akademi award in 1979 for his short story collection *Sakthi Vaithiyam.*

Developments in literature invariably reflect social and cultural changes that have an impact on ideas of morality, identity and spiritualism. The Manikkodi movement in Tamil literature brought in new ways of writing, with an emphasis on craft: well thought out plots, nuanced characterisation, evocative language and subtle humour. These writers were influenced by the Modernist movement in England in the nineteen twenties and thirties. The Manikkodi writers followed the deliberately pared-down style and psychological explorations that were the hallmarks of the English modernist writers. T. Janakiraman belonged to this Manikkodi group of writers that included luminaries such as Puthumaipittan, K. P. Rajagopalan (Ku Pa Ra), Pichamurthy and L. S. Ramamirtham (La Sa Ra). The work of these writers established the foundations of modernism in the Tamil literary firmament. Another common factor among these writers is the fact that although they wrote at the time of the Freedom Movement, they collectively moved beyond its homogenising tendencies to explore regional nuances and class hierarchies.

The very mention of Thi Jaa's name conjures up the emerald green fields, the fragrance of the rich soil and the distinctive Tamil dialect of the Kaveri delta that he managed to imbue with so much emotion in his works. The use of specific cultural idioms and linguistic devices in Thi Jaa's works lend them a unique regional flavour and help in the creation of a characteristic style. This makes the task of a translator even more daunting, for the carrying across of the nuances of the Thanjavur brahmin register is no mean task.

The Czech critic Kamil Zvelebil believes that Thi Jaa is the best representative of the prevalent realistic, humanistic, and mildly progressive trend in modern-day Tamil literature. This makes his writings widely accepted and popular, with the possible exception of the most radical anti-brahmin individuals. Zvelebil highlights the one outstanding characteristic of Thi

Jaa and his writing: 'his honesty and the absence of any kind of pretense' (Zvelebil 1968). He notes that Thi Jaa's style is vibrant, flexible, his language distinctive and colourful, though never shocking or crude. He often employs in his dialogues a written version of the brahmin colloquial, which he uses with the ease of a native speaker.

The Manikkodi writers focused mainly on familial issues, with a particular emphasis on women, although they were predominantly men and theirs was a male gaze. The central characters in Thi Jaa's best known novels—*Mohamul* (The Thorn of Desire), *Amma Vandhal* (The Sins of Appu's Mother) and *Marappasu* (Wooden Cow)—are all strong women who face life's challenges with courage and fortitude. In an era when ideas of feminism were not widely prevalent, he showcased women of strength and resilience who were able to hold their own in the face of social disapprobation and censure.

Like his contemporaries Jayakanthan and Ramamirtham, Janakiraman was a serious writer, devoted to the craft of fiction. Whereas Jayakanthan wrote with an eye on the future, seeking to shock his readers out of their complacency, Ramamirtham was obsessed with the mystique of the word, with problems of style, language and writing technique. Janakiraman was the most balanced of the three, careful about the themes of his works as well as the language he used to express his vision of the world.

Thi Jaa remained the best at his chosen genre—realistic, humanistic, fairly progressive fiction. His narratives are rarely concerned with social reform; he describes socially unacceptable behaviour with restraint, leaving readers to draw their own conclusions. His forte was his ability to effortlessly evoke the milieu inhabited by his characters, the single narrow street of a small town in Tamil Nadu, the house with a courtyard and a *pyol*, and the interweaving of Carnatic music into the interstices of everyday life.

Thi Jaa was gifted with deep knowledge of Carnatic music as well as a passion for it. This is reflected in several of his fictional works. In *Marappasu*, Gopali is an exceptional singer of Carnatic music. For him, Tyagaraja, the saint composer is paramount, far above his family. His philandering ways are for him a mere diversion—Carnatic music is the central *raga* in his life. Unsurprisingly, it is his superlative singing that draws Ammani to him. She is captivated by his singing even as a child growing up in Annavasal, which is Gopali's birthplace as well. Part One of the novel delineates Ammani's growth from a precocious child to a luminous, spirited young woman.

Ammani is the narrator of this pathbreaking novel; it is through her consciousness that the events are reflected. The opening line of the novel, 'Almost anything makes me laugh' (p. 3) is a good indication of her nature. Confident, beautiful and wilful, Ammani is the only child of a poor secretary of a wealthy brahmin landowner. Irreverent from childhood, she is disdainful of social proprieties. Her despairing parents give in to her demands for higher education, sending her to her father's elder brother, her Periappa's house in Kumbakonam.

While in high school, Ammani's headstrong nature coupled with her intolerance of injustice results in her being mired in controversy yet again. When her alarmed parents try to marry her off before the scandal ruins her chances of marriage, Ammani's aunt, her Periamma steps in and stops their plans. Ammani's Periamma and Periappa adopt her and they lovingly encourage her ambitions. Emboldened by this, Ammani moves through the poorer neighbourhoods of Kumbakonam, spouting communist philosophy and railing against the unjust treatment of the poor by the government.

However, her mercurial nature is revealed when she balks at the ordinary match her Periappa arranges for his daughter. In the hope of making the wedding ceremonies more memorable, Ammani boldly invites Gopali to perform at the reception on the strength of having met him at Annavasal. Hoping to impress this beautiful young woman, Gopali enchants the audience at the concert, refusing to accept any payment for his performance. But Ammani pays a heavy price nonetheless, for Gopali's charisma draws her into his ambit.

On the pretext of furthering her higher education, Gopali takes Ammani to Madras, where she enrols in a college to pursue her B.A. He also arranges for her dance lessons and moves her into a house he buys for her. Ammani is initially distraught, but she is beguiled by the attentions of the famous musician and his followers. The simple life at her Periamma's home is a thing of the past; she now has a comfortable lifestyle supported by Gopali. She rejects marriage as a bourgeois concept but she accepts her hedonistic new life, much to the distress of her Periamma and Periappa.

At the same time, somewhat paradoxically, Ammani is not a fickle-minded, capricious woman. Her laughter serves as a cover for her complex inner life. Her laughter is subdued when she stands before the mirror—it is a moment of introspection for her. When she first begins her involvement with Gopali, she assuages her guilt by imagining herself to be like Kunti, the mother of the Pandavas in the *Mahabharata*. When she was young, Kunti had been given a mantra by the rishi Durvasa, by using which she could have a child by a *deva*, a celestial being, without a pregnancy. She decides to test this boon before her marriage, and Surya the Sun God appears. She asks him to return to the heavens, but Surya says that he is compelled to fulfil the boon, and a child, Karna, is born. When Ammani observes people who follow their chosen path in life with conviction, her laughter is muted. Her Periamma and Periappa, Maragadham and Pachiappan and Pattabhi are characters who have an impact on Ammani, ironically through their silence and restraint.

In Part Two of the novel, we see Ammani as a woman of the world, divested of all her connections with traditional brahmin society. Trained at Gopali's behest as a Bharatanatyam dancer, Ammani travels the world, giving performances. This strains her relationship with Gopali when he realises that he is not her only male companion. Having seen the atrocities perpetrated on young widows in orthodox brahmin society, Ammani is wary of marriage, which she sees as a lifelong imprisonment.

Now her many romantic entanglements provide her with a different view of the man-woman relationship. She enjoys the freedom and comforts of her new life, although she is still supported financially by Gopali. Notable among her many male conquests is Pattabhi. This impoverished young nephew of Gopali comes to live with her and pursue his studies. He shows his devotion to her through his unobtrusive efficiency. They become intimate at Ammani's behest, the involvement becoming quite serious. However, Ammani is loath to marry him, revealing her somewhat perverse nature. She laughs her trademark laugh when Pattabhi proposes marriage, wounding him deeply. Her wayward character is seen at many points in the novel: her attempt to pose as a streetwalker in London; her sardonic assertion that she is and yet is not Gopali's wife on the train journey; her stubborn rejection of socially-sanctioned relationships with men.

Readers are not privy to Gopali's inner compulsions, but they are given an extensive view of Ammani's thought processes. They see her grapple with issues of self-worth and pay the price for flouting tradition. Her decision to continue her relationship with Gopali is astounding in a woman of her caste and class, in the era in which the novel is set. Contemporary critics have remarked that it is a blessing that Thi Jaa wrote in a more tolerant time, for such a progressive theme could cause widespread protests in today's society. Thi Jaa's mastery and sensitivity as a writer are evident in his delineation of the layered and complex character of Ammani. One cannot help but think that perhaps she also represents a subtle dig at armchair communists who spout Marxist philosophy but cannot exist without the luxuries of life.

The unconventional narrator in Ammani can be juxtaposed with the other women in the novel. Noteworthy among the 'minor' characters is her Periamma who shows her mettle in insisting on her further education. When faced with Ammani's liaison with a married man, Periamma is initially shocked, but she recovers her equanimity and cooks a tasty meal for Ammani, as if to underscore that this is her child whom she has raised with so much love. Periamma returns to Kumbakonam with her dignity intact.

Far from adhering to the caste and class hierarchies and morality, prevalent then and now, Thi Jaa is pioneering in his portrayal of strong women who live by their own convictions and who remain true to themselves, despite social censure. Another character who captures the readers' attention is Maragadham, the wife of Ammani's manservant, Pachiappan. What is remarkable about Maragadham is that she makes her presence felt through her silences and a few chosen words rather than through her actions. When Ammani first hears that Pachiappan plans to marry, she warns him of her perception of the flawed nature of the man-woman relationship and conveys her cynicism and bitterness. Pachiappan just smiles and introduces her to his bride, the dusky beauty, Maragadham. Ammani is struck by her statuesque looks, but does not have much hope for the marriage. However, Maragadham, with her devotion to Pachiappan and Ammani as well as her self-possession and integrity, wins her mistress over. Observing this couple, Ammani realises that a man and a woman can also be true soulmates, and this renews her faith in the institution of marriage.

Ammani is by no means a unidimensional character; her consciousness reveals itself to us in many different ways. Once when she is in Gopali's house in Madras, she sees the sunlight filtering through the window and the leaves of the tree and falling on the floor in shimmering dots: 'The scene wheeled in discs of gold maturing into silver, vanishing, only to reappear in silver circles. Then again they would temper into a tender gold and fade away' (p. 58). As the translator Lakshmi Kannan observes in her introduction to this volume, when Ammani is in a certain state of mind, the dots of light seem to spread out like a dappled deer, and in other moments, the same dots growl and roar like a spotted leopard. 'This metaphor fans out with profound implications', says Kannan (p. xxxi). Another significant metaphor is that of the wooden cow. One day Ammani notices people avoiding a dead cow on the street. This leads her to a momentous insight about her choices in life—she has avoided the messiness and chaos of married life, but she has been as worthless as a wooden cow, just a decorative piece. The real cow has provided milk and borne calves for her human owners; her life has been useful. But when the cow dies on the street, people are wary of the unpleasant business of disposing of the carcass. Ammani realises that while she has successfully sidestepped the disorder of marriage, ultimately she has been merely a shining curio that has not been of any real value to others.

Lakshmi Kannan is an acclaimed bilingual poet, novelist and short story writer who writes in Tamil and in English under the pen-name of 'Kaaveri'. This is her second translation of *Marappasu* after a gap of forty-one years. She has also translated Indira Parthasarathy's *Thiraigalukku Appal* (Through the Veils).

This translation of *Marappasu* differs a fair bit from the earlier one, particularly in certain sections of the second half of the novel. In the earlier translation the narrative moves somewhat erratically, especially in Part Two, leaving the reader at times flummoxed. This has been carefully rectified in this translation without deviating from the original; Ammani's bold choices are also conveyed with tact, insight and sensitivity. One other notable change is the retaining of original Tamil words, which allows the translator to evoke the flavour of Thi Jaa's narrative and his use of the Thanjavur Tamil dialect in English translation. Kannan's remarkable ability to suggest certain nuances of feeling with delicacy to describe Ammani's unconventional relationships with men is testimony to her rich experience as a bilingual writer. That she does this without any verbosity or prolixity is an extraordinary achievement. Thi Jaa's technique of interweaving the mellifluous strains of Carnatic music with his pathbreaking themes helped to ensure his place in the great tradition of modern Tamil fiction. Kannan's translation is able to beautifully recreate with verisimilitude the dusty streets of Kumbakonam and the sylvan tree-lined roads of Mambalam in Madras that Thi Jaa describes so well in Tamil.

With her poetic sensibility, her economy of expression and her command over Tamil and English, Kannan is perhaps an ideal translator of Thi Jaa's works. Her close personal friendship with the author adds another layer of authenticity and insight to the translation. Global promotion of the wealth of Indian literature in the regional languages is an enterprise whose time has certainly come. This is more than evident in this sensitive and painstaking retranslation of T. Janakiraman's trailblazing novel, *Marappasu*.

Reference

Zvelebil, Kamil. 1968. 'The Tamil Short Story Today: Jeyakanthan, Janakiraman, Ramamirtham'. *Mahfil* 4 (3/4): 37–45, Tamil Issue, Spring and Summer. Asian Studies Center, Michigan State University.

A Dappled Deer or a Growling Leopard?

Lakshmi Kannan

Marappasu, the Tamil original of *Wooden Cow*, was by all accounts a rather disconcerting novel to translate. But something compelled me to take it up as a creative challenge, and I first translated it way back in the late seventies. It has a certain intensity that cuts through our reservations. Translating the work of the powerful iconoclast T. Janakiraman was a wholly different experience altogether. His ideologies, his delineation of love, music, passion, the sensuousness of the body and the feminine spirit shook the Tamil ethos by its foundations. *Marappasu* has all the guiles and capricious use of language that are characteristic of Janakiraman's birthplace, Thanjavur. It has a surface that ripples with cunning and half-spoken innuendoes that are challenging to capture in English. Equally, his piquant sense of humour is as effortless as it is mischievous, catching you by surprise in your most unguarded moments.

There are two persons living inside a writer—one who lives in a very different realm when he/she takes up a pen to write, and the other who lives his/her life like any other ordinary person. The writer holding the pen feels free of the shackles of conventional, habitual thoughts that run in a groove in predictable ways. While writing, the writer's allegiance is entirely to the themes governing the work being written and to its protagonists, all of which may or may not conform to the norms of his/her everyday life. The other person is the one with whom the family, the community and professional peers at work interact with on an everyday basis. This is not to falsify one or the other. There are writers who can skilfully strike a harmonious balance between these two persons and are quite poised in their balancing act. Still, the two may not always be on comfortable terms with each other. The writer may experience emotions ranging from conflict and doubt to a firm conviction that, having set his/her artistic goals, he/she is on the right path. Since I had the privilege of getting to know Janakiraman as a person during the time I was translating his novel, and later when he evolved as a mentor, I found him amazingly in control of his life. He could write those explosive novels that sent readers into a frenzy of admiration, shock, or bitter criticism, and he could still be a kind and caring human being, pleasant to know and interact with. I would like to share glimpses of Janakiraman the man later, after I have elaborated my experience of revising this translation of *Marappasu*, and why it was an exciting challenge.

Since the time I first translated this novel, I have been in and out of conferences and workshops on creative translation in both national and international forums. In many, I have spoken about the need for creativity in translation, and the need for readability with an eye to the contemporary reader in English, even if one is translating the sensibility of a culture and the ethos of a people who do not speak English.

In most of my talks, I drew upon four main factors that conditioned me as a writer and as a translator: a) my experience in translating my own stories and a novel into English, and revising them for the reprints, each time with a different editor; b) my experience of translating other Tamil writers such as T. Janakiraman, Indira Parthasarathy and the reclusive 'Mowni' (S. Mani Iyer) tucked away in Chidambaram, whose fiction is enigmatic, recalling some of the stories of Alexander Pushkin; c) my experience of having my works translated into other languages such as Hindi, Marathi, Urdu, French and German; and d) the experience of reading many books in translation. This multi-layered experience has shaped my work as a translator. I was constantly learning, and un-learning. I was also avidly reading good critical books discoursing translation as a creative activity and cultural communication. They further alerted me to not just the act of translating *per se*, but to this unnameable reader of a translated work who could be from any cultural background.

Time and trends move at a relentless pace. In all these forums, I found myself citing examples that were more recent, while *Wooden Cow*, my first translation of a novel, receded into the background. I felt very, very sad about that. Somewhere it hung heavily on my conscience. Here I was, travelling back and forth to articulate my views on translation, while *Wooden Cow* was languishing, desperately in need of a revision. I was itching to revise it, and yet I wasn't able to do so. Twice in the early and later nineties, there was a proposal for a revised translation of *Marappasu* from the editors of Orient BlackSwan. But for some inexplicable reason, it never quite materialised. And then T. Janakiraman returned in a big way when a group of scholars, writers, critics and readers formed a committee for the centenary celebrations for this much-loved author, who was born on 28 June 1921 in Thanjavur. Members of this committee contacted me to say that the celebrations would be spread over a year, from 2020 to 2021, in both Tamil and in English, and that there were plans to hold webinars, discussions and talks, along with the publication of articles in the media. That was when things came together like they were ordained.

When I wrote to Vidya Rao at Orient BlackSwan to inquire if they would re-issue *Wooden Cow* in a revised translation, she readily rose to the occasion. I thank her immensely for this opportunity. Thanks also to the very timely nudge from the Centenary Celebration Committee for T. Janakiraman, and everything falling into place, I finally got the '*Gita muhurtham*' to take up the revision.

Translating a text is one thing, but revising an existing translation is an entirely different proposition altogether. The language of a translation done so many years back would expectedly be archaic. Words have their own mortality. They grow, flourish, dry up, perish, get revitalised and flow on with time. Words change in connotation, and time in turn deposits a new colour or sheen, or the dust of obsolescence on the same word. Words also wear themselves out with the sheer fatigue of use or overuse. They drown and then re-surface according to the changing trends in how writers use them, together with the current drifts in academia and quality journalism. I have experienced all of this first-hand when my published translations in English went through several reprints, and I have worked with different editors each time. We had to drop certain words used in the older editions of my books.

Translations in English are crucial, not just because they reach a wider readership at home and overseas, but equally for the valuable feedback from each reader in English who comes from a distinct cultural and linguistic background, and thus makes us aware of the multilingualism that is the *zeitgeist* even in our deracinated times. I have to be very conscious of this reality in order to be in step with the synergy of this atmosphere.

Translation is a risk taken willingly to leap into a trans-lingual zone where I render into another language something that springs from the living culture of a different language. I have come to like the challenge, the pain, the tedium and the solitary punishing hours in rendering the mood behind the lines, and the occasional reward. Translation keeps me on the brink of a creative experience, forever uncertain, forever tentative about the 'finality' of a chosen word. A sobering thought that no translation can be deemed 'perfect' guides me along. Gregory Rabassa, one of the most honest critical voices on the art of translation, declares:

> With this in mind, we should certainly not expect a word in one language to find its equal in another...A word is nothing but a metaphor for an object, or in some cases, for another word. (Rabassa 1989)

When I take up a work for translation, I realise that I first have to forge a relationship with the original text, and nurture this relationship till the very end. I have to follow the speech patterns, the rise and fall of a tone. With an original like T.

Janakiraman's *Marappasu,* I have to absorb the silences of the unsaid, the echoes and sighs that wrap around some words almost imperceptibly. The silences in between words and sentences fascinated me even more. The challenge here is how *not to translate* these silences, but to re-create them within my translation.

After her initial shock on learning of Ammani's relationship with Gopali, Ammani's Periamma decides not to waste any more words in arguing with her beloved niece, and instead cooks a fabulous farewell meal to express her indestructible, unconditional love for the girl she raised so tenderly as her own. And this is despite Ammani's stubborn refusal to leave everything and come back home with her. Our respect for this extraordinary Periamma deepens on seeing her unspoken gestures. There are other instances too, such as Maragadham's quiet communication; Pattabhi's silent interludes when he lets the thoroughness of his work speak for itself and express his loyalty and affection for Ammani. All of these silent actions speak more eloquently than spoken words. *Not* translating these silences, but just allowing them to enter my translation is what I strove for.

I was also drawn to the ways in which Janakiraman uses language. Tamil is a lush language with rich reserves. It is fascinating to see how he uses it differently for different people and situations within the novel. His main protagonist Gopali is an acknowledged genius in music. Janakiraman, himself gifted with a deep knowledge of music, carries this passion as he straddles two realms—*music* which can only be experienced aurally; and *words* which are his chosen medium for a novel drenched in music. Gopali's intense merging with music had to be conveyed verbally. Janakiraman rises to this challenge with his superb diction that often borders on poetry. Along with his mesmerising music, there is Gopali's persona and compelling stage presence that attracts the young and old alike. In Janakiraman's description, Gopali is not just attractive, he is also entirely unselfconscious about it: '*adhanuda udambaisutri veesugira kuzhandaitthanam*' (...the way his body exuded a child-like innocence). Ammani, who initially seeks to learn music from Gopali, ruminates on a widely held observation about her eminent teacher: 'It is said that Gopali is like an *aalkanda samudhiram* (He is like the heaving ocean when he sees his audience). Ammani is overwhelmed when Gopali rises like an ocean even while singing just for her, a humble, solitary disciple: '*adhu samudhiramaga pongum*' (he rose like an ocean).

However, as the novel unfolds and there is a growing intimacy between Gopali and Ammani, she prefers to use the neuter gender '*adhu*' (literally 'it') for Gopali, instead of 'he', 'him' or 'his'. This expression of affection, reserved only for two people who are very close to each other, was untranslatable in English.

Janakiraman also shows a remarkable economy in his use of words in *Marappasu*. Both the narrative and the dialogue are marked by a brief, terse style that can turn staccato, making the impact of the words more explosive. It can also easily slip into a cheeky, irreverent way of speaking that characterises most Tamil people. And then there are moments when words take a back seat, making room for implicit meanings to curl around the words silently. There are silences in between words and sentences, and a lot that is left unsaid in a conversation. How effective these silences would be for theatre, I thought. They will hang on stage like gossamer and make the audience wait in anticipation for the next move.

One such instance is in the midst of a stormy, violent scene when Ammani's Periappa is so infuriated with Gopali for ruining the life of his adored niece that he slaps him hard, and then rips off the pictures of saint Tyagaraja, Rama and Krishna that are hung on a wall. Gopali commands Periappa to collect all the pictures and replace them on the wall or make them recline against the wall. Periappa silently obeys. Gopali then tells him quietly, his voice low, 'Now come and thrash me. I will take it without a word' (p. 78).

Then there is the newly married Maragadham, Ammani's maid who is as beautiful as a sculpture, who catches

Gopali's predatory glad eye. The purity of her being, her total commitment to not just her husband but to what she perceives as the essential femininity and integrity of her Self, and the respect she has for the institution of marriage—all are expressed in just one terse phrase when she declares to Ammani: '*Nan kuditthanakkari*' ('I am a married woman'). With that, Maragadham gives it straight from the shoulder that she doesn't like the amorous advances of her 'master'. In my translation I added, 'I have a family' (p. 183), because it is implicit in the word '*kuditthanakkari*'. Just saying 'I'm a married woman', I felt, would not have conveyed her sense of being accountable to her family.

The spoken language reflects the speech patterns of the region, with all the verbal idiosyncrasies inherent in the very genius of the language. The dialogue is often peppered with a punchy style and a cheeky nonchalance that characterise the speakers of this language. Humour—that ranges from the dry, the wry, the caustic, the satiric, the savage, to a cunning, naughty stance that delights in absorbing details even in a blink-and-you-miss second—ripples through the narrative and the dialogue in the most unexpected of places.

There is a certain sensuousness and physicality in the novel, a tactile quality that is rare among Tamil writers. The human body, skin, physical appearance, the emotions evoked by them, the sensuousness of trees, plants, flowers, their colours and fragrance—all of this makes for the totality of the rich sensory experience in Janakiraman's fiction.

Ammani awakens to her own sensuousness early on, as a small child. Sure enough, she is misunderstood by most people in her community. When she relocates to her Periappa's house in Kumbakonam, a cruel scandal is generated around her in school just because she rubs a headache balm on the forehead of a boy, a batch mate who was unwell. As a little girl growing up in Annavasal, Ammani observes her own tactile responses to the people around her. The elderly Kandu who has a body that feels like a ripe mango. The tall, attractive Sheerali, the maid with a lithe gait who toils hours on end and still looks fresh; the knowledge that Sheerali, married to a scrawny, puny fellow, soon finds a manly paramour and has a stormy relationship with him only draws Ammani further to her. Later, as an adult, Ammani is deeply attracted to Gopali, and how he is completely oblivious to his own physical charm, but she cannot separate his charisma from his mesmerising music. She is also attracted to young Pattabhiraman, who is not conventionally handsome, but everything he does sings the harmonious tune of a work done well and with genuine pleasure. And lastly, her attraction to her beautiful maid Maragadham is on a very different plane. Ammani feels fiercely protective of this young girl and instinctively seeks to guard her purity and all that she stands for. There are other instances where Ammani looks at people and the world through the eyes of an aesthete, but people in turn only look askance at her.

Being a man, Gopali, on the other hand, is above all censure. While people know that he is a proven philanderer, they think he is entitled. So does he. He is credible, our Gopali. We see this all around us, all the time. Whether a man is a genius or just an ordinary womaniser, he escapes censure.

Gopali and Ammani, the two main protagonists, live life on their own terms, defiantly, each asserting their fierce independence. Drawn towards each other, because they are both disdainful of traditional morality and have scant respect for the institution of marriage, they are also equally torn apart by their individual proclivities and their relationship is naturally volatile, tumultuous and fraught, but it always remains credible. There are no value judgements provided, no authorial sermons, as if the author is telling his reader: 'I have written this novel. Now draw your own conclusions if you must.'

Music is Gopali's calling. Janakiraman follows the curves of Gopali's quest and his emotions, noting astutely that his predatory ways with women are clearly less important to him than his music. He is a supplicant to the only god he knows and reveres—the immortal Tyagaraja. It is not clear if Ammani finds the same kind of fulfilment in her pursuit of dance.

The so-called 'minor' characters of the novel—Ammani's Periamma and Periappa, Maragadham, Pachiappan, and Pattabhi—they all appeal to us in the way they lead simple and sensible lives governed by values, affection and emotional attachment. All of them, imperceptibly, also make Ammani return to the lost beauty and simplicity of life.

As a child, Ammani is precociously intelligent and mature. As an adult, she at times comes through as an improbable woman. Yet, during the period that I was translating this novel, I met many potential Ammanis in real life. In Jadavpur University, Calcutta, and in Delhi University, it was commonplace to find young idealistic people with strong Marxist leanings, as also the kind of armchair Marxists who come to visit Ammani. My women colleagues smoked king-size filter cigarettes, wore expensive sarees and dresses, zipped around in cars (while I commuted by bus or auto-rickshaw); they took flights to visit parents in their home towns and went to exotic places on vacations (while I went to quiet hill retreats, saving my hard-earned money, and was content). Well-versed in Marxist spiel, these women and men maintained a carefully cultivated public posture and persona, vehemently denounced *other rich people* as 'feudal and bourgeois', and advocated sexual freedom as a possible means of living an independent, unshackled life. A few of them were, however, self-destructive and led skewed lives, while a few others ended up as drifters.

I shared this with Janakiraman during our occasional interactions in Calcutta. I also told him that I was translating his book at a phase in my life when I was studying the 'Self' in the solitary protagonists of Saul Bellow, on whose fiction I was then writing my Ph.D. dissertation, and that this impacted my understanding of Ammani's character. Janakiraman was immediately interested and wanted to know how Bellow deals with the 'Self'. I told him that Bellow's protagonists observe and reflect deeply on the life and people around them, so one gets to see everything through their eyes and their consciousness. Although this entails a risk of solipsism, even narcissism in some cases, as readers we don't feel 'trapped' within their consciousness. Bellow's Herzog, Henderson, Sammler and others give us insights into the social, political and cultural paradigms taking over the new world order; so one gets a kind of world-view—an expansive vision that can be illuminating, even epiphanic. For a writer, this was a literary and philosophical triumph, I said. Janakiraman absorbed all this with a healthy intellectual curiosity.

When I further shared that despite the US being his adopted country, Bellow's literary models were Continental writers who were steeped in Western philosophy and the existentialism that pervaded globally after the World Wars, Janakiraman told me that he too had read the works of some German philosophers such as Arthur Schopenhauer, the first Western thinker to draw upon Buddhism, Martin Heidegger, Karl Jaspers, and the Danish philosopher Soren Kierkegaard, all of whom had an abiding influence on post-war thinkers. We then had a most stimulating discussion about these philosophers as we related their work and their vision to creativity in fiction.

Inevitably, we talked about Ammani. I said that for a woman who professes that everything makes her laugh, her laughter often borders on tears, or perhaps it is a strategy to quickly divert her anger or pain. Laughter also seems to be her defence and her ammunition against the extreme ironies of life. On her introspective and reflective moods, I also mentioned that while we are allowed to enter Ammani's mind and her consciousness, with Gopali, the narrative does not admit us inside his thoughts. I revisit here our brief conversation.

'What could you get out of Ammani's reflections?' he asked.

'There are many that pertain to a woman's sensibility. For now, I remember just one line that stayed in my mind, which reveals how we perceive things, depending on our state of mind.'

'Do you remember the line?'

'Yes. Ammani likes the room in the house in Madras where the sunlight filters through the leaves of the tree and falls on the floor as luminous dots: *"Sunlight scattered in dots like the hide of a dappled deer. At other times, it growled like the hide of a leopard*" (p. 58). This metaphor fans out with profound implications. It is a deep, inward-looking consciousness; still it can draw within its vortex the signature of a hundred other subjectivities that resonate with people. Then how can one call it narrowly subjective?' I asked.

Janakiraman did not answer. He was deep in thought and looked remote and withdrawn.

A few weeks later, I received a gift from him. It was a deer skin, the spots glowing yellow and gold on a soft surface. He said he bought it for me when he went to the Andaman and Nicobar Islands. Since only *rishi*s are eligible to sit on it, we hung up the lovely deer skin on the wall of our prayer room.

During his next visit to Calcutta, and in his periodic letters, he would solicitously inquire about my research, the progress of my dissertation, and if my professional problems were sorted out. Jadavpur University wouldn't relieve me in time to join another university in Delhi, and the Delhi appointment wouldn't wait beyond a limit. In addition, there was much tension on the home front. My husband had, upon his transfer, already joined his ministry in Delhi, and I was still in Calcutta, soldiering on, while desperately trying to arrange for the transition of our two small sons to good schools in Delhi. My travel bags were already packed for Delhi. That was when Janakiraman revealed the other side of him, the gentle, fatherly person who would first inquire if I found enough time for my work, and if the translation of *Marappasu* was not a huge strain on me at this time of transition. So caring was he that he said, 'Lakshmi, do this translation some other time. It can surely wait.' In this, he stood in sharp contrast to other writers who demanded that I translate their works, and turned harsh and hostile whenever I said I don't have the time. They were most dismissive about my professional and personal commitments. Janakiraman, on the other hand, was surprisingly aware of every little detail: 'How is your elder child? Has he recovered from bronchitis? Where will you stay in Delhi on arrival, at the government guest house? Let me know if you need anything. My wife Rajam and I will help.'

To me, *this* is what qualifies a writer as a considerate and compassionate individual. Janakiraman was a wonderful human being, and a gentle mentor who brought out the best in his juniors. He made me take up my Tamil pen seriously, waving aside all my protests that 'I cannot write in Tamil and I've always written only in English'. 'Just plunge in and write!' said my literary father. I did, and discovered first-hand that the more I wrote in Tamil, the more I enjoyed my mother tongue.

Janakiraman, a 'formidable writer' to many, was a relaxed and relatable person to his family and friends. He loved good food just as much as many of us do, loved talking about food, and the good things of life. He was very fond of *thalirvetrilai*, a special variety of tender betel leaves that are flown all the way from Chennai and supplied to the south Indian temples in Delhi. After relocating to Delhi, we visited Janakiraman's house several times. I once remarked that Rajam Mami, his wife, had a voice to match her sweet nature. He then told me that she sang Bharati's songs and *kilipaattu* very well. After retiring from All India Radio, he and his wife moved down south to Chennai.

We were shaken and devastated by his early death, which happened soon after he relocated to Chennai. I so longed to see Rajam Mami and to spend a few quiet moments with her. I had such wonderful memories of her—she was kind, warm, and utterly hospitable always. I grabbed the first opportunity to visit her in Chennai. It was she who comforted me. 'My husband is a *chiranjeevi* who will live on in his works,' she said with a smile. 'Lakshmi, both of us remembered you a lot,' she said, adding a metaphor from the realm of music again, 'You were like a *swaram* in our lives.'

Reference

Rabassa, Gregory. 1989. 'No Two Snowflakes are Alike: Translation as Metaphor'. In *The Craft of Translation*, eds. John Biguenet and Rainer Schulte. USA: The University of Chicago Press.

PART I

1

Almost anything makes me laugh. The marriage *pandal*. The bride, head bent in bashful decorum. I laugh at the groom, broad-chested, firm-hipped, and smooth-skinned, pouring ghee onto the sacred fire. I laugh at the middle-aged and the old, taking in the scene. At the man with the *nadaswaram*, oblivious of the noise around, his lips chewing the teat of the pipe, brandishing the instrument between heaven and earth. He is the real laugh. Why does he have a frown on his face? Those puffed cheeks! Just look at him, caressing the holes of the instrument with studied attention, painfully struggling for some perfectly chaste note. The profiles of all those gathered for the wedding, all the rows of teeth, the brows, the folded legs, the smiles, the eyebrows raised in worry, the chalky whiteness of powdered faces, the toddlers immersed in their soliloquies, the kinsmen meeting after many years—why should he shut his eyes to all this humanscape and opt instead for the ordeal of his pipe?

I have the same laughter when confronted with death. An uncle died. Everyone wept in the passage. My aunt, prostrate on his chest, was wailing and shrieking out at regular intervals, 'How could you leave me like this? How *could* you? What did I ever do to you?' But uncle was right there! Where had he gone? Each time she cried out, I laughed. Twice I even remarked, 'Aunty is lying.' But no one understood me.

'Go away!' hissed Vembu Aunty. Her son Muthu came close.

'You ought not to be laughing now,' he said.

'I *will* laugh,' I said.

'I'll slap you hard if you do.'

'I'll slap you too!' I said still laughing.

'Be quiet, darling,' said my mother.

'No, I won't be quiet. Why are you crying?' I asked.

Rolling her eyes gone bleary with crying, Amma gathered me in her arms and went to the backyard. Putting me down beside the well, she said, 'Don't be foolish. You ought not to be laughing now.' She pinched me. That hurt. The pinch was intended to make me cry. But it made me laugh again.

For a moment it looked like Amma was going to laugh too. 'Why did you have to be born to me!' she said, pushing me out of the door. 'Go get lost somewhere—the Perumal temple, the pond, the tamarind grove—go wherever you please and come back,' she said, exasperated, and slammed the door on me.

That was when I was a child. If you ask me, it's pretty much the same now. I feel like laughing not only at death or marriage, but at everything. At a story or a play, at those who hold that the world is in contradiction or askew or crippled or illogical. At the fictions they study and the fictions they create, paintings, dramas, reviews, the coloured shirts on their backs and the colourings of their minds, the bear-like shagginess, the impotent anger, and so on and so forth. Take Komalamma, for instance. She believes that she and her family have been endowed with exclusive faculties for ruling the earth. She feels elated when she meets a person lower in the social ladder, and thanks the Lord for the difference. That is why she thought it her husband's privilege to build and beautify their small bungalow enclosed within a garden, with building materials stolen from those purchased for putting up a ten-storeyed office building. It was especially funny when she wept with gratitude to God, as if she was one of the chosen few, like the Jews—herself, her husband, Suresh, Seema, Bhama and Lalli. In the midst of it was her anxiety about her own health. She washed down with water eight varieties of tablets, some of which she chewed, and studied the x-ray exposures and ECG charts spread out on the teapoy. Instead of marvelling at the cubism and surrealism that existed in our bodies, she worried about it. Laughing at her was the appropriate thing to do.

I recall the four girls I once knew. They didn't tie up or braid or even trim their hair. They would descend on me at any time of the night or day and leave just as unexpectedly. I had befriended two of them in Paris and the other two in East Germany. They would hold forth for three hours at a time about the impossibility of eradicating poverty, class and injustice in this country without an armed revolution and then make short work of all the food in the house before they dashed off in a car. I have never seen any of them wear anything other than Kanjeevaram, Bangalore and Benares silks. They used to dress the same way for the revolutionary underground meetings. They commuted only by car. They smoked only filtered King-Size cigarettes. They suddenly announced one day that they were all going back home. The father of one was an oil millionaire in Gujarat. The father of another was a tycoon selling machinery. The father of the third revolutionary was a moneylender to big industrialists. The three men got to know each other only through their daughters. It was much later I came to know that all three girls had flown back to their nests following a stern warning by their fathers that they would be disinherited if they did not return home immediately. The fourth, tiring of empty revolutionary talk, concluded that no revolution would ever happen in this country and joined a factory as a legal adviser. I had quite a laugh over the way this clique of female Marx, Che Guevara and Castro scattered so abruptly!

Another was a boyfriend. Forty was the age when his instinct for love sprouted. He used to turn up at dinner time.

'Will you eat?'

'I've just washed my hands.'

'Where did you eat?'

'Over there.'

'At Vidya's?'

'Yes. She insisted. She threatened that if I don't eat she would serve me raw lady's fingers in sour, unsalted buttermilk. I said I would even eat tamarind-*bhath* prepared in crude oil.' Remembering this, he would chortle, much amused, and I would laugh too. He had savoured his blessed singleness for twenty years. Now, the poor thing...

I am amused by a whole lot of other things. At people who drive around in cars, at those who travel by air, at those who gaze fondly at their refrigerators, charmed as they would be with a baby. People who would bathe and caress their cars as they would a baby, at youth fatally wounded in war, thirsting for water in an alien land, at those who print their photographs in newspapers and sing a requiem, at garlanded middle-aged leaders who grin and appropriate all the glory for themselves.

This compulsive laughter, does it imply that I have schizophrenia or some kind of mental illness? Maybe. But that you'll have to judge for yourself. Who are you anyway? Are you someone given to dropping names like Freud, Jung, Camus, Sartre, Pinter, Adamov, Brecht, Ionesco? Or someone who swears by Kamban, Milton, Shakespeare, Tagore, Bharati? Or a business executive or a politician relaxing with an Ayn Rand, Irving Wallace, Harold Robbins? Or do you sport long hair, broken spectacles and shop around for alienation? Or are you a housewife, grateful for the three-day rest during her menstruation as she accumulates old unread magazines and story books? Or are you the sad sack, the butt end of highbrow jibes and curses who reads the weeklies and monthlies from cover to cover? A thinker who prizes intellect as life itself? In that case, what kind of a wise guy are you and with what kind of money do you count your days? Eagle money? Bear money? Dragon money? Are you the sanctimonious cat who closes his eyes to the source of money?

What does it matter who you are. Listen if you like. Or call me arrogant, jealous and close your ears if you like, but I'll keep laughing.

If you're the male of the species, you won't just walk away like that. I'll tell you a story. A true story. It happened when I was a girl of twelve. There was a large pond in front of our house. The pond was enclosed by streets on its four sides and on each side a flight of steps led us down to the waters. It was holy water but very clear. People used to come and bathe in it. Storks and eagles would be wheeling around for fish. Perched on the *pyol*, I would watch it for hours on end. One evening, a big crowd collected on the bank of the pond and I ran out to look. A woman, completely nude, stood in the centre of the crowd, shouting, with a baby on her hips. Rolled around one arm was a green saree. I knew this woman. I've seen this Aiyangar woman, a teacher in a primary school, dark but with a full figure and a broad face, rounded and sturdy limbs, her torso, thighs, arms and legs—all looked like they were custom-designed. The poor woman had lost her husband and had gone mad.

Four houses across was Poondi Mama, the rich man of the village who had set up a home there for the schooling of his children. 'Will you cover yourself up this minute? Or else I'll cane you and draw your blood all over!' he shouted, flourishing his whip handle. 'Who are you? Are you my husband to order me around?' she screamed back at him. Poondi Mama flourished the whip handle but did not hit her. If only he had, perhaps she would have put the baby down and covered herself up with the saree. I for one felt that Poondi Mama as well as the crowd were more anxious that she might really cover herself. I laughed at the lecherous look in their eyes. They were all men, except for the three little girls like myself and the two old women selling vegetables on their way home.

You may ask me, if her dark nudity could be so attractive, what are you then, an *apsara*? Well, I haven't seen an apsara. But I have with me, roughly, some four hundred love letters. About forty people wrote them. They later wrote me another four or five hundred letters. They don't read like love letters. Yet the rapturous metaphor of each one of them is a looking glass in which you can peer into me. I look at them and have a good laugh. Whenever I tire of looking at myself, I turn to these letters.

My only laughter-free moments are those that I spend in front of a mirror. Inverting the parting of my hair from the right to the left, the saree pulled from my left shoulder over to my right, the mirror tells me you are very beautiful, so very fair, and there is nothing to equal your smile...! The mirror flatters me and makes my head reel. It scares me. Very often, to stop my laughter, I plant myself before a mirror. The face vanishes and admits memory.

A four-year old girl, soft as a fruit all over. A stage when you couldn't predict whether she would be fat or slim, long-limbed or short, slender-waisted or thick in the middle. Thick hair curling at the ends, defying the comb. A silk cord tied around the waist. The constantly misplaced *arasilai* would be solicitously drawn back to order again and again by Amma and Appa. Every time I threw away my skirts and *pavadai*s, Amma's eyes would roll and Appa's eyebrows would contract in a frown.

Laughter would well up from within. I would laugh as if I missed the point of their chagrin.

'Idiot! Laughs at everything. Everyone will make a fool of you, silly goose!' said Amma.

Clothes and costumes were never my friends. Only the breeze was. My choice then was unspoken, unreasoned. The words belong to now.

Before pushing me away, Amma would adjust my chemise and my skirt. The moment I discarded both in the passage, my precious body would come into its own. I would swear enmity towards the clothes. On reaching the front of the house, the breeze would caress my face and the peepul-leaf *arasilai* would again get displaced.

'He and his *tambura*, like a little girl and her misplaced peepul-leaf pendant!' That was Gopali's metaphor. 'It's only a factotum. He'll never achieve harmony, not if he is reborn seven times!' That was how Gopali described the unlucky singer who was tone-deaf.

Sometimes he, Gopali, would study himself in a mirror as eagerly as a four-year old girl. Even in his self-absorbed admiration, his eyes wouldn't lose their captivating allure. Large dark-lashed eyes as if drawn with kohl, but his was the real thing though. How many afternoons and nights I have lost myself looking into those eyes...But selfish to the core he was. 'How did the full moon sprout arms and legs,' he would wonder, staring at me. Will the filtered rays of the moon soften the darkness of the room? Even in the haze I could see the darkness in the corner of his eyes. You waited submissively while he went over your face and figure, but his thoughts would be elsewhere, and his voice would be humming a *raga*, huskily. I didn't know much about music but I believed fanatically that music was only what *he* sang. I've known the middle-aged and the old swear that the music of all others ranked far behind his...I'm still waiting. The low, sweet notes are the only things that matter. I would give anything for that huskiness, oh that unparalleled huskiness!

The night before I left Hungary, I was told that a gypsy was to sing in a hotel in Budapest, and I was taken there. She could even sing some Indian film songs. Mike in hand she sang, dancing from one table to another. When I heard her sing, at first I was thrilled. It was the same kind of voice—Gopali's husky, private voice! Was she Gopali transformed? There could only be two such voices in this world. 'How could the full moon sprout arms and legs!' For someone who never knew what it was to cry, grief overwhelmed me. I was furious at the thought: does another creature have the same kind of voice? Glass after glass was filled with wine. I still don't remember how I got back to my hotel. It seems I threw up in the taxi. The flight was at seven in the morning. I woke up at six, to the sounds of fists pounding on the door. I felt dizzy. Couldn't see. Couldn't pack. Hastily they gathered and stuffed my clothes, cosmetics and books into a bag, dumped me into a car and saw me off at the airport. I've a vague memory of muttering something by way of farewell. I was in a temper even after reaching the plane. 'How did the full moon sprout arms and legs!'

On reaching home, I told Gopali about her, the gypsy. The only response I got was 'Was she pretty? How old was she?' I could've slapped him.

'I thought all your manliness has dissolved into your husky voice to make you impotent, hmm...but I seem to have dissolved myself, melted, and here I am, blabbering something.'

'Don't get angry. I've always been a woman inside. Or else I wouldn't be able to touch the delicate nooks and crannies of ragas, seeking their sensitive spots and separating them. Instead, like a dog I would've rolled all over you.'

'Oh yes, I am a woman, and so are you! This raga then is the only male principle!'

'Don't chatter. All this is beyond me. You are educated and can talk about geometry, philosophy and what not. You roam the wide world. I'm just an illiterate singer who can't even sign his name. All right, tell me something...I've heard that women in Germany and Japan are not beautiful like you. I believe they look like shaven yam. Was this gypsy also like that? What are you thinking? Would you call me a yogi or a *bhogi*, an epicurean? Only a thin line separates the two. I've heard that is how North Indian orthography is written. Yogi and bhogi will read alike if written hurriedly. It was Motibai who told me that. Let that be...You said you remembered me while downing the wine. You could've brought a pint for me!'

I couldn't help but laugh.

'Go ahead and laugh. I'll also laugh with you. Only in name are you the daughter of Annavasal, the place that feeds everyone. If I'm thirsty for a peg, I would have to beat out a *tala*!' I stopped Gopali's mouth with my fingers.

I don't like anyone talking about Annavasal, the place where I was born and brought up. Old wine is one thing, but stale buttermilk is quite another.

2

Annavasal is like vintage wine when I think about it, but it is rancid buttermilk when *others* talk about it. Gopali's talk is a cocktail of the two, a mixture that has lost its element.

Annavasal had its Shankara Jayanti. And Mariamma's. And the Arunagirinathar festival. The Vishnu temple festival was a sticky affair. And then there was the ritual wedding of Radha in the *agrahara*. Each was an annual excitement, held every three months.

Gopali would never fail to turn up for the Shankara Jayanti and the Arunagiri festival, even if the calendar missed it. People flocked from ten miles around to hear him sing. They would listen to him suspended from every nook and cranny, and from rooftops opened up especially for them. Spending the night on the street and on temple platforms, they would return home by cart or on foot the next morning.

The town is not all that big. All put together—the farmers' lane, the backstreets, the fisher folk's lane, the slums, the agrahara and the corner diversions—it may add up to only about four hundred units. But a furlong to the west of the town, the river Kaveri's tributary divides, flowing into the northern and southern bounds of the town. Arable soil of two rivers, a soil rich in surfeit with a shady canopy of groves all around. A furlong to the east, both tributaries separated and lay back in exhaustion like an enceinte woman. The shade and fertility extended to the point where the boundary of the town was drawn. The name Annavasal may have come about because of this fertility. A Nayanar, an Arunagiri must have sought its shelter and sung there before moving on. Ages before the Nayanars, Shiva, Perumal and Mariamma had set up their abode here. Sixty years back, an archaeological expert, looking at the Linga in the sanctum of the Shiva temple, had declared that the temple belonged to the Chola times. Was there a *padhigam*? Without losing more time, a Nattu Kottai Chetty had renovated the temple, clearing the thorns and peepul roots that had penetrated the walls. In this same sanctuary of the Devi, there was a small structure on the ground for the *khundam*, the sacred fire. A follower of Shankara said that the Devi's presence was so fiercely manifest here that Adi Shankara established a *yantram*, and that was the *khundam*. This inspired Kandu Sastri to start the Shankara festival.

Kandu was the first to declare, 'Music is only what Gopali sings! He alone has the true voice of a singer.' All manner of scholars attended the Shankara Jayanti. The old and the new, the young and the veteran. They regurgitated about *advaita* with its doctrine of *maya*, ignorance about metaphysics, well-known metaphors such as the serpent and the rope, the pearl and the mother-of-pearl and so on. But the stage was set for only one event—Gopali's concert, and nothing else.

I'd heard him singing ever since I'd worn an arasilai, snuggling on my father's lap or on my mother's in my pavadais. I also heard him later, in a full saree of six yards.

Did I hear or did I see?

Gopali's easy grace as he settled down on the stage. I would see him coming and taking his seat, but not how he sat—like a mynah alighting on a branch.

His big broad face, his skin the colour of a *maruda* tree, neither light nor dark. A crown of wavy hair. If his voice could rush into my ears and turn me crazy, would the man also get into me like this? He was not really handsome. None of his features was. You could even say some were ugly. But put together they not only harmonised, they could fascinate you like a dream. How could a mother create him like this? His eyes could transmute the commonplace into something extraordinary. Eyes that seemed touched with kohl, eyes that teased, or turned remote even while studying the crowd. What nonchalance in the way he sat! What arrogance. He seemed to mock everyone, as if he was sworn to snub the bigwigs of Annavasal. As I grew older, I seemed to know better. I was happy. Anyhow, he was the pride of Annavasal—particularly of those in the agrahara—that someone like him took them into account once in two years.

Annavasal's agrahara, with its seventy or eighty houses, was shaped like the Tamil 'Ta' (L). Eight of these houses belonged to the landowners. Majority of the rest were middling. The remaining were clerks of the former. Every day, a Vaishnava priest, a couple of pandits or some twenty people would take a cart to go to court. They would loan money at multiple rates of interest and keep filing suits on it. Seven of them made money by playing three aces. Two of them went to Madras every week without fail to watch the horse race. When the Madras season ended, they moved on to the race in Bangalore. Consequently the moneylenders were embroiled in litigation with half the people in Kalla Street and in dispute with half of Velala Street over lease. At least once in two years, in a twilight hour on the fields, these disputes ended in mugging a Natesa Iyer or a Chidambara Iyer. Stabbings were followed by bail-outs. Kalla Street and Velala Street were thus preoccupied in fighting and filing suits. The occupants of four houses in Salia Street, grown numb and anaemic from working the loom, wove sarees and dhotis for the whole town.

Annavasal abounded in feuds and fights. But everyone curled up tamely on the day Gopali performed. Half of Velala Street kept away from the Mariamma festival. Half of Kalla Street was restrained. Only the Arunagiri festival and the Shankara Jayanti united the town. Rather, it was Gopali who united them.

Gopali claimed that he once told Ahorapillai who organised the Arunagiri festival: 'The entire lot in Annavasal violated their mothers. Everyone except you and Kandu Sastri.' Gopali told me about it later. Did he think that he made me happy? *Me*?

Only I truly understood Kandu Sastri.

My father worked on his farm. Every day he went around Kandu's spread of thirty acres with an arched bamboo under his arm, stepping over each bramble and twig, keeping a close watch over the land. I was the one who, in my peepul leaf nudity, would suck my middle finger and ring finger, my eyes fixed on Kandu, and take in every word of his, laughing.

Kandu was considered to be as expansive as advaita. His brain was sharp as a blade of dry *kusa* grass. A quick mind and an imagination swift as lightning were his natural gifts. As I reached the age of comprehension, I observed the several shades of his mind, and they registered in mine. But what arrested me first was his physical appearance. He was of medium height and a yellowish pallor. Large eyes, steady in their expression. The smile showed on his cheeks and lips, as did his annoyance and thoughtfulness, leaving the eyes unchanged. Only his mouth and cheeks crinkled. A balding crown, with a small tuft of hair at the back like a looped silk cord. The baldness would last only a day, though, and in a couple of days his head would be covered with stubble. It was the same with his face. Three stripes of ash on his forehead. Three yards of cloth woven in Salem draped around his chest. Five yards of the same draped around his waist, tucked in at the back. In the front yard of his house there was a smooth back-rest of red cement. In the mornings he would sit there, propped up on his right hand. As soon as Amma finished brushing my teeth and rinsing my mouth, I would head straight for the cement seat and stand in front of him, watching. I often felt like sitting on his lap, dangling my legs down and hitting his chest with the back of my head, hug his chest and back with my arms. He would not call out for me. Unlike others, he would never lift my chin up with his palm, never caress me.

I followed him everywhere, to his bath, to his dinner, when he was at the puja, when he reclined, legs stretched out the length of his armchair, discoursing to his disciples, till he was about to climb into the bullock cart ready to take him out of town. Once, sucking my finger, I saw him reclining on a chair. A disciple in a dhoti and upper cloth stood a little away, talking to him. That was how everyone talked to him. The lessons over, no one remained seated. They kept standing. Or they would go and sit on the cement platform to study. That day, Kandu lay reclined, his body like a ripe shining fruit. The soles of his feet were dirty with walking. I ran to the well, dampened a rag, brought it back and rubbed it on his feet before he could even look at me.

'Aha!' he said, quickly withdrawing his feet. 'What are you doing?'

'There is dirt all over your feet.'

He got up, his eyes wide. Suddenly he lifted me up. I looked at him, holding on to his chest, laughing. It was like hugging an enormous ripe mango. Cool to the touch. He went to the kitchen. Mangalamma looked at him in surprise. 'What's this?' she said. 'How strange!' I could not understand it then. I can now. I heard that he did not lift his own children.

'Do you know what she did? I was reclining on the chair. She ran into the backyard and...'

He finished and then looked at me. Putting me down, he kept looking. How long I squirmed under that gaze, looking away. Why did he look at me like that? Why is that gaze still alive within me today?

'Is there some rock candy? Give her a piece. Let it be the first *prasadam* today.'

The rock candy came.

'Isn't there a bigger piece?'

A bigger piece came.

'I hope this doesn't become a habit,' said Mangalamma as she gave it.

Kandu turned around sharply. I could see the woman's back. She was replacing the jar of candy on the shelf.

'Go, my daughter-in-law, run along now,' he said, pushing me away gently.

I reached the courtyard and stood in a corner beside a sandalwood grind. Outside I could see sunlight filtering through a creeper and falling on the ground like coins. A silvery dust whirled up to the coconut thatch above. Putting the candy into my mouth, I blew at the dust.

Kandu came out after a while and went into his room, staring at me.

Later, I dreamt about this some four or five times, that I was perched on the ripe mango of Kandu's body against which I repeatedly cooled my cheeks, burying them on his shoulders.

When Kandu went out of town, everything became desolate and I couldn't pass the time. I rested against a plant and listened to the rhythm of the oil press. Listening to it made me dizzy. Or I felt like laughing. When the oil press stopped, I would pass the time looking at Salia Street and the front yards of the four houses where they set up the handlooms.

Now and then Kandu's youngest son Balan visited us. As the son of the landlord Kandu, he received special respect. Only when I neared ten I understood. Amma would suddenly get embarrassed. Balan resembled Kandu in complexion, and he would go around in a thin dhoti of one and half yards, his smooth chest bare. His back looked as imposing as his front. That was funny.

One day suddenly, all this turned bitter.

Kandu's youngest daughter was eighteen. She came home one day with her husband who was newly appointed as an engineer in Madras. A week later, he was laid down with a chill. They said it was bilateral pneumonia. On the sixth day he died.

The town was hushed and I was in a panic. I could not see Kandu reclining in the front yard. Every now and then sobs would be heard from the house. There were bullock carts with people coming and going without talking. Everything moved like in a silent film.

On the tenth day there was a crowd on the river bank. About two hundred people had turned up from the neighbouring towns for condolence. Besides, there were children and women from Kalla, Velala and Salia Streets. Despite Amma stopping me, I followed the wailing procession. Handpicked roses from the town, jasmines and leaves of the evergreen were strung on the hair of Kandu's daughter. Vermilion was streaked all over her brow in crazy lines. Two widows in white with shaven heads led her, accompanied by a bevy of women. Behind them was a surging crowd of men. The crowd from Kalla and Velala Streets was already waiting at the river bank. Near the river bank was the peepul tree that stood protectively over the stone serpents and Pillaiyar. Three months before, the tree was aflame with coppery leaves. Now it stood a dark green, each leaf fanned out like a serpent's hood, hissing in the wind.

The women of the town took turns to smear turmeric on the girl's cheeks and stepped away. After that she was given a bath. Two persons sought out Kandu who had fallen down limp on a heap of sand, and brought him. The pandits pleated a white saree of nine yards, twisted it and handed it to Kandu. Kandu staggered towards his daughter.

A shrill voice abruptly cut through the hush like a knife and sent the vast riverside trembling.

'Sastri Sir, I'd asked you to cut this out.'

It was Kandu's youngest son Balan, the same boy. Tears dropped like pearls of fire from the corners of his eyes. His arms were stiff, fists clenched. Kandu turned around and held his son's gaze for three long seconds. Then he turned back and walked on. He draped the white saree around his daughter's shoulders, and the girl was led away from the river bank.

The boy kept glaring at Kandu, his teeth set on edge. Suddenly he lunged forward without warning. A few people restrained him and dragged him homeward.

The Kalla folks, who traditionally swore by staves and knives, witnessed it all like subdued kittens. Velala Street stood on, looking anaemic.

Kandu walked back alone, stoic and silent.

I trapped myself at home.

Three days later, unable to contain myself any longer, I went to their house. The girl, swathed in a white saree, her head completely shaven, was curled up as if in a swoon. Mangalamma slammed the door on me.

I returned home and lay down. I felt like laughing when I thought of Kandu Mama. I wanted to take the dust of his feet and rub it all over his body. The agrahara that indulged in ferocious litigation, the Kalla Street, the slums, the Salia Street—I felt like trampling over everything wildly like Kali, cackling and baring my teeth in demoniacal laughter. I enacted all this in my mind.

That year, all the teachers had enlisted for the war; the three classes above the fifth were therefore closed down. I was taken to my Periappa's house in Kumbakonam. Before going, I did not take leave of Kandu.

3

Periappa's house overlooked the pond. There were streets on the four sides and a temple on the opposite bank. Every house had a two-tiered platform. There was a wooden trellis near the lower platform. Time just flew whenever I stood there, holding on to the trellis, looking out. There were so many noises. The calls of the women selling vegetables, the call of the kite, the screech of the herons, the calls of the water birds, the bells of the carts jingling towards the train station, the ceaseless squelch of clothes being washed. At sunset, the streetlights from the three sides would be elongated as their reflection floated on the waters. As one listened to the notes of the temple bells, the nadaswaram, the drums, I just felt like closing my eyes and stretching myself out on the cement slab.

I felt proud that I had not said goodbye to Kandu. I imagined that Appa, Amma and others chided me in turns for this. I must have made Kandu very sad. I was triumphant. 'Good! Let him boil over!' I exulted.

Amma turned up once. It was Appa who came every week. A female cousin of Kandu came. And two of his disciples. That not one of them should ask me about it!

Instead of being asked, 'I believe you didn't even say goodbye to Kandu?' I was asked the insipid question, 'How is school?' Perhaps Kandu Mama was not really bothered.

After all, I was only a poor employee's daughter. Who cared if a commoner didn't say a proper goodbye? If I were you, I would've taken a cart and come specially to ask, 'How could you go away, my child, without talking to me?' What's the use of all your big learning? The world celebrates you as a great scholar. Your disciples prostrate themselves before you. But you couldn't even shed tears for your own daughter. You couldn't see her shaven bald, draped in white, curled up inert in a room.

Will *you* be my father-in-law? Never! A girl from a poor family, she has such a full face, nice chiselled features and a lively disposition. 'If we take her in as a daughter-in-law, we can keep looking at her, make her a slave.' She, on her part, would work herself to the bone, grateful for this rare generosity. You would also have another talking point then: 'Money is not everything for us. What matters is the individual and her character.' *That* would make you one of the elite and then you could brag, with or without so many words, about your generosity!

This was my mental exchange with Kandu as I stood, one arm on the wooden trellis, studying the reflections that wriggled on the pond.

Kandu will not come, nor will he ask about me. If he did, I shall insist that his girl grow her hair again.

'What are you standing there for? You think no one will notice you in this town? Be careful, or the gossip may reach the Kandu household,' Amma warned me once, while on a visit two years later, when I started wearing a *dhavani*.

'Kandu is your master. What is he to me?' I retorted, and that made Amma tremble all over. There was no one around and she had only spoken in a low tone. Likewise, I too had replied keeping my voice low.

'Rolling your eyes doesn't settle anything,' I added, staring at the pond. *That* was the way to bait Amma. She flared up when you didn't talk to her face to face, when you talked to her with your face averted.

'So that's how it is, is it?'

Silence.

'And you've learnt all this in just these two years? It'll do you little good to have so much pride!'

'Why not? Supposing this son also dies three years later, I would have to surrender my hair to his spirit and, in a swoon, be discarded somewhere between the tamarind pitchers and the pickle jars in the store room.'

Two minutes passed without a word. I stared on at the pond, laughing within myself. The amber sunlight of dusk fell on the water, bathing the moss in gold.

'Your schooling finishes tomorrow. It's enough that in two years you've learnt to utter so much devilry.'

'I'm on a full scholarship and rank first in class. They have even given me some free books and copies. I'll do well. And afterwards I'll marry some poor hotel hand who reeks of bengal gram flour and sweat. I can offer tuitions. I will sport a bare yellow thread around my neck, but I won't enter the

Kandu household to be fettered by chokers and heavy *kaasu maalai.*'

'He is a godly person, so is the family. Don't talk so sneeringly. The family is blessed by Shakti. Take care, or else your tongue may freeze.'

'Yes, yes, I can see that. They already have a Goddess Shakti in the house, fully shaven.'

'I'm going right back tomorrow,' said Amma, getting up. Turning around in the passage, she whispered, 'You may study well, marry a tramp and carry on with your yellow thread,' before she went in.

Some five months later, Appa came one day, just as he did every week. It was a day of *Amavasya.* The provision shops were closed. Periappa was free from his accounting work. Appa, who always used to go about his work briskly on his employer's lands, looked sluggish and distraught.

The two of them sat on the cement seat and talked. After throwing the remains of the dinner in a garbage bin, I washed my hands and settled down in a room near the cement seat and opened a book.

Appa was saying: 'My mind has been disturbed for the past two days, Anna.'

It seems four days earlier, Kandu Mama, who had been sitting on the *pyol* of the front yard, abruptly rose and went in, and wrote something in haste on a piece of paper. 'Viswam is coming down the end of the street. Hurry up and give this to him,' he said and giving the piece of paper to Appa, he went upstairs.

Appa walked briskly. Stopping Viswam halfway, he gave him the paper saying, 'Aiya sent this for you.' Viswam promptly pulled out the spectacles tucked at his waist and put them on to read it. Suddenly, his face registered shock, as if he was insulted. For a few moments he looked confused. He stood there for a while, looked around and then without a word, he turned back and walked out of sight.

Appa went upstairs and later reported this to Kandu. Appa didn't know the contents of the message. It was in Sanskrit.

'He studied under me for five years, visiting every week. I poured the sap of my learning into him. Later on he might have studied with others. Last month, when someone addressed him as my disciple, he replied, 'You could put it like that. I have burrowed through books with him for a long time.' If he is so ungrateful to his guru, and embarrassed to admit that he is my disciple, why then should he set foot on my doorstep? In the message, I asked him not to show his face to me hereafter. If he comes here in future, in my absence, you would be within your rights to forbid his entry,' Kandu said to Appa.

Listening to this exchange made me feel like I was watching a movie strip. Viswam was perhaps three or four years younger than Kandu. Elderly disciples such as Dakshinamurty vouched for Kandu Sastri's scholarship and enlightenment. I could imagine Viswam blanch at the message.

I wanted to run up to him and massage his heart. Holding his palm in mine, I wanted to stroke his shoulder with my other palm. Who is the guru, and who the disciple?

I shall now proceed to touch and hug one and all, and I shall talk to them only through touch.

The scene of poor Viswam's disgrace often comes in front of my eyes. How could such a thing happen? It happened on a morning when the cool, yellow sunlight had not yet matured into white heat. There were coconut palms on either side of the road. And rosewater trees and neem trees in front of some houses. Trees that received the hopping, screeching birds, the tailor birds and the chirping house sparrows. In the burrows of eaves in one or two houses, these sparrows chattered, making sounds that were neither speech nor song. It was the time when the doves cooed in the woods, the oil press groaned. A time of cool, gentle breeze. A time that melts your senses. At a time like this how could someone steel his heart to a man coming to visit him and order him not to come, order him never to set foot on his doorstep again? How? How could he be so oblivious of the morning sounds? Didn't he feel the soft warmth of the morning sun on his eyes? Feel the cool breeze on his skin? Only someone insensitive to all this could have such hatred in him. How could he do it? Has Kandu dried up and grown desiccated by the holy advaita?

Repeatedly, I see the image of Viswam turning away, crestfallen and crushed by the smouldering anger and hatred in the letter. But there was no anger on his face.

Something tells me that I should touch everybody.

I do keep touching of course. There is no one I haven't touched. I've caressed thousands of people. Schoolboys, girls, relatives. College students, girl students, teachers, lady teachers, gardeners, taxi-drivers, governors, waiters, ministers, pandits, shopkeepers, sweeper women. I've lost count.

If anyone holds his hands in greeting on being introduced, I feel like giving him a hard slap. What is this folding of hands? Why can't he shake hands? Why can't he hold the shoulders and hands, and talk?

Once, some six or seven years later, I had been to a temple in Kerala with Gopali. The priest offered puja with a damp cloth around his body. After finishing *arati*, he brought the prasadam of coconut and flowers. 'Take,' he said. Everyone stood, holding the loose end of their sarees or top cloth. The priest tossed the prasadam all around. It was our turn for the puja, and after the camphor arati, our turn for the prasadam. Before the priest could toss the prasadam, I did not hold out my saree. I held both his hands in mine and then took the prasadam.

He glared at me fiercely. I laughed.

'I'm giving it to you,' he said.

'What, are you mocking me? Why are you laughing?'

'You experience the deity by repeatedly touching Him. I thought I could at least touch *you*.'

Perhaps the priest had some life in him. He smiled condescendingly, as one would at someone foolish and ignorant. The next moment his brow creased in a frown, as if he had weakened unnecessarily. Then he went down to have a bath.

Gopali asked me, 'Why couldn't you tell him that you touched him by mistake? Why tell him that you did it on purpose?'

'But I touched him on purpose. Why should I hide it?'

'Of all the people, why did you have to touch *him*?'

'Why shouldn't I? Until I touch somebody I don't feel I have seen him properly. Why just him, I touch everybody, and I will always do so.'

'Have you vowed to touch a certain number of people?'

'I don't have a specific count. But I want to touch everyone born in this world at least once. I want to shake hands with them.'

'All right, touch, shake hands by all means. But what's it for? What's there in it?

'Nothing. Touching is quite enough. What more should there be?'

'Are you going to give everybody the touch of benediction?'

I didn't reply.

My silk-clad revolutionary friend once reviled me. 'Come now, do you think you're bringing about some new revolution by touching everybody in this world? That you'll pour affection all around, that the whole world will ooze with love...Do you think you can bring about a revolution of the heart by madly hugging everyone? You are preaching as if you've discovered some great philosophy! I don't like these fake stands.'

'Bala, I'm not philosophising at all. Nor am I preaching nor am I pretending. I never talked about any revolution of the heart or the body. I only expressed what I felt. I wonder if like you I have a heart or an *atma* at all. All I have is this body. I do feel like touching everybody. It satisfies you to look at people or to smile at them. Not me. I'm satisfied only if others touch me too. If anyone talks to me without touching me, I feel lost, as if there is something wanting somewhere. Where do you see a revolution or pretence in this? It is a need. I didn't say that you should be like me.'

'How can that be? If you touch me, how can I be untouched!'

I could not answer.

Whenever I met her, I touched her too. I talked holding her hands. It was like touching wood. Or like touching something feverish. Bala had good looks. The kind of conventional good looks that women cherish, slimness, an occasionally noticeable femininity and bashfulness. But I knew it for a fact that at least twenty men who had initially intended to court her had abruptly fled. They even solemnly swore never to see her again. To me, it looked like male sparrows breaking their beaks pecking and caressing a stone sparrow, mistaking it to be a female sparrow. Warm and alive to her ideal of eradicating the hunger of the poor and bringing a revolution that would wipe away want from their lives, Bala scared away her lovers, who perhaps wondered if they had run into a Joan of Arc.

4

The snubbing of Viswam haunted me for a week and it hurt. Did I expect Kandu not to repeat something as awful as shaving off his daughter's hair? Few have the right to insult anyone in the middle of a street. I could not sleep. If I dozed for a while, I dreamt I was being trampled by a stray cow. Dreamt that the zodiac sages Guru and Shukra practised maledictions on Viswam by casting *dharbai* grass over him and that the same grass, transforming into serpents, coiled around him.

I recall that clearly. After a fortnight of torment and bad dreams, I woke up one morning and listened to the herons circling over the pond. In that half-asleep state, their noise sounded a note of encouragement. It was like looking at myself in the mirror. My eyes and complexion had a new lustre, as if I had recovered from a long illness. I remembered Kasiraman, a boy in my class. He was absent from school for a month and a half. They said it was typhoid. Then he came one day, thinner, darker. Examinations commenced and ended, and a vacation was declared. Kasi came again when school reopened two months later. But it took me some time to recognise him.

He had doubled his weight and was bursting at the seams of his shirt and pants. He had also grown a bit taller. I wondered about this for three days.

It was as if I too had a rebirth of that kind.

Someone touched my forehead. I opened my eyes. Periamma was sitting beside me.

'Do you have any pain in the body, Ammani?'

'No, Periamma.'

'I asked because you don't usually sleep for so long...Have coffee.'

'I'll have it after I brush my teeth, Periamma.'

'That's alright. Have it.'

I held Periamma's hands and pressed them to my eyes and face. Periamma's daughter and her five-year-old son came and sat beside me. I stroked them. The boy smiled. When I reached out, he held my hand in his. I also took the girl's hands in mine. It seemed as if I had been born like Kasiraman. Periamma and her children seemed to touch me in a new way.

From that day on, I linked my fingers with Periamma's whenever I went with her to the temple or for shopping. In school too, touching was magic, a way of communication. Why had I not touched anyone all these days? If I had, I would've befriended many more people. I could've discovered many more things through my hands.

I could not touch the boys. There were separate rows of benches for boys and girls. Suddenly I thought, why are these benches separated like toilet seats?

'Why do you hold hands when you talk?' asked Kamini. She was the daughter of a judge. She came to school by car and went home the same way.

'You are a judge's daughter after all. I thought it would be useful to cultivate you. If you don't like it, I won't,' I said, withdrawing my hands.

'You're angry.'

'Me? It's you who got angry because I touched you.'

'Shut up!' shouted the girl and embraced me the next moment. Then she said, 'Come to my house.'

'Why?'

'My father is a judge. You can fawn over him. If you see my father once, instead of fawning, you might perhaps break his limbs.'

'Oh dear!'

'Yes, ever since he became a sessions judge, my father thinks he is God. He acts like a judge even at home. I've seen him at court. He took me to some big courts. In one such court, I saw a lawyer barking loudly, as if he had sighted a thief on the street. Seated opposite were five or six judges, looking this way and that. One had closed his eyes like a cat, another was chewing a pencil. Yet another had piles, so he twisted and squirmed on his chair, his face contorting as he listened. It was funny to watch them look so complacent, like they had the most superior career in the world and there was nothing to surpass them. My father is also like that.'

'Why do you talk like this about your father? Does he scold you often?'

'He doesn't scold me, but he scolds my mother. Not really...I mean, whenever my mother talks, he just glares at her. Mother gets confused and wonders if she is saying something wrong. That makes her falter and blabber all the more. I often wonder how a judge's job can make him so vain.'

I had touched this girl just once, and she has thrown up such a lot. Since that day, she became a good friend of mine. She was angry with all judges because her father harassed her mother. Going through the morning paper every day, she would take up a judgement and comment with a laugh, 'Look, all these nuts have been appointed judges!'

I have touched girls like this, and they have opened up. At last I also found a boy. He used to sit on the last bench in my class. He was rather naughty, though he wouldn't do anything objectionable. He would just sketch anyone he saw. Caught in the act one day in class, the lout Gopala Iyer tore up his copy and made him stand outside for a whole day. The boy did not come for a week, and when he came, the master, beckoning him to come nearer, slapped him on the cheek for not giving a proper answer and made him stand on the bench. The class gave over in ten minutes. Everyone dispersed for lunch except the boy. Face down on the desk, he sat there with his eyes closed.

I went near him and watched him closely. The veins on his temple throbbed. Touching his temple with my left hand, I held his hand in my right.

He opened his eyes. Seeing me, he withdrew, scared.

'Why are you sitting here? Aren't you going to eat?'

'No. I have a headache.'

'Because the teacher beat you?'

'Yes. Last week I had measles. That's why I didn't come. Only the day before yesterday, I had a bath and washed my hair. With this thrashing, my head throbs painfully.'

'Why don't you lie down on the bench? I'll press your head for you.'

'I'll be all right soon.'

'No. I'll get the headache balm from the first-aid kit in the Headmaster's room.'

'No, it's all right,' he said, looking at the classroom door and smiling apologetically. I followed his glance. A group of boys were looking at us, smirking. At the next window stood two girls from my class. One of them was the judge's daughter Kamini, looking like a judge herself. I beckoned to her. Excusing herself from the group, she came in. I spoke to her and ran out and got the headache balm.

I rubbed it on his temples in the full gaze of everybody.

'He has the right nickname, Gopala Iyer, the Lout. Why do such characters come to teach? They could rightly join the police and hang around my father's court,' said Kamini.

The boy had had enough of it and distanced himself bashfully. He was worried about the onlookers.

'Does the master know you had measles and that you had a bath?'

'I don't know. You don't write letters when you have measles. It might carry the infection. So I didn't send a leave letter.'

'It's a small matter. Anyhow, it would be good to inform the Headmaster lest another boy gets thrashed too.'

'Please don't.'

'Why not?'

'No, no.'

'Shall *we* go and report it?'

'No.'

The judge's daughter looked at me and pouted.

'Why?'

'He may yell his head off again that I complained,' he said shyly, revealing a set of large white teeth.

That was the end of it.

But not quite.

When the lout of a master sat in his afternoon class, he looked at the girls' benches and said, 'So, we have some troublemakers here?'

At first, I stiffened.

'Why no answer? I'm asking you, Madam Ammani.'

'Me, Sir?'

'Yes, you. Are you doing the job of a Narada or a Naradess?'

'A nurse's job, Sir.'

The boys laughed.

'That's right. Then why follow it up with a Narada job?'

'I did nothing like that.'

'But you provoked it, didn't you?'

'Yes Sir.'

'What do you mean, Yes Sir?'

'Yes Sir. I did it so that you don't thrash someone again and get sacked. I heard that teachers could be dismissed for beating boys just because they don't study properly. That's what scares me, Sir,' I said pouting solicitously.

'Is that so?' said the Great Guru, looking at me intently. Then he said, 'Okay. You may sit down.'

I sat down.

Alternately looking at me and at the teacher, the boys sniggered.

A neighbour's elbow nudged me. A note slid in my direction. '*Come to my house. I want to see you talk to my father like this,*' the judge's daughter had written.

Three days later, when I went to school, I saw groups of boys near the compound wall, amusing themselves with something. A couple of girls and I went to see what it was about.

'*Shanmugananthan is Ammani's keep!*'

'*Shanmugananthan is Ammani's gigolo!*'

'*Have a headache? Ammani will rub it away!*'

The three messages were scrawled in coal tar on the walls of our compound, outside our class and the rear wall.

Something suddenly burned within my stomach. My eyes stung. I went into the toilet and sobbed. I sobbed a lot.

A voice called out repeatedly, 'Ammani!' It was the judge's daughter. 'Open the door!...Don't do anything drastic, Ammani.'

'Ammani!'

The tin door shook.

'Ammani!'

'Hm.'

'Open the door!'

When I opened the door, four more girls were standing outside. Their look seemed calculated to tease me so that I would cry. Seeing that, I instantly wiped my eyes and briskly walked past them. I went straight to the Headmaster and said, 'Sir, I want a change of section. I can't remain in that lout's class.' I didn't shout, I growled.

'What does that mean?'

'It means just that.'

'What?'

'Change my section immediately. Or else, I'll implicate you as well. It's because of your incompetence that the lout could write like this.'

'Do you imply that he is behind this?'

'Not with his own hands. But through the boys and peons that he sent with the tar that he bought.'

'You cannot slander anyone without proof.'

'I didn't come to you for proving this, Sir. I want to change my section.'

'Go and sit in the section of whichever master you like.'

The tone in which he said this, I wanted to shout back at him. That when I married some day and had children of my own, I would never allow any of them to take up teaching for a livelihood, and certainly not anywhere in our district. I could have bitten off his nose!

All through that year there was chaos. Within my mind, in our house, everywhere. An inquiry was held, and even the judge took time off from harassing his wife and set the police on the lout's trail. The Education Department conducted its own investigations. The lout was thrown out of his job.

At Annavasal, my reputation blew around in tatters. The old and the very young, everyone drooled on seeing me. At school, it wasn't only the boys. Even the teachers, when they caught me alone, gave me a sly thin smile. If I stood in the front porch, a few boys would talk among themselves, all the while looking at the house opposite ours. The established practice was to marry off girls 'like me' in secret haste, in a temple or a marriage hall in some godforsaken place, to some middle-aged clerk from Hyderabad, Delhi or Bombay, or to the son of the 'same kind' of woman, and whisk her off in a train before an anonymous letter made its way to the family.

Periamma stood up to it like a queen. She told my mother, 'Now look here. This child has grown up with me. Whether she has to be married or not is my lookout. She is going to continue with her studies. You can consider that you have given her to me in adoption, and you can go back home.'

Amma and Appa left for home. The music of the oil press ceased. Kandu Sastri's face faded. Celebrations, *bhajanai*, everything vanished.

I slept soundly, holding Periamma's hands.

5

It always amazed me to remember the spirit and the determination with which Periamma said that.

'You can consider that you have given her to me in adoption. And you can go home.'

She didn't say this loudly. There was no distortion on her face either. Only in her eyes, for a bare second, there was a piercing light. At nine in the morning every day the doctor's horse cart would speed past our house. Sometimes, for a split second, the steel hook holding the lantern of the cart would catch the sun and reflect it brilliantly, piercing my eyes as I stood in the front porch. Blinded for a moment, my eyes would smart. There was that kind of flash in Periamma's eyes for that one moment, and the next moment it had vanished. Not just that. Periamma had smiled as usual. Perhaps it signified the triumph of the moment's intensity.

After Appa and Amma had left for home, I said to Periamma, 'Before leaving, they would always say, "Child, be good, will you?" This time, they didn't.'

'If it was their child, they would be worried about her behaviour in someone else's house. Now, why do they have to worry?'

Again, the same smile. A smile that acknowledged me as an equal. Those who haven't heard Periamma's laughter are very very poor indeed. One could laugh like that only if one didn't discriminate between the small and the big, the petty and the lofty, the high and the low. It took me a long time to discover this.

For me, laughter was the only companion. I had laughed ever since I remembered things. But Periamma's laughter was a natural one. It had no meaning other than happiness. I think that's why Periappa was free of worries.

Periappa was not very educated. Had studied up to the sixth. 'It's the lot of being born a brahmin that I sit in the

Chettiar's shop, doing accounts. Otherwise, I could've tilled the fields,' he said.

Periappa's income was meagre, of course. But he was the wrong example for every economic principle I studied. That is, he wasn't an accomplished man. He had no need to be. Didn't have a wide knowledge of anything. Didn't think of starting a shop on his own with the experience he had gained. Had no plans to build a house of his own. After his morning bath, he would spend most of his days doing *japam* with his eyes closed. Some days he demanded coffee soon after his bath.

'Is the japam over?' Periamma would ask.

'I'm not doing it today.'

'Why?'

'Why should I trouble Him every day? I'm worried He may turn sour towards me.' And saying this, Periappa would wink at me.

After closing down the shop for the night, on his way home, he would enter a second-hand book shop and buy himself some crime fiction in English for half an anna or one anna. He finished them over a couple of nights. This way he built up his knowledge of English. If I brought home some heavy-reading books, he would read them too. If I asked him why he didn't get such books from the second-hand shop, he would say, 'Why should I pay for such things? If you wanted tragedy, you have to first study our Chettiar. The last *Adi*, he had solid twenty lakhs in the bank, but I've never seen him without a frown. His first son is insane. The wife of his second son drowned herself in the river. The third son can always be seen in Sarangapani Street, dead drunk. He has filed a suit for his share of property. The Chettiar is fighting back that the son has no right to it, and that it is all *his*, the Chettiar's, self-earned property. The Aiyangar lawyer has made enough out of this dispute to buy a new house. I don't have to buy books for comedy either. There is your Periamma for one thing, laughing all the time,' he winked. He had a habit of winking for everything.

When Periappa gave his first daughter in marriage to a shopkeeper like himself, I was a bit disappointed. I even asked him about it.

'Why do you say he is like me? He is a salesman in a cloth shop.'

'Couldn't you get a better match?'

'Only this man was inexpensive. What can I do? He was the only one who said, "Just give her to me in marriage. That's enough." If his father was like my brother-in-law, your Periamma's elder sister's husband, who has a son in the IAS, would he accept her? He would've said, "Give me a neat thirty thousand, a car, a refrigerator, silk sarees for the girls. Collectors, secretaries and ministers would be there for the reception. So make arrangements for at least two thousand people. My brother-in-law's son is a collector. Yet he can't find a girl of his choice. Perhaps it is overwork or whatever, but he can't find the time for all this. He said "Yes" after seeing the girl and the horoscope was checked. You may settle the rest with my father and mother, he said like a good docile son. You should've seen the way my brother-in-law and your Periamma's sister crushed them like a sugarcane press. It rained refrigerator, cash, jewels, five sets of dresses and silver. From where would I get all these things? The boy looked to be a good man, so I decided for him.'

'Just look at this, Periamma! Your sister's son is a collector. And your son-in-law is a salesman in a cloth shop.'

'Well, whenever I visit his shop, he'll display a hundred sarees without a frown. We can take a good look at them and make a selection. Even if we don't buy any, he won't get angry,' said Periamma.

'Did you hear that?' said Periappa and winked at me.

'Hear what? After all, my Akka's husband is a teacher. And he coached his son and made him get into the IAS. He's had a hard life. So he forked it out of his *sambandhi*. Do you think his son will be like him? When a son gets a son, he won't demand all this. The girl's people will give everything on their own. Do you think the big officers in government service will expressly ask for anything?'

'Got that?' said Periappa.

'What do you mean *got that*? Isn't there any difference between the demands of the new rich and those of a son born to someone rich?' I asked.

'The third generation ought to be more interesting, more enterprising.'

'Why should the children know that their grandfather was a teacher and that their grandmother was a teacher's wife?' said Periamma, laughing.

'All this is empty chatter. I'm going to print the invitation. And I'm not going to attach a separate slip for dinner. Nor am I going to say that there'll be dinner only for those who get the slips. The Chettiar has generously offered to provide all the food items for the wedding. "I'll send you as many things as you want, don't stint on the food," he said. Isn't that enough? Okay. Let it be. Don't listen to all this and misjudge my brother-in-law and his son. If he is posted in this district as a magistrate, I can request him not to haul you up, and he will listen to me,' said Periappa.

'What! *What* are you saying, Periappa?'

'You do speak against the government in all the meetings you attend in the slums and in the lanes of the peasants, don't you? Should the police arrest you, my brother-in-law's son will see to it that your case is thrown out. That is what I'm saying,' said Periappa.

I was shocked.

'Am I right?' said Periappa.

'Why should your brother-in-law's son feel so obliged? He can do his duty,' I said, knowing full well that I'd stepped on a knife.

'What!' said Periamma. 'What's all this, Ammani?'

'There should be no poor people in this world, she says. And that you should grab the money and property of the rich and give it to the poor. You know these 'excursions' Ammani goes on every month? This is what she says in every city she goes to. But if you get a salesman in a cloth shop, she feels let down!' said Periappa.

I thought there was no point in enduring any more ragging.

'If you don't like it Periappa, I won't go,' I said.

'Why're you scaring the poor child?' said Periamma.

'Child? She is going to herd up the rich, tie them up like a bunch of coconuts, chop off their noses and ears, and give away their wealth to the poor! Wouldn't we also gain by that?' said Periappa, chuckling.

'Like the demon Rakhtabija, the more you lop them off, the more they will spring up in greater numbers. What'll you do then?' Periamma said to me.

'What's that, Periamma?'

'Devi Chamundi slew Rakhtabija. From every drop of his blood that fell on earth sprang another Rakhtabija. In the place of one demon, there were now a lakh. Then another Devi drank up the blood so that it may not dribble down and multiply into more demons. That put an end to it. What's all this mad talk? Three years back in Wardha, someone murdered a man and threw money at the witnesses and the police. The witnesses talked some arrant nonsense which confused everyone, and then he got away. Finally, everyone joined him,' said Periamma and suddenly she laughed.

'What's this? We started talking about marriage, and now it ends with Rakhtabija!'

'It was you who brought him in,' said Periappa.

'No, it was you,' said Periamma.

Periappa winked.

6

It was night and I was staring at the book by the light of the hurricane lantern in the courtyard at the back. The printed lines blurred into my thoughts. How did Periappa come to know all about my journeys to the slums? He talked about it so casually, without calling me aside for a separate session of scolding. Did he approve, or disapprove, I couldn't tell. It was disquieting to know that he found out without my telling him. Unlike his own children, I wasn't under any parental control. I had the freedom and autonomy only an adopted child enjoys.

I looked at the lizards licking insects off the wall and munching on them. Another lizard made a loud clicking sound somewhere in the courtyard. I remembered Amma. She would tap on the floor with her finger for every tapping note the lizard made. These days Amma does not come here often. It's been four months since she last visited.

'It seems you're doing well at school, scoring lots of marks,' she would say, looking at me. She had the habit of staring at me. Even when she was talking to others, her eyes would be only on me. My skin and my back would also be aware of it. She would narrate all the news of the village to Periamma, but her eyes would rest on me as I sat studying.

'The marriage of Kandu Mama's son has been finalised. The girl also holds a big job like him, as an accounts officer or something.'

More than wanting to see Amma's eyes, I wanted to see her midriff to see if a flame burned in there that made ashes of all her desires to see me in her place.

'Don't know what *punyam* she did to be so blessed,' said Amma. She gave us other news too, which I remember with much fear and agitation.

A girl used to come to our neighbour's at Annavasal to winnow the paddy in their backyard. Their courtyard was designed more or less like the one in Periappa's house where I studied. That's how I remember her so clearly. She was quite dark. People called her Shirali. She was very tall. I used to be captivated by her legs and shoulders, the smoothness of her skin, her hair coiled in a bun. She had such a sculptured body. She walked taking long strides. Her long legs and thighs would be tucked in when she squatted down to winnow the rice. She had expressive eyes that said several things in one glance. You could keep on looking at her as she came in, ducking her head to avoid hitting the door frame, one elbow holding on to the basket. A few glass bangles on her wrists. Earrings set in green stone on her earlobes. If she sat down to work in the morning, she could clean two or three sacks of rice without a pause, meticulously separating the paddy husk and the powdered rice, then leave as fresh and vibrant as she came in. That was some vitality! They got her married to a local sad sack, a thin, short fellow who couldn't even speak loudly. I wondered how such a puny man could be born in a Kalla family. Within three months of marriage, she acquired a paramour, a farm labourer in the house next door. In six months, the news had spread all around town. But she wasn't bothered. Neither was he. The community accepted it as the fault of those who had fixed up such an unsuitable marriage.

One day, these two, the paramour Marudamutthu and Shirali were talking in the courtyard while she was seeding a basket of tamarind fruit on the sickle-stand. No one knew what transpired between them or why they fell out, but the man suddenly snatched the sickle from her, brought it down with force on her wrist and ran away.

The wrist snapped and the hand was left dangling, suspended by a tendon. 'You killed me, you son of a whore!' she screamed. Holding the severed hand, Shirali walked up to the street, got a cart ready and reached the hospital. She lay in the cart in a swoon, got off holding on to her mother and went and lay down on the hospital bed. She had been wounded for two hours. Blood was spattered all over the cart. All over the veranda. For her iron determination alone, the hand should have been saved.

Seeing that it was lost, the doctor amputated the hand, dressed the stump of her wrist, gave her a shot and prescribed bed rest. Within two months, she reported back for work again. What a woman!

Amma deeply lamented the incident as she narrated it. Shirali's beauty and strength were not something one could forget. With a little grooming, she would have easily made it as an inspector general with the police. In my mind, I would picture her in all kinds of situations—how she bathed, how she slept, served food, or when she was with that Marudamutthu. If only I had that kind of power and vitality which knew no fatigue! If only she had some education, how accomplished she would've been, with her manner of speaking, her strength and that face!

As soon as the town got wind of her affair, people in both streets, the Kalla street and the Agrahara, the young and the middle-aged, especially the middle-aged, would stand and gape at her and crave for her. Some would even boldly accost her. But about three days later, in the fields at dusk, they would receive a sound thrashing at the hands of Marudamutthu.

Raising the flame of the lantern, I sat staring into space and thinking about Shirali.

'Are you still studying?'

I looked up, startled.

'There are still three months to go for the examinations. Why don't you settle down to sleep?'

'I have to study a bit more, Periappa.'

'Study you must. I have no objection to that...' He was about to say something more, but didn't.

'Who told you?' I asked abruptly.

'Told me what?'

'That I address meetings?'

'Was *that* the "study" you were doing? Were you thinking about that?'

'I should have told you myself, Periappa, but couldn't.'

'You can talk, my child. Only it shouldn't upset your exams and studies, see. That is why I mentioned it.'

His voice seemed to be asking to be forgiven. I laughed. That is, I changed the emotion that was choking my throat into laughter. I thought of others who would have been tearful. Who have I taken after—Appa, Amma or Thatha?

Sixty years ago, it seems my *kollu* Thatha's landlord had pestered him for more paddy when there was hardly any yield from the land. What he had was barely enough for the family to eat. Thatha promised to add more in the next instalment, but the landlord did not relent. 'All right then, come along,' said my kollu Thatha. When they reached the pond, he lifted up his landlord bodily, threw him into the pond like a ball, and came back. Did my tough fibre come from my kollu Thatha?

Periappa continued, 'When Gandhi called upon the children to abandon their schools, we had alien rule. Since that is no longer the case, we must be more careful and apply ourselves to studies.'

'I will study properly hereafter,' I hurried to reassure him.

'That's not what I meant, my child. I know you'll top the records. That's not it. I was looking at the books that you have here. I cannot understand a word in them! Do you go to address the poor illiterate in the slums after reading these? Ten years ago a man came to the Chettiar temple to give a discourse on the *Ramayana*. He said I'm not going to tell you the story like a grand aunt, about how Rama went to the forest and how he chased the deer. The *Ramayana* is truly one vast ocean of philosophy. Then, for five days the man sat and expounded on Rama's ethics, Sita's ethics, the Dandakaranya allegory, Parasurama, Ayodhya and so on and so forth. By the sixth day, only the Chettiar and his shop assistants were there to listen to him. And there was old Yogambachi, Ganesan Pillai's mother, who sat there reverentially wiping her tears with a wet cloth. The fraternity you read about is somewhat like that. If you read all this stuff and then go and lecture them, when will the poor folk in our town eat and when will they belch?' Periappa finished with a wink.

I so wanted to laugh. I told him, 'I don't understand all these books either, Periappa. We talk to them in very general terms, and we get away with it. If anyone plies us with questions, we have no answers. We talk to them in a way such that they don't ask us any questions.'

'All right. Now go to sleep. It's getting late.' Lifting the lantern, we drew the latch on the back door and went inside.

Periappa lay down on the bench.

I lay down beside Periappa, on the floor. I didn't feel sleepy as yet. What he said was amusing. Why did it take me so long to understand Periappa?

Ten minutes later, I softly called out 'Periappa...?'

'Hmm.'

'Chettiar asked you not to skimp on the food. I want you to arrange for a *kacheri.* Will you?'

'A kacheri! A court kacheri?'

'Oh Periappa!...A music kacheri.'

'A *music* kacheri? Everyone will mock me and laugh at me, saying, 'Just look at the man's pretentions!'

'Are we here to stop their laughter? We can go about it according to our status.'

'What is it then, a dance or *tabla* or a cards kacheri?'

'Gopali's music kacheri.'

'Issh! Be quiet now and go to sleep. Gopali is a top artiste now. If he's approached to sing at a small village wedding like this, he will snigger, and that will kill us!'

'I will slap him if he sniggers.'

'What!'

'Yes. I'm going to ask him. My Periappa's daughter is getting married. Will you sing for us, I'll say.'

'This is not your slum, Ammani, where you're free to go and talk as you please. Nor is it a temple kacheri.'

'I will ask him anyway. Let's see what happens. I'll tell him, you sing every year for all the rich lazybones of Annavasal. My Periappa is poor. Won't you sing for him?'

Periappa was snoring loudly. A fake snore.

7

A street running alongside river Kaveri. My sandals pressed into the soft soil. I didn't remember all that Periappa had said, and even if I did, I didn't worry about it. I'd got used to it. Ever since my first years in college, I was the invariable choice for secretary, deputy chairman, treasurer or vice president for some committee or the other. So I had mastered the knack of getting in and out of people's houses, be it a lawyer, doctor, municipality member, professor, lesser-known musician or shopkeeper.

On entering the street, two women directed me to Gopali's house.

'You want to see *him*?'

'Yes.'

'I wonder if he is in town,' said one.

'Most of the time he is not,' said the other.

'I'll take a chance. Perhaps this is one of the days that he is in town,' I said and walked on.

'Who is it? Who is asking for him?' said an old widow in white from the upper platform, chanting her beads.

'I want to meet Gopali.'

Oh God, pray let him be in today, said a voice in my head.

And what if he isn't?

It was evening. On each of the pyols in the front porch there was a woman, a couple of girls and old women, their faces scrubbed with soap and water, their hair loaded with flowers. The soft yellow light wasn't necessary to announce the evening: the pyols in the porch did. I was a stranger to this street. Several pairs of eyes probed me.

A small fear fluttered within me. Not because of those eyes. It was something else. I felt my throat suddenly going dry. What could it be?

I ascended the steps, removed my sandals, went past the passage and peeped in. In a corner, dangling her legs down into the lowered courtyard, a woman sat, brushing her hair with a wooden comb. Is that Gopali's wife?

'Is he in?'

'Who are you?'

'I study in a college.'

'Silu!' she shouted, without taking her eyes off me.

A boy scampered in from a front room.

'Go and tell Appa there's someone from a college. She wants to see him.'

The boy ran upstairs. 'Why do you want to see him?'

'In connection with a kacheri.'

'In the college?'

'No.'

'Then?'

My legs dragged me to the front door. Couldn't she have told me that he was out? I hoped the boy would return and say, 'Appa can't see you now. He asked you to come another day.'

The boy returned. 'He asks you to come up,' he said.

'Please go in. Show her in, Silu.'

'Please come.'

Climbing up the stairs, we reached the first floor. Then up another flight of stairs, and we reached the second floor. In the midst of all my apprehensions, suddenly laughter seized me. From such a wife, why one or two, one had to be seven floors away! How could Gopali marry her? How does he even look at her, approach her, get close to her, his breath upon her face? Does he shut his eyes?

The woman's face had simian contours. Also a touch of the lion. A face that rarely smiled. And when it did, it became more leonine. It shocked you at first. I found myself staring at her face in astonishment even as I cautiously responded to the few questions she asked, studying it carefully all the while. What a face! Was he saddled with her in his years of innocence? As I climbed up the stairs, did I laugh, or was I disturbed as if a worm wriggled inside my head?

'Please go in,' the boy gestured with his hand, and went back down.

Across the open terrace, a room. In the middle of the room, a swing. On the swing sat Gopali, dangling one leg.

A woman was seated on the floor, a tambura resting before her. A boy stood near the wall opposite, snipping betel nuts into a plate kept on the swing.

'Do come in,' said Gopali.

That was it. His eyes were all over me, penetrating through my skin. Unable to withstand his gaze, I stared at the tambura, which had, I noticed, stopped in the middle of a song.

'Did you leave your shoes and socks downstairs?' asked Gopali.

'What? But I wasn't wearing shoes.'

'Did you come by cart?'

'No, I came walking.'

'Surprising! Your feet are so clean, even after walking through the dusty street.'

The woman—she must've been around thirty-five—discreetly covered her feet with her saree.

'That doesn't mean *you* have to conceal your feet. But anyhow. I didn't ask you: so do you study in a college? I feel like I've seen you somewhere.'

'I'm from Annavasal.'

'From *Annavasal*!' his eyes dilated.

'I'm the daughter of Kandu Mama's secretary.'

'Kandu Mama's secretary? Then you must be Natesan's daughter. Excellent! With such an introduction, you can't be so standoffish. Are you a secretary or something? Come closer, come and sit here.'

'That's all right.'

'That's *not* all right, even if you say so,' said Gopali. He walked up to me and, with an arm around my shoulders, gave me a hug. Then he made me sit with him on the swing and lean against him, squeezing my shoulders lightly.

'Natesan's daughter, all grown up! Think you're a big woman now!'

I couldn't disengage myself. I was also afraid to do so.

'Don't stare. I've known her from this age,' Gopali told his disciple, indicating by the palm of his hand a level lower than the plank of the swing.

The disciple returned a look that said, 'Did I ask you?'

'You! Go down and get some coffee for her,' he told the betel snipper. The boy ran downstairs.

There were inquiries one after another. 'So you're at your Periappa's house for studies? You've been here all these years, and you thought of coming only now? What are you studying for your B.A.?'

The memories Gopali was fussing over, his gestures, his questions about my age, it was all a lie. I don't recall him ever even looking at me properly. When I was older, after I'd discarded my skirts and pavadais, on my visits home I had heard him singing at a kacheri from a distance. He called me 'child', but his arms weren't hugging me like I was one, though I couldn't say for sure.

I edged away and looked up. The body and the eyes that had foolishly embraced me were no longer there. I could only see the sublime ecstasy with which he sang, obliterating all the people sitting in front of him. That leonine air, lording over his audience without so much as glancing at it. Once at a kacheri, distracted by the chatter at the back, he'd turned around twice or thrice, anger smouldering in his eyes. The loud whispering subsided for a while, then it was audible again. This time Gopali burst out, 'Should I sing today or not?' Then, finishing the other half of the song in haste, he'd hurried on to the finale, *Bhavamana*. The performance had barely lasted half an hour. He'd bowed to Kandu and said, 'I beg your pardon. There was a loudmouth at the rear, so I finished it. I apologise.'

The next morning, with the same instrumental accompaniments, he sang in the *pujai* room of Kandu's house, dissolving himself in his music. I was then in my pavadai phase.

'Say something.'

I laughed.

'What?'

'Once, you...' I began and recalled the incident.

'Were you there then?'

'You made me sit here as if you remembered me a great deal.'

'That's right. Give it back to him, just give it back!' said the woman disciple.

'Natesan would never snap at people like this!' Gopali said to me.

'That helps when you're stumped for a reply. "The father is so fine, so is the mother!"' teased the disciple.

'You should know who she is,' said Gopali. 'On the way to the market from your street, you'll find a grimy sign with the inscription Somesa Iyer, High Court Lawyer. The carts of some of his clients would be parked there, unyoked. But this one here doesn't demand any fees for talking, and is forever ready to give her very life for music.'

'What he's implying is that I'll learn music only after I give up my life!' said the disciple, getting up.

'What?'

'It's getting late. I'll come tomorrow,' she said.

'I think I interrupted the session,' I said.

'Good lord, now don't you slip out too!' said Gopali, pressing my knees with his hands. His ring, an emerald set with diamonds, pressed into my knee cap.

'He went to get coffee. Has he gone to buy a cow or something? He takes his own time about it. Please, can you find out?'

'That's also why I got up,' said the lady. She crossed the open terrace and went down.

'I remember that incident very well,' said Gopali. 'It was sacrilege to abandon a concert just because I got angry at some backchat. I couldn't get any sleep that night. Why this arrogance and ego when you're singing for God? Does it matter if someone listened or didn't? It was two in the night. I got up, went over to Kandu's house and knocked on the door. "Who is it?" he asked through the window. "It's me," I said. He hurried to open the door. I fell prostrate at his feet. "I'm going to do a kacheri in the morning, if you will kindly permit me." "Is that why..." Kandu started saying something politely. "I've already disturbed your sleep. We'll talk about it tomorrow," I said, and came away. The next morning, after an early bath, I prayed: Lord Krishna, annihilate me, and then settled down to sing. That day I sang *Devagandhari* and *Mohanam*. Did *I* sing? No. The ragas unfolded on their own. They trampled over me and sang on by themselves. Otherwise, which man can sing like that? Can *this* man sing? In the courtyard, passage, backyard, veranda and kitchen, there were heads everywhere. I had to close my eyes from time to time. It was mid-day. But there was no fatigue, no exhaustion.

'Aha! Aha!' cried the entire crowd deliriously as one that day. After Devagandhari, Gopu played the violin. And how he played! He just squeezed out the song from the violin, made it weep. "Gopali, you are the very incarnation of Gopala. I cannot play anymore. Please do not embarrass me," he said, wiping his eyes with his gold-bordered *angavastram.* What he said was true. It was indeed Gopala who sang.'

Could it be Lord Gopala who was speaking even now? I thought I too had found a refuge, in becoming one with that annihilation.

The next moment, I felt as if a spirit from a closed, inapproachable universe had stepped out, to admit me inside, and to reveal all its secrets to me. Once I dreamt that Lenin and Dostoevsky visited our house, dined with us and then stayed on for a chat with me in the backyard veranda. Even Nehru had come in my dreams once. He had talked, sitting on an aqueduct in a street lined with coconut trees on the way to the fields. All those were dreams. What I am experiencing right now is with my waking eyes, my ears, my body. This, after all, is my very first encounter. For him to touch me, make me sit down with him like this as if we have an ancient relationship, and then to open himself up to me—who am I?

'After that day, I have never been able to lose myself like that,' said Gopali.

I reached for his hands and pressed them in mine.

Perhaps ten minutes passed. He was looking at me. Then he stood up. He gently pulled me to him and made me stand up, his touch firm yet soft. We walked towards the door. My body felt sheathed in his hands. They slid down my back, straying, pressing against my skin. My eyes felt moist. Dry lips moistened, spreading the pungent smell of cardamom.

I struggled for breath. My chest ached. Extricating myself from his arms, I escaped to the open terrace and stood there. Out beyond the backyard, the Kaveri flowed. Limpid green waters. Clumps of hyacinth stalks and flowers. A banana grove. The new bridge to the west, and the old bridge to the east. It was winter. On the opposite bank, beyond the spread of hyacinths, smoke curled up from huts. The sound of beetles vibrated the air. Two boys swam noisily in the river, shouting at each other, shaking their thick wet hair. I saw their white teeth.

Gopali came out of the room, looked down the stairs and shouted, 'Are we getting coffee or not? Silu! Kunjali!'

Coming towards me, he muttered, 'Dumb idiots, so sluggish! Kundalam had that rare briskness.'

I turned to look at him.

'Kundalam has your looks, though she is a little shorter. How old are you?'

'Getting to be twenty.'

'Kundalam is twenty-two. One never comes to know that she's working, but anything you ask her for gets done in a minute. When she cooks, there's no mess, no clang of ladles. In fact one hardly knows that she's cooking. It's said that a clever woman gives birth to a daughter first. That way, my wife is clever. Only I'm the fool here. To get my daughter married, and then wait forever on the open terrace, letting my visitors vainly hope that coffee will come!'

He went near the stairs again and shouted 'Kunjali!'

Some sound came from below in reply.

'Is it coming? When?'

Gopali has a daughter who is married and is now with her husband?

'If you ask me, I'll reverse the saying: the clever one begets a girl as the last child. One should have a daughter in one's fortieth year, so that she stays on till one is sixty. Having a daughter when I was twenty-five, I have to keep shouting like this, for a sip of coffee.'

'Here Anna, here's coffee.' The betel-nut boy came, holding a silver jug covered with a cloth. He placed a pair of tumblers on the swing and started cooling the coffee.

Forty-seven years? I did a mental calculation.

'Do you sing?' asked Gopali.

'Why should I?'

'Then how will you get married?'

I curled my lips and made a face at him.

'Unless you ruin at least two compositions of Tyagaraja, how can you qualify for marriage? Or you should at least learn a *thai-thai* from a dance master and prance all over the stage in a theatre or two. Else, how can you face the ritual *saptapadi*?'

'I'm not an officer's daughter. And besides, if I knew how to sing or dance, I would never have come here. I would have myself danced for my Periappa's daughter's marriage.'

'Periappa's daughter's marriage?'

'Yes. That's what I am here for.'

'Why?'

'My Periappa is a great soul, but he earns only two hundred rupees a month. It's just a small-scale wedding. I wanted you to come and sing. I told Periappa. He was shocked. Gopali is a top artiste, on a very high pedestal, he said. He'll only sneer at us and say, "You want *me* to do a concert, for *you*?" I will lose face, Periappa said.'

'So you promised to persuade me and told him that you'll drag me along? When is the wedding?'

'In the month of *Chithirai*.'

'Kittani, go down and get the diary.'

Kittani shot out like a field sparrow, his sweaty feet squeaking on the floor.

'Which day of Chithirai?' asked Gopali.

'That hasn't been decided yet.'

'So whichever date it is, I'll have to come and sing?'

'We'll keep a date when you don't have a kacheri.'

'Don't talk so glibly. They won't keep the wedding on a Saturday or Tuesday just for my sake. Will your Periappa pay me? Not for the kacheri. But at least the fare for an ox cart from this street?'

Finishing the coffee in quick gulps, I reached out for his hands and clasped them. This time it was I who hugged him. Periappa is a touch-me-not. Even if a finger brushes against his, his whole body recoils. The food that I ate in his house all these years, Periamma's laughter, the faces of her children—I wanted to bury the weight of all these in this body that I held.

'The diary will come any moment,' said Gopali.

I detached myself.

'Wedding in Chithirai. Your examinations will also get over by then. I suppose you'll go home.'

The diary came. 'Make a note of it, Kittani, there's a wedding in her house in Chithirai. Just put this down generally. The other engagements will give way to her day.'

'What address shall I write, Anna?'

'Just write, I say! Put it down as the wedding in Periappa's House. I can't write. I can read, though.'

'I know.'

'What do you know?'

'Once at a kacheri at home, you received a note asking you to sing a particular number. You looked at it, creased your brow and, claiming long sight, passed it on to the violinist, asking him to read it aloud,' I said.

'I can read printed matter. Handwriting is all loops and hooks, you see, so I can't make it out...Have you noted it down?'

'I have, Anna.'

'Right. Then go and keep the diary.'

Kittani went down.

'Satisfied?'

I didn't reply. Didn't shake my head. Just looked at him. Then a brief dialogue took place in my mind, in whispers.

'Who is that woman downstairs, combing her hair?'

'That is her. Who did you think it was?'

'But she can't be your wife?'

'I started giving performances from my sixteenth year. Even before I had done my tenth kacheri, I received a lot of adulation from people. "Here's a lad, a prodigy!" they said. Young people surrounded me saying, "This is what style is all about!" My father got worried. A big man came forward, offering his daughter to me in marriage. She was decked and displayed in diamonds and gold. That settled it. Is she really as ugly as you think?'

'Not ugly. Her figure and limbs are quite all right. Only the face...couldn't it be a bit more pleasant? A face usually turns ugly in anger or it blooms in joy. But with her face one can never

tell if she is happy or in sorrow or in pain, or just weary and exhausted. There's such a perpetual animal grin or scowl on it!'

'How does it matter what the face is like? The body is taut! There's little difference between people below the waist.'

'I don't agree. If there's a difference above the waist, there'll certainly be a difference below the waist as well!'

But my last unvoiced words came out of my throat as laughter.

'Are you laughing wondering how I learnt all these *kriti*s when I can't even read or write?'

'Yes.'

'I quite like the way you lie, with a "Yes". When I see someone swallow a mountain and then look perfectly innocent, as if she's merely sipped water, I like it...Why did you laugh?'

'Oh, it's nothing. I'll tell Periappa that you have consented. He'll not sleep for four days out of sheer happiness.'

'I'll take the blame for that. But you're slipping away without telling me why you laughed.'

'I'll tell you another day.'

'Why be so shy about it? When will you tell me?'

'Can we put it on the invitation card, that you'll be singing?'

'Certainly. Also write a letter that you are happy I agreed. Supposing I don't turn up, you'll need an affidavit, won't you?'

'All right. May I go now?'

'When do we meet again? What'll you do after your B.A.?'

'I wish to study further. For that I would have to go to Madras, Tiruchirapalli or Chidambaram. But where will I find the money for my stay and my food? I don't know what Periappa will say. If I can't study, I'll look for a job. Why worry about it now.'

'That's what I was about to say.'

'But I don't worry. I've left behind all that in Annavasal. Every year when my Patti's *shraddham* is due, my mother worries about it three months ahead. She keeps saying "The shraddham is coming" three times a day. Why so much fuss about feeding a couple of brahmins and sprinkling rice and *til* seeds on their heads, I asked. The shraddham is something to worry about, my mother replied. From that day, I have stopped worrying about everything.'

'You have no worries then?'

'No.'

'That you should pass, get a job, get married?'

'I have no worries.'

'Even if something untoward happens, you wouldn't worry?'

'If someone told me that my life will end tonight, I wouldn't worry,' I said with a sweet pout.

'That's enough. I thought you were smart. Go along now, it's getting late,' he said, giving me a gentle push from the back.

I went down the stairs. As I passed the central room, Gopali's wife gave me a stony stare.

'Kunjali, this is the daughter of Natesa Iyer of Annavasal. See, she's so much like Kundalam. Only a hundred times naughtier—she has just now fixed up a kacheri for peanuts!'

To me it looked more like the Kunjali woman was gnashing the peanuts between her teeth. I quickly averted my eyes from her face to her body. I could study her better now that she was standing. An ordinary figure. Fair skin. Suddenly I heard the whispered dialogue bubbling up inside my throat. Going to the backyard on the pretext of cleaning my feet, I let out all the laughter that I had till then contained within myself. Then I opened the door and stepped out into the street. It was, like they say in stories, blind providence. I walked on, philosophically mocking God that even he could make such mistakes. When God proposes, shouldn't we too have our own take on that? I'm not the one to give up.

8

It often happens at concerts at wedding receptions that the musician drones on like an orphan. Everyone listens to everyone and everything else except him. But at the wedding in Periappa's house, no one had eyes and ears for anyone except Gopali. After the first two numbers, Gopali gestured to the tambura and violin accompanists to stop. Looking around, particularly at the women and children, he said, 'I have finished. Now you can name your requests. If I happen to know them, I'll sing them for you.'

There was complete silence, as if no one understood him.

'Come on now...!' he said, encouraging them with a raised hand.

The children looked at one another. The women looked at other women, smiling shyly.

'You too can ask,' Gopali said looking at the women. 'You boys, what would you like me to sing?'

Silence.

Gopali laughed. 'All right. Then I'll start singing some songs that you won't even understand!' he threatened.

'*Kanne Pappa*...' a little girl piped up, smiling.

'That's the way to ask!' Gopali said, delighted, signalling to the instrumentalists with his eyes to get ready. 'Kanne Pappa, Kanne Pappa,' he sang, 'I'll bring candy for you!' It wasn't just his lips that sang. His eyes, head and hands all joined in and sang, and with proper *abhinaya*-like gestures too. The song lasted about ten minutes.

When it ended, all the children promptly sprang up with requests. Gopali did not know one or two of the songs, but he sang almost all the others. The women would not be contained any longer. They frowned at the brats. 'If you keep singing for the children, then when do we get to ask?' protested a cousin of Periamma.

'But I'd asked you first, Amma.'

'*Mamanga Odam*', '*Mangalamma Unjal*', '*Kavadi Chindu*'... and so the requests kept coming, like Draupadi's saree. Every song was sung with the same expressiveness of gestures, the same sparkle of the eyes, the same softness of melody. The women were charmed, delighted. They sat blissfully unaware of their men, unbothered by their presence. Gopali did not ignore the cart drivers and servants either, who had come all the way from Annavasal and stood huddled in a corner.

It was hardly like the usual music concert. It was as if the adults had found an excuse in the bride and groom to indulge in their own revelry. The boisterous audience vibrated with sounds of laughter and applause, and lapsed into an enraptured silence each time that Gopali sang. When a song ended, a river of voices rose, as if some ten windows had been opened onto the street together.

Gopali didn't seem to care much for the men. Only the women and children drew his music, his mind, his eyes, his everything. As it went on, he changed his sitting posture to an angle that gave him a vantage view of the women and children. There was weariness in the eyes of the men, an annoyance that they hid with effort. One stood up, smiled vaguely and went out. Only Periappa, the Chettiar of the shop, the shop assistants, servants from Annavasal, four cooks, men past their middle age and the old men were enjoying the music and laughing along heartily. Chettiar was even beating out the *tala.*

The fun had begun at six in the evening. It was now eleven. Gopali looked at his watch. 'Aren't you hungry?' he said, looking at the crowd.

'How can there be any hunger when there is music?' said a woman's voice from the audience.

Flourishing his index finger enthusiastically as if to say 'Indeed!' Chettiar kept nodding like a doll for a few seconds.

'Very true. But what about the children?' Gopali asked.

There was a small din. And then Gopali sang his concluding song, about the hunter woman's message to the deity Kanda.

After dinner, Gopali chatted with the family for a while. Out of deference, the accompanists who played the violin and the *mridangam* sat a little away from him. They kept looking at him now and again, as if to say, after all, he is Gopali; he can do as he pleases; who are we to comment, much less, understand. The children were gathered around him. The women sat a little apart, talking to him and amongst themselves.

'I've never heard a kacheri like this before,' said Periamma.

'I've never rendered one like this either,' said Gopali. 'I wonder if I ever will...Only if you celebrate another marriage and invite me! You will call me, won't you? This is how a kacheri must be done. This is the only way. But who does it? Can one sing like this if a concert is organised like some kind of a contest?'

Gopali finally rose to leave only around one at night. Receiving the silk dhoti and gold-laced *angavastram* presented by Periappa, he gave them away to the groom with betel leaves and betel nuts, with an apology to Periappa. He kept his word and took his fare of three rupees for the ox cart, giving a rupee each to the violin and mridangam men, and got into the cart. Two bigwigs who had come from Annavasal fussed over him, offering him a lift in their cars. 'The only transport I wanted today is a cart,' said Gopali as he got into the cart and placed the metal rod inside its hook.

Periamma and I were the last to retire. Halfway up the stairs, Periamma hugged me tightly and said, 'All this was only because of you, darling.'

In the big building hired for the kacheri, the guests slept on a huge carpet spread in the hall upstairs. Some were breathing hard, others breathing softly. Finding a corner for myself, I lay down amidst a profusion of bodies, knees, feet and crushed jasmines.

I closed my eyes. I thought of Gopali, the children, the women. The famous musician who sat in kacheris, always aloof and arrogant, was today like a child amongst children, a woman amongst women, losing himself in their play. Like Krishna with his *gopis* and goatherds. The men in Vrindavan barred their wives from meeting Him and locked them up. I thought of Jesus, and how the women and children would swarm around him. 'Die! Die!' said the men who nailed Jesus to the cross. I saw many such faces in today's gathering. Gopali's face—the waves of his hair, the beauty of his brow, his mouth, his physique, the way his body exuded a childlike innocence, the force that drew people to him—I witnessed all this for myself today. The men of Annavasal were like so many sheep caught in brambles, I thought.

Gopali will never do a kacheri like this again. Except when there is another wedding in this house, and he is invited! I could've laughed. Whose marriage...as long as there were surly men of this kind in the world? Who will marry when men locked you up or nailed you to a cross?

Are these the thoughts of my half-awake mind? Children, women, laughter, mirth, music, the cross, the flute, the clang of the metal rod being hooked, the click of the locks, the sound of rivets, the crash of hammers, the open terrace of Gopali's house, the flowing river, the fidgeting body, the surly simian face of a woman gnashing peanuts between her teeth...

Was I half-asleep or half-awake? For the next few days I was in a similar dreamlike state.

Three days after the exertions of the wedding, I went to thank Gopali. The lady disciple was present as before.

'Anna is very sad,' she said.

'What about?'

'There was a concert last night at a temple near Tiruchirapalli. He said it didn't quite turn out like the one at your Periappa's daughter's wedding,' she said. She had also attended the wedding.

'I didn't say that, but she is more or less right,' said Gopali.

'He couldn't get an audience like the one that listened to his virtuosities on the *Kanne Pappa* number!' said the disciple.

I asked her if she was being serious or sardonic.

'I'm not being sardonic. I just spoke my mind,' she said.

I wasn't quite sure. I said, 'I couldn't sleep that night. Everyone, every single servant was bursting with joy and gratitude that he sang whatever they requested him to. And they remained ecstatic for the next two days.'

'Yes. I too felt so and I thought, was this a new *avataram*? I even told my husband. He had come for the marriage ceremony in the morning, but left soon after. He didn't come for the kacheri because he was expecting a litigant. I told him about it. He enjoyed it immensely and said, "Who else has such generosity and courage? Such a pity I missed it" The man is so perceptive,' she said.

'Aha, what wifely devotion! I'll tell him that you said so! I'll also tell the judge,' teased Gopali.

I glared at him.

'Are you in her camp now?' he asked me.

'I say something with good intentions, and you spoil it all with such remarks,' said the disciple, looking offended.

'Oh, I'm sorry. What did you think? What was your opinion about the kacheri? After all, you're a B.A.'

'One doesn't have to be a B.A. for this. That night I was thinking about Krishna and Jesus Christ.'

'Is that so? Then you could consecrate a temple or a church for me. Krishna lived with ten thousand wives. Fearing that every youth will take after him, the priests built a temple for him. "He is an avataram, a free spirit, but don't *you* go about philandering!" they said, and kept you, me and others outside the temple. Now if someone asks me who I am, my answer will be: He is a strange character. Don't let him in! Make him sit in a pandal, let him sing, pay his fees and send him off! Isn't that so, you lawyer's wife?'

'Things are not so bad now,' said the lady disciple, making peace.

'Bad or sad, things will always be like this. Is there an escape? Amma belongs to Appa. Appa belongs to Amma. Someswara Iyer belongs to you, and you belong to him. Kunjali belongs to me, and I belong to her. The man who belongs to Ammani...Oh, I see you're still single.'

I pouted and made my usual face.

'Gorging yourself on comforts and pleasure is not the right thing to do. Savour everything drop by drop on the tip of your tongue. But the lawyer's wife in you will contradict this. It was Krishna who discoursed on the *Gita*. Not Rama. Because Krishna, who emptied pots and pots of food and butter, was characterised as an ascetic. Then in great haste, Rama was created. If saint Tyagaraja hears me, he will crush me. I'm making a living by singing his songs. Now this Kittani has stayed back in Thanjavur because his father is ill. Can you please get some coffee for Madam Ammani?' said Gopali.

The lady rose to her feet and went down.

'Didn't you tell me that you can't read properly?' I said.

'What's this suddenly?'

'A mockery creeps into your tone as soon as I begin to say something.'

'What if I don't read? I'm also a derelict like Krishna. And that's why I feel Krishna is the right one for me. Can't comprehend Rama. Who needs a big education for all this? It was you who started talking about Krishna. Adding on to what you said, I developed the *alapana* and *pallavi*, and ended up here. Some skill!'

'You nearly looked for a match, for Ammani!'

'You're talking like Kunjali!'

I couldn't understand how I reacted to that—with anger, pity, or was it just indifference? Suddenly I went limp from within and without. Gopali gathered me into his arms, crushing time itself with his hands, his lips, his body.

Even within this burial, I couldn't help thinking about Periappa, Periamma, Amma and Appa.

'I don't need anything,' he whispered in my ears. 'You don't have to go and stand on the open terrace,' he said.

Without asking why, I looked up.

'The house in Madras doesn't have a terrace. There is no Kaveri there, no river bank on the opposite side. Only the compound wall and the road. I've bought this house in Madras. Every musician has settled down there. What can I do here all by myself? I'm not a Tyagaraja or a Purandaradasa, with a bowl slung over my shoulder, eating whatever I get as alms,' said Gopali, and sat down on the swing.

'Come and sit here. I've bought a house in New Mambalam. It has an upper storey. You can stay in it and study. Or you can learn music from the master of Someswara Iyer's wife. Gopali's life and living is music. If you say you want neither and want to stay on in Periappa's house...'

I closed Gopali's mouth with my hand.

'I will tell Periappa myself. That I will see you through your education.'

'I can't sing.'

'I haven't heard you sing!'

'I think I can learn.'

The stay at the hostel did not last very long, what with the daily commute between Tiruvallikeni and Gopali's house. The music lessons started when my studies were completed. Then the drama began.

A long street that branched off from Pondy Bazar road and turned left. A house with a compound wall. Living accommodation on the first floor. A large hall after you climbed up the stairs from the front. Two rooms on either side overlooking the front and windows on three sides of each room. Leafy clumps of a jackfruit tree and a neem tree brushed the window of the left room. A *sapota* and a mango tree reached up to the balcony and the window on the right. Sunlight scattered in dots like the hide of a dappled deer. At other times, it growled like the hide of a leopard.

9

Except at mid-day, sunlight stayed in this room morning, evening, forenoon and afternoon. The scene wheeled in discs of gold maturing into silver, vanishing, only to reappear in silver circles. Then again they would temper into a tender gold and fade away. I was confident that the circles that faded and vanished would appear as certainly as the next day.

I watched the circles of light and counted them obsessively. I had a belief that new rays of sunlight appeared and that new circles spilled over the room when I wasn't looking. There were ellipses, full circles and irregular blotches resembling small leaves. There were circles like cheeks that were pulled. And circles that were reduced to half, as if someone had pressed them.

By a day's reckoning, the circles in this room equalled the number of men who were sleepless after sunset, sleepless even after the noises of day had slept off in the night. I counted forty-four. When the leaves at the window swayed, two silver circles pushed the shade to the centre and merged into a longish circle. After a while it divided, one circle uniting into a second one on another side—an absorbing sight. A third circle waited to pluck out one circle from the union and absorb it within itself. Waiting in the room like this, ever watchful and wild, all spread out, I wondered did they take after me? Or was it I who learnt from them? A needle of sunlight pierced my eyes through the leaves.

In the afternoons I would observe the direction from which the circles appeared. One day, the passion of Kunti Devi possessed me and completely took hold of me. Though there was no open terrace in this house, there was an open space, enough for two people to sleep. It was meant for washing one's feet and hands. Walking up to it briskly, I sat down. Spreading the pallav of my saree, I lay down on my back. As if Karna himself was forming within me, solid and firm as a banyan seed, my cheeks, neck, chin, thighs, stomach, everything stiffened and went limp. I swelled with a vast desire that leapt over the sky, that if anything happened it should come from the sun, and that the fruit of it should be Karna.

The doorbell rang. It was discordant with the chatter of the birds that was in harmony with the sunlight. I didn't feel like getting up. I squinted at the sun, perspiration pouring down my back to my ankles. Still I kept lying there, watching the red sky and the sun that waltzed around a black dot. The bell rang again...and yet again...

I rose slowly and called out in vexation through the iron grill in the front veranda: 'Who is it?'

An outline materialised, the figure stepped back and looked up. It was Gopali. I went down and opened the door. Standing near me on the stairs, he looked at me from head to toe. I climbed up ahead of him, laughing. He came into the hall, his eyes going all over me again. Then going to the space at the rear, as if he wanted to wash his feet, he quickly looked down the back stairs.

'Satisfied? Got over your suspicion?' I asked.

He touched my hands, looked at the beads of perspiration. Looked at my warm damp body.

'Where were you?' he asked.

'That is no answer to my question.'

'What?'

'Why should you hide your annoyance and look at me that way?'

'Now who is suspicious, me or you?'

'Then why did you go there and look as soon as you came in?'

'Now you'll say I was looking under the bed!'

'I won't, but you might as well have.'

ଓ

That happened six months after I moved into this house.

Higher studies at college during the day, music lessons at Tiruvallikkeni in the evenings. For that I had to come to Mambalam every day. With so much of commuting to and fro, my studies got disturbed. I didn't know which was more important, music or my studies. I also didn't know why I was studying.

The music class lasted for an hour or two in the evening, at Gopali's house. For about four or five months, I used to sing after him, repeating what he sang. I was merely experimenting.

One day, he abruptly interrupted my singing and said, 'There are two ways of teaching music. One is your present way of learning, the *bhajanai* way. That is, I sing, and you follow. The other way is for me to sing and for you to listen with full concentration, to listen with your mind and ears and eyes. Then you sing a little, I correct you. Later, you go to your room and sing aloud. You also sing with your mind. Which would you like?'

'The second way.'

'You are a wise one. I knew you would say so.'

I laughed.

From the following day, Gopali sang by himself. Selecting a raga, he sang for about an hour, pointing out the notes. I have heard it said that Gopali is like an ocean that rises and swells up at the sight of people. Before an audience of four or five thousand, he swells up like the sea. But in a gathering of a hundred or two hundred people, particularly if there were ministers and officials, businessmen and retailers who own shops sitting in the front rows, he would go into regular labour pains. Otherwise, when he looked at a big crowd, anonymous and classless, he closed his eyes in a gesture of profound reverence.

Even I in my singleness seemed to be transformed into a large faceless audience for him. He rose like an ocean that swelled and performed for the people. Closing his eyes in ecstasy, forgetting himself, forgetting this one-woman audience, he would be transported elsewhere—remote and replete in his solitude, oblivious of my presence. In between, that is, after finishing an *avartana*, he would open his eyes briefly and look. For a few moments or for one long minute. In that look, there was a monumental gratitude.

Gratitude directed at whom? One couldn't say.

Sometimes I would appropriate it for myself. But a contrary thought, that Gopali was no small fry, would hit me hard on the head. Returning to my room, I would look at myself in the mirror. It would contain two faces.

I was beautiful, of course. I knew for certain that Gopali was aroused by my sensitivity, my fun-loving nature, by the answering ecstasy that danced in my eyes when he sang, all of which drove him on. Yet, beyond all that gratitude, there was also a wistful longing that I could understand.

One evening on the Tiruvallikkeni beach, when my first summer vacation was about to end, Gopali said, 'I can't wait anymore. Enough of your M.A. studies. What are you going to achieve by studying?'

'I don't know.'

'Do you plan to get a job?'

'I've no idea at all. I'm being taught, so I study. I'm being taught music, so I sing.'

'I hope you won't get angry?'

'About what?'

'You're not made for concerts.'

'But I never thought I was.'

'You can learn how to dance. Probably excel in it too. The professionals who've been dancing for generations think that only they know how to dance. They believe that the ones who marry a man, cook for him and bear his children can't move their eyes, let alone do an abhinaya. Sheer vanity! "What do *your* women know of dance?" Sarada would remark. "They can only fix a butter-milk stew. When you give away your daughter, they'll stand beside you and receive holy water in their hand." She is so conceited! I have a wish to present you before her. That'll hit her on the head. If she accepts you as a brahmin dasi, it would be worth a hundred M.As.'

I could've laughed loud enough to startle those who were out on the street. But in the noise of the waves, my laughter would have run away like a *chittira kullan*.

'Are you angry?'

I laughed.

'It is difficult to interpret your laughter. Is it out of anger, happiness, approval or disapproval, sarcasm or candour. It is impossible to know.'

'Go on.'

'I'm going to select a house for you. A flat on the first floor. Come and see it. I haven't given the down payment yet. If you like, you could move in there. If you can commute for your classes from Mambalam every day, go ahead and study. If not...'

'Become a brahmin dasi!'

'Yes. If you go to some big Chettiar houses in the George Town area, and ask if the Chettiar is in, his wife will come out and blithely announce that he has gone to his mistress! Let Kunjali say the same thing, but with more dignity.'

I was in truth not really upset. That was how Gopali talked. But what I saw was the rhapsodic countenance that sang, with me sitting in front as his disciple.

Perhaps I was impatient too.

The house was fixed up in two weeks, and Gopali moved me into it. A room at the rear of the top floor for the servant, who'd await my bidding and do the house work. I was my own cook. My approval of the house was mainly because of this room. That day, late in the afternoon—it must've been four—the sun and shade were scattered in dots like the spread hide of a dappled deer. I stood in the centre of the hall and looked around. At the rear and front of the room, blue and green panes were fitted alternately on the windows. I peered through the tinted glass at the coconut fronds, the leaves of the mango tree at the back and the branches. They captivated me like some primordial memory.

'If I see a place like this in my dreams, I won't open my eyes,' I said. I went to the front rooms on either side again to look, my eyes lingering on the sunlight patterned like the skin of a spotted deer. I voiced my thoughts.

'For rishis who live alone in retreat, the deer skin is the refuge,' said Gopali.

There was furniture even before I moved in. Two beds, a dressing table with a life-size mirror, in the hall four mats spread wall to wall, a few mattresses, a big water container, cooking utensils, boiler, table lamps, bedside lamps. Everything was already in place on the day I moved in. Velayya came the same evening to begin his dance lessons and to beat out the steps with the wooden sticks.

My meal came from the hotel. Gopali joined me and did not go home. The scent of *javvadhu* rose from all over his body.

'If Kunjali Mami were to be asked for the Chettiar, I mean the music master, what answer would she give?' I asked.

'Let the servant go to sleep,' was the soft reply.

'What are you scared of? When Mami can say so, why can't you?'

The servant fell asleep. His shrill snores came through the fastened door and reached me through the window. I didn't sleep. Gopali didn't either. The cricket on the wall didn't sleep. The white clouds didn't sleep. The leaves of the tree didn't sleep.

The tree went to sleep after midnight. The crickets were silent. When the tree slept, Gopali also went to sleep, lying on his back exhausted.

I didn't sleep. I was wide awake in a kind of stiff wakefulness. I turned around to look. The fragrance of javvadhu wafted from the sleeping body. Gopali has a daughter two years older than I. Also a son. It was an early marriage. The scent of his javvadhu told me all that, and it tickled me.

When tickled, you laugh, just for the sake of it. But actually, you're vexed.

It was past midnight. There was a dull moon. An oppressiveness in the breeze. It was the sea breeze of the afternoon returning to the sea, leaving behind a residual oppressiveness.

Discarding my saree in the washroom, I drew mug after mug of water from the *anda* and poured it over myself. Having emptied the anda of all the water, I dried my hair with a towel and changed into another saree. The breeze felt a little less oppressive now. I stood in front of the mirror and tied the ends of my hair into a knot.

I had a sudden urge to say a prayer.

I have never prayed. I gave it up in school. In college, the egalitarian fraternity that accompanied me to the slums used to harangue us on the purpose and manner of prayer. The poor are the only gods, they said, the common people the only deities. At fifteen, the invocation to Pillaiyar, the *Soundarya Lahiri*, the *Tiruppavai*, the hundred Kanchi hymns sung to Devi Kamakshi that made the mute speak up, all the gods who variously rode the bull, the mouse, the peacock, the Garuda, the lion, the lotus, all the gods who tenanted with Periamma—I made a bonfire of them all and fed them to the flames of the poor people's hunger. In their place floated the smell of burnt wood and smoke.

I came back to the front room. The odour of Gopali's thirty years of marriage blended with the scent of javvadhu.

The municipal trucks dredged soil and garbage from dried-up ponds and lakes and made a thousand trips to tipple the loads in front of residential areas. Day in and day out, the rubbish piled up, giving off a miasmic, repulsive odour.

Gopali came once in three days. He would sing. He would come around the same time as Velayya in the evenings and stay through the dance lessons. He would open the bottle and drink whisky. Eat dinner, sing and play around with me and fall asleep. I would stay awake, bathe, and remember the smell of dry pine in the prayers of Periamma. Sleep eluded me. This amnesia has come to stay. Angry, I would sit up and watch the sleeping Gopali. It surprised me that I didn't hate him.

After tuning up the *shruti* one day, why did he forget to play, I wondered. I've been to so many concerts with Gopali. I've seen musicians who wouldn't even let their students carry their instrumental cases or a stranger touch their flute, much less play it. But I haven't seen anyone tune up the shruti and then forget to play! It was funny.

Six months passed.

Unable to sleep, I was lying in the sun one afternoon, as if to give birth to Karna, as if I was embracing the Sun God. When Gopali came and pressed the doorbell, I didn't get up. What I felt, lying there in the full glare of the sun, was neither laughter nor hatred. A firm obstinacy took hold of me. Let me see what you do.

10

Obstinacy was not part of my nature, though it had now begun to grow like a banyan sapling rising from a chance seed that had lodged itself in a sparrow's dropping from a crevice in the wall. It must've been Periamma who planted it.

When I failed to write to her twice a month, Periamma felt that the ground under her feet collapsed, and that she was suspended mid-air. Periappa and Periamma spent their good money to make two trips, to visit me here. I too went home and stayed with them for my Christmas and summer vacation. During summer vacation, I stayed there only for ten days and rushed back, so I don't miss my music lessons. I thought Gopali had spoken that way because he couldn't bear our separation even for ten days.

After moving in here, I waited for a month and then wrote to Periamma.

Dear Periamma,

My namaskaram and regards. I've now moved into another house. Please visit me once. It's enough if you come alone. There's absolutely no need for Periappa to come right now. In your reply please let me know the train you will be travelling in. I'll receive you at the Mambalam Station.

I felt a mild tightening of the chest when I posted the letter, as if my heart was squeezed and had squirted out all its fluids and then hardened into stone. Periamma had helped me renounce Amma and Appa. I had cut off both of them with a pair of new scissors as it were. From then on, Periamma and Periappa became everything to me.

Instead of a letter, I got a telegram in reply: *Periamma leaving tonight by Fast Passenger. Meet her at Mambalam Station. Periappa.*

In Madras, as soon as one got up in the morning, there was this peculiar humidity. This is the only reason that made me dislike it. What a city! Deep-frying her citizens as soon as they woke up in the morning! Or was it perhaps the stuffiness in my heart that surrounds me with this damp air and a stifling humidity?

Even before she alighted from the train, Periamma called out, 'Here I am, my child!' The train was still slowly coming to a halt when I heard her voice ring out, as if offering an *abhayam*. I turned around—there she was, looking out of her window and smiling. In three long strides, I was there before her.

She got off and, looking me up and down, asked, 'Have you come alone?'

'Who else will come with me?'

'What's the matter? When I saw your letter, I was confused for a moment and just slumped down on the wooden bench. Couldn't get on with cooking either. My stomach felt queasy. I prepared *rasam*, offered it as *naivedyam*, and straightaway made for the shop. I called Periappa aside and showed him the letter. He was nearly in tears. "All right, you better leave tonight. I'll send her a wire," he said. All through the way I thought, Oh God, Oh God...What has happened, dear girl?'

'Nothing, Amma, don't panic. Let's go home first.'

'Did you say *nothing*? Oh, do say that again!'

We got into a rickshaw and reached home. Climbed the stairs to the top floor and went in. I opened the back door, called the servant and sent him to the market. I also directed him to go to Gopali's house and report Periamma's arrival. He would take an hour to return.

While I made coffee, Periamma was looking around the house. She stood in front of the twin beds and the life-sized mirror. Stood in front of the dressing table attached to it. Opened the wardrobe and looked at the silk sarees suspended on hangers. Opened the lids of everything kept on the dressing table—the vials of sandalwood essence, the musk, the lipstick, the rouge, face powder, face cream—opened the jars and tubes and sniffed at the contents.

I placed the coffee tumblers, the coffee, biscuits and *burfi*s in the central hall and called Periamma. Even from the corner of my eyes, I could see that she was bewildered and puzzled.

'Coffee, Periamma.'

'It's a lovely house,' she said, sitting down.

'Do you know Gopali's story about all this, Periamma? He tells everyone that I'm his adopted daughter.'

'What do you mean by "his story"?'

'One can be born to only one person, and one can be an adopted child to only one person. Come on, have your coffee.'

I didn't continue till she had eaten a burfi, some biscuits and had coffee. If I'd told her beforehand, it would have nauseated her. Periamma finished her coffee and kept the tumbler down. I began my circumvention.

'One can be born to only one person. It was Balarama who grew in the womb of two women. The story goes that he was in Devaki's womb for about seven months. Then God extracted the foetus and transplanted it in the womb of Rohini, the first wife of Vasudeva, who was living in Gokulam under the protection of Nandan. How is all this possible for ordinary mortals?'

'But you used to deny both God and the devil.'

'That's what I'm saying. I'm an adopted daughter to you and Periappa. How can I be the same to Gopali? He goes about declaring morning, noon and night that I'm his adopted daughter! He gets his wisdom only after it is dark.'

'That you're *not* his adopted daughter?'

'Yes.'

'Is that wisdom?'

'It's the truth.'

'Can truth be the same as wisdom?'

'Wisdom lies in realising the truth.'

'May he be burnt to cinders!'

'Burn me too along with him.'

'What are you blabbering?'

'He has set me up like this and thrown dust in your eyes, knowing very well that I like living like this. I too have been deceiving both of you. It's only for this reason that he sang at the wedding concert in our house. Remember, you hugged me on the stairs and said, "All this happened only because of you...?" At that time, I didn't want to tell you and upset you. The plan is as old as that.'

Periamma stared at me for some time. It was like how Amma would look. Her eyes pierced me and went on pricking me like a splinter.

'Thank God you had the good sense to write that Periappa needn't come.'

Silence.

'You don't seem to be the least bit troubled.'

'I am, Periamma, every now and then. I made up my mind very early in my life. Ever since I saw the shaven head of Kandu's daughter. Ever since Kandu sent a letter to his disciple through Appa, saying that he doesn't ever want to see his face again and snubbed him in the middle of a street. I hardened my mind. I knew there is no meaning in marriage and all that sham in the name of respectability. What's the great bliss you got by marrying Periappa? What bliss did Amma get by marrying Appa? Marriage is like a thief tied to a pillar—a woman with a man-pillar, or a man with a woman-pillar—what did anyone ever get out of it? Even if you bind a thief, the fact is he has stolen, isn't it? Where's the certainty that he won't steal again? I don't wish to steal, but I wish to live on my own terms. I wish to be independent. All of us are born to be happy. Gopali is there for me. If I don't want Gopali, there will be someone else.'

'Those who talk like this should live in an isolated street so that they don't become an eyesore to anyone.'

'I live in a separate house. I've actually been alone here for a month now. I've always been alone. I don't wish to live with anybody. I have myself, my body, my mind and my *atma*.'

'So you do know that you have an atma?'

'Whatever it is, Periamma, I am happy. I'll keep smiling. I have my thoughts. When alone, the mind understands everything, one by one.'

'You've gone crazy, my child, blabbering on like this. Nothing that you say strikes me as true. Rest your mind for a while. Let bygones be bygones, and come back with me. Right now, the town is not yet reeking of the scandal. I am telling you, just come away with me. If you get married, all your troubles will be cured. You're deeply disturbed because your Appa and Amma let you down. You are troubled because you wonder whether Periappa and I, who have brought you up, will also turn out to be the same as your Appa and Amma. That's why you're tormenting yourself like this. Let me tell you, Ammani, my own children are not as important to me as you are. I hold you far above them. My body thrills to see you as if you are my own flesh. I have never been indifferent to you even for a day. Even for a moment. I cannot be. Sometimes I feel you are my very own daughter. There've been so many nights when I've thought that our friendship goes back a thousand years and that we've bonded birth after birth. How can I bear to see you suffer like this, my child?'

'It is you who say that I suffer.'

'When I look at you, I'm unable to think otherwise. Can looking at this mirror and these beds give you happiness? I cannot believe it, my child.'

'Periamma, don't keep calling me a child. Don't you see the two beds here?'

'For that reason alone, will you cease to be my child?'

'Periamma, listen. You said that such people should live in an isolated street. You can take it that I too have come away like that. If you step into a place like this, your *dharma* and tradition will be different. People who look at us from the other side would be furious. Or they may console themselves that ours is a different world. I can't find any difference between the two. Three-fourths of the people stay on your side, but mentally they live on both sides of the street. The whole trouble starts because there are isolated streets. Just think about it for a moment, Periamma.'

I don't know what she was thinking. Silent tears flowed down her cheeks, falling on her lap. Hanging from her chin. She didn't even wipe them with the end of her saree immediately. I remained silent. It must've been a familiar sight to me. Like the day her daughter went to her husband's house last year. And today...

I remembered all kinds of things. Once Periamma had taken me to a place near Tiruchi. A sanyasi of a *mutt* there had chosen a junior guru to be his successor. I believe it was a small mutt to which Periappa's family was devoted. The old sanyasi had chosen a boy of ten for grooming. The boy had lustrous looks. A flower-soft skin that spoke of his tender age. They shaved his head, asked him to bathe in the pond and stand on the steps of the pond, with water lapping at his feet. Then the old sanyasi gave him saffron clothes, a staff and gave him the *deeksha*. The sight made me weep. From then on, the boy couldn't go home. Couldn't see his father and mother. Couldn't attend school. Couldn't play. Must eat only what the old man gave him. Must bathe three or four times a day. Couldn't go to the movies or plays. Couldn't walk on the street. Couldn't visit a shop. Couldn't carry money or buy himself candy or chocolates to eat. Couldn't even touch money. More than all this, the way the boy lost his hair, his white dhoti and shorts, his childhood just shook me up.

Periamma pulled herself together. When the boy climbed on to the bank, she ignored his tender years and prostrated before him on the muddy street. I too prostrated. 'That's the boy's mother,' she said, pointing to a lady standing in a corner of the street. Periamma prostrated before her, tears pouring down her face. I too prostrated.

Perhaps it is the same kind of tears that I see now in Periamma's eyes. The tears of parents who dedicated their daughters to be the brides of Christ, as nuns who joined the convent. The more she wept, the more my mind hardened. All these lamentations are beyond the wall now, on the other side of the river. I have come over to this side. These tears belong to another era. I don't wish to dampen my body in them or expose my mind to them. Even her protracted tears can't touch me now.

I pushed aside propriety and said gently and decisively, 'What do parents say of a girl who has run away? That "She wasn't born to me". Or that "She is dead for us". Take it the same way, Periamma. Or think of how that little boy was given saffron clothes, and how it made you weep so much.'

Periamma gave me a blank look for a few minutes. Then she said, 'All right. I'll think of it the same way.'

'And for that reason, please also don't go away without eating,' I said.

'Why should I be angry? I'm going to cook a good meal for the two of us, serve you and eat with you before I leave.'

A proverb rose to the tip of my tongue: 'There's no one who hasn't eaten a worm along with his rice, or who hasn't eaten food served by an adulterous woman.' But I bit my tongue and pushed it back.

Periamma cooked elaborately. She made very tasty *rasam*, *kuzhambu* and other things. She served me and she had her meal. Then she slept soundly in the afternoon. Before we left, she asked, 'Is there a temple in this place?'

I took her to a Shiva-Vishnu temple, and waited outside. It took her ten minutes to come out. Then I took her to Egmore station to board her train. Having got into the train, Periamma said, 'Why don't you carry on? There are still forty-five minutes for departure. Why should you wait?'

After hesitating a bit, I said goodbye to Periamma and left.

11

On the way home in the bus, the breeze blew around as usual. Everything was the same with the people seated opposite—their dhotis, shirts, trousers, sandals, bodies, faces, expressions, everything. Still, everything looked new to me. The breeze, the noise of the bus, the chatter, the aroma of jasmines from a girl's hair—everything looked like it was born anew. Even my body felt new. Madras had become unrecognisably new. From now on, I could think of anything and do anything I wished. Everything—yesterday, today, the morning, the noon, evening, Periappa, Periamma, children, the bank beside the pond, Kandu, Appa, Amma—they all seemed remote already, like dreams from the past.

The next morning, I sent for Gopali and told him all that had happened. 'Last evening, a woman of the older generation in the form of my Periamma took a train and left for good. From now on, this is the place of my birth, the place where I grew up. And from now on, I have no relations either.'

'This man seated like a rock, don't you have him?' said Gopali.

I held his palm and pressed it. I held on to it. I don't know what he felt. He started singing softly in his low, beguiling voice, and went on singing until lunch time. I listened to him while I prepared *vatral kuzhambu* and a dish of vegetables.

He had a bath and put on freshly laundered clothes that I had kept for him here.

'Oh ho!' he said, standing up suddenly as if he'd forgotten something.

'What?'

'Usually, after my bath I stand in front of my shrine and recite *slokas*.'

'So what can we do?'

'Please go ahead and have lunch. If I can, I'll come and eat. Otherwise, I'll come in the evening and eat,' he said and, briskly slipping into his sandals, he walked off in a hurry.

'But I've cooked for the two of us.'

'Keep them in warm water after you've finished eating. I like *vatral kuzhambu*, rice soaked in water, *vadu manga* pickle and all that,' he said, hurrying down the stairs.

He must be hungry. He had been singing for nearly four hours. Even if it was sung in a soft, subdued voice, it was music that fanned the flames.

The doorbell rang at four in the evening. Paying off the rickshaw man, Gopali lifted a parcel and came up. He untied the strings of the parcel. There was a portrait of Tyagaraja, one of Rama and one of Krishna.

'Hey Pachiappa? Where is he? Pachiappa! All right, a hammer. Get a hammer. And get some nails!' he ordered. I could only get a large pebble.

Running to the courtyard at the back, he pulled out the nails from the wall on which the servant's washing line was strung. He hung Tyagaraja's portrait in the middle, flanked by Rama and Krishna. Then he prostrated before his deities on the wall.

'Are you wondering at the smaller size of the gods? That's how it is! The *bhakta* is larger than God. These two boys should be like props to him. That's why I chose a smaller size for them. Rama and Krishna are great for the world. But the greatest one for me is this bard with a brass bowl for alms. You don't have a god, I know. You don't have to look at them. You can put a curtain around them. You said you have no relations at all. That's why I put them up on the wall here. Tyagaraja is a closer relation to me than you are,' he said with a smile. The usual captivating smile. Goodness, what beauty! Then he sat down and sang a couple of compositions.

'Lord Rama, Lord Krishna, just like you live in my house, you must also live in this house always,' he said, and patting his chest he repeated, 'Just like you live here always, you must also live *here*.' Then he stood up. 'I can't stay today. I'll come tomorrow morning, around ten. I will offer some flowers and sing a couple of songs,' he said, and he left.

That night I dreamt of Marx and Lenin who came to Pondy Bazar and confronted Tyagaraja wearing a turban, with the brass bowl for alms in his hand, singing along as he walked. The two men placed a roll of newspaper beneath his legs and made him trip over.

The doorbell rang at nine in the morning. Just when I was getting ready for my bath. Gopali said he would come at ten. I went down and opened the door.

Periappa!

'Please come in, Periappa.'

'Here I am,' he said with an unnatural smile. A smile that neither touched the heart nor made the face pleasant. It was like the dark glow from the smoky glass of a hurricane lamp.

'Come in, Periappa.'

12

Press together some twenty rose petals and pierce them with a needle. How long does it take to pierce one petal? Periappa looked at me just that long, and looked away. That's the full comparison. Not just for that split second, but equally for his eyes. The coolness of rose petals, the anguish, the anger, the cruelty...

Even after coming up the stairs, he didn't look at me. Like Periamma, he looked around the house, at the rooms, the trees, the dressing table. The beds.

'Please be seated Periappa. I'll get some coffee.'

'I've had coffee.'

I called Pachiappa, gave him two rupees, asked him to go to the market, and also made a sign for him to 'go there' and give him the news. Then I went in to make coffee. After all, Periappa has come to talk it over.

'Ammani, come here...I'll have to get going soon,' he said.

'I'll just bring the coffee.'

'But I said I have had coffee. Look here, Ammani, you will come away with me this instant in just this saree and blouse that you're wearing. Whether you secure the house or leave it unlocked is no concern of mine. But you will come with me right this minute, just as you are.'

I stood there with my head bowed, silent.

'Get moving. Didn't you hear me?' It was a command.

'Are you coming or not?'

Silence.

'If you want to stay alive, you will move this instant.'

'But I'm not alive after all, Periappa.'

'What!'

'I told Periamma. I told her that she should consider me dead.'

'Did you tell her only that?'

It was almost as if Periappa had been fitted with a new pair of eyes. Eyes I had never seen before. Until now. It wasn't twenty but just a single rose petal that the needle was insistently pricking. Just a single petal it was tormenting repeatedly.

I was silent.

'Are you going to talk to me the same way that you spoke to Periamma?'

'What more can I say? I have to speak the truth.'

'What did you say? So you're speaking the truth, are you? *The truth?* Are you speaking the truth?' Every 'truth' came closer and closer and resounded in hard slaps on my cheeks. Again. And again. And yet again. On my cheeks. My head. My back. Periappa rained blows, each blow accompanied by the roar of 'The truth? The truth?' He held my hair tightly in his fist and shook my head hard. Bringing his face close to mine, and in a hoarse whisper so it doesn't go past the wall, he growled 'The truth?...The truth?' Baring his teeth set on edge, he made a sound like the lowing of cattle. For some time I could only see the whites of his eyes and his teeth.

I didn't make a sound. I didn't even moan.

He pushed me backwards to the corner of a wall and encircling me within his arms suddenly, he just crushed me. My ribs, chest, shoulder bones, everything bunched up together as if they would crack. I was released from that crushing embrace equally abruptly. He stood back and glowered at me. 'Come now!'

I shook my head silently.

Dhritarashtra in his rage thought he was crushing Bhima, but crushed an iron pillar instead. The pillar broke. But he didn't embrace Kunti or Draupadi.

Despite my dishevelled hair, despite the painful impressions of his fingers on my cheeks, despite the choking of my lungs, heart and ribs, I wanted to smile just once. Oh no! It was affection that had whipped him up like the devil. That thought turned my smile into ashes. I went into the wash room, washed my face, ran a comb through my hair. I quickly changed into a new saree and applied a vermilion dot on my brow.

The doorbell rang. I ran to open the door.

In a flash, Periappa caught hold of my hair and pulled me back. 'I will open it,' he said.

'No, it is I who will open the door,' I said, struggling. Periappa clasped my throat with his hands and pressed.

'The master has come. Let me go, Periappa!'

The doorbell rang again, with urgency. Periappa just flew down the stairs. I ran to the balcony, bent over the banister and looked.

'Oh, it's you? When did you come?'

'Just now.'

Before I heard the door shut, Gopali came up, followed by Periappa.

'What brings you here all of a sudden?' asked Gopali.

'This!' replied Periappa and he slapped Gopali hard on both his cheeks.

I did not interfere or try to stop him.

'Huh! What's this!' Gopali was stunned. The leaf-wrapped packet fell from his hand. 'Ammani, what's all this?' Gopali asked again, his eyes bloodshot.

'What do you mean *Ammani...Ammani*? Talk to me! What a fine girl she was. How did you have the heart to turn her into a prostitute! Is this what your Guru taught you? In that case, why on earth should *he* be here?' said Periappa, leaping up again. It must have been the sheer force of his anger, or else the picture of Tyagaraja wouldn't have come off with a mere jerk of his hand like that. The next moment, the pictures of Rama and Krishna were also plucked out of the wall. One flew to the kitchen and the other to the back courtyard.

'You grocer!' Gopali snarled in a low tone.

Periappa made a move as if to hit him again.

'Don't you dare come near me,' he said glaring at Periappa. Gopali's eyes were naturally large. Now they stood out like black circles detached from the eyelids.

Surprisingly, Periappa held back.

'I have done you wrong. I have deceived you. But not this girl. Only you. For that, I took the beating you gave me. Now put these pictures back in their place. Or just collect them with respect and recline them against the wall. If you don't do that right away, I can't vouch for what may happen. Only one of us will be alive here. The temper of my village runs in my body. The brahmins in my village have practised *silambam* with the men from the Kallar Street. Two brahmins from our previous generation took stale rice in butter milk on a new moon day and went out as dacoits with flaming torches in their hands. They were just one house away from us. It won't take much time for that trait to skip a house and come to me.'

'Are you saying that it hasn't come to you yet?'

'I asked you to be decent enough to hand over the pictures to me. Didn't ask you for a reply.'

I went to get the pictures.

'Ammani!' Gopali glowered at me. 'It is he who must make amends for his offence. What he tore and threw were not pictures.'

I looked at Periappa.

Periappa walked towards the pictures, his feet thudding heavily over the floor. He picked them up and made them recline against the wall, one over the other.

That done, Gopali told him very quietly, 'Now come and thrash me. I will take it without a word.'

'It was a mistake. It was a sin to have touched you. Ammani, aren't you coming?'

I shook my head.

'Ammani won't come. I know I'm a depraved person. But she is not living with me for that reason. You won't understand all that. You only understand tamarind and pulses.'

'*Chhee*! Shut up!' said Periappa. All his wild anger had died down. His face was instead suffused with an intense loathing. He no longer cared. I was scared now.

He said, 'Ammani, what you said was right—yes, you *are* dead for us. I am going to bathe in the sea before I leave for my village.' Then he picked up his bag and left.

I did not feel like going down to bolt the door.

Gopali rushed into the wash room. Three minutes later he emerged, dripping wet. He dried his hair, opened the wardrobe, pulled out a white silk dhoti and draped it around his waist. He hung up the pictures on the wall again. He picked up the leaf-wrapped packet that had fallen from his hand when he was slapped, and opened it. He adorned the three pictures with garlands of jasmine. Then he stood in front of them and started singing '*Rama Rama inti thathaga*'. He couldn't sing the *anupallavi.* His voice trembled and fell. He stopped for a few minutes. Then he started singing again.

I went into the kitchen, put some water to boil to cook the rice, and settled down to make a dish of vegetables and *kuzhambu*. The singing had stopped. After a while, I heard footfalls. Gopali came in and sat down. He looked at me.

'What's this!'

I looked up.

'Your cheeks are all swollen. Were you also given the honours?'

'Ten times more than you. Only now, my body has started aching,' I said and laughed.

Gopali also laughed. He came nearer and stroked my cheeks. I rubbed them with my fingers and felt as if I was touching an old woman's cheeks.

'I've never seen a Periappa like this. You can cut the vegetables later,' he said, pushing away the sickle-stand. He pulled me to him and made me rest my head on his lap. He caressed my swollen cheeks. 'Such wrath!' he marvelled, looking at them.

'No. It is love. It was only today I realised that Periappa could love me so much. He just didn't know how to show it all this time. Given this situation, he was driven to express his love for me this way.' A teardrop rolled down my eyes. The sun and the earth can be trapped in a drop of water. In that drop which was invisible to me, Periappa, Periamma, their children, their house, the pond, that wedding, the trust they had in me—all stood reflected as images. I wanted to sob my heart out aloud. I buried my face in his lap. My back shook. Gopali ran his fingers through my hair in gentle strokes. He didn't know how to console, but the inside of his palm sang sweeter than all his songs.

I got up, blew my nose, washed my face and returned. Sat down with the sickle-stand and the vegetables.

'Should I return to my village, as Periappa and Periamma want me to?' I asked him with a smile.

'Should I keep my head on your lap now and cry?'

Then I remembered. 'You told Periappa, "Ammani is not here for that reason. You won't understand all that". What is *all that*?'

Gopali didn't reply.

I could hear Pachiappa's voice. He had returned from the market.

PART II

1

Can there be a dance without a debut in a public performance? Gopali ordered his friends, his disciples, his circle of fans and the bigwigs who admired and idealised him to write about me in the media. He made others spend lavishly, just as he himself squandered money carelessly. These people wrote about me for the sake of writing. They wrote whatever they felt like writing. They wrote the truth. Having written their stuff, they then took to circulating around me. People who used to earlier come with Gopali now visited me on their own. Sometimes they came alone. Old men, middle-aged men, the young ones, all of them now visited me separately. Do I sound like an old woman when I talk of the 'young ones'? But I think of what an old woman would experience. Several pairs of friends who were known to be 'inseparable' now visited me separately. Having come, they would linger on and talk endlessly.

A girl living in a big sprawling house all by herself can, within a year, witness all that an old woman does in a hundred years, listen to all that goes on around her, think about many things and experience myriad sensations. There were so many kinds of people, with all their phobias and desires!

There were young men who sat quietly. They too would visit me alone. They'd get apprehensive if the doorbell rang. They'll turn sheepish or look disappointed or camouflage their annoyance with a smile. 'Is *he* closer to her than I?' was their gnawing suspicion. People who spoke garrulously when I introduced them spoke thoughtfully, in a measured way. Some mouthed philosophy, others proclaimed atheism, a few spoke about art. A professor of Sanskrit, a couple of lawyers, secretaries of music halls, college students, and students learning painting and sculpture...Those were the days when they didn't keep their hair long, when filthy or torn clothes did not necessarily signify rebellion. Only a sharp goatee beard could occasionally be seen as a fetish for the arty types.

Initially, they came in twos and threes. Even on a second or third visit. Then they came alone. Not one of them failed to speak on the status of women. One would hold forth like this: 'It is a man's world, whether it is the whites, the blacks, the yellow-skinned or the brown—whichever country it may be, the power is with men. Likewise, the laws and customs are all for their convenience.' Another would say: 'You've done the right thing. As a single woman, you are not in anyone's clutches. You really are a smart one! Actually, Appa and Amma are the source of all my troubles. I wanted to be a school teacher. But Amma wanted me to own a car and Appa wanted me to be an engineer. If I do well in mathematics, does it mean I have to be an engineer? Is a teacher's job so lowly? But I couldn't protest. So I carry my engineering education like a donkey's burden. You have rightly shaken off your Appa and Appa to be on your own!'

'If you are an artist, you can't be bound to anyone. A husband is a manacle, so is a wife. Even if you can avoid lighter manacles like a mother-in-law, father-in-law or sister-in-law, you'll have no say when it's a heavier handcuff,' was the logic of a lawyer. That meant: You are clever. You haven't submitted to wearing the manacles of marriage. All their talk invariably ended on this note of independence.

I could see through their hearts and minds, their muscles and flesh like one can see through glass. I could see their great urge to probe me, to strip me naked, but in different forms. Some were smoky, some had pent-up feelings, while some burned like a flame.

I would introduce them to Gopali. 'Happy to meet you,' he would say. There were several undertones to this 'happy-to-meet-you'. After saying this, Gopali would sit there silently, waiting for that man to leave. Then he would look at the clock and abruptly ask me, 'Aren't you ready yet? But I sent word through Pachai this morning that we'll have to leave at 5.30?'

I couldn't very well ask him 'Where are we going?' or say that Pachiappan hadn't informed me.

The man would say, 'Looks like you have to go out. Let me make a move, then.'

'That's all right. You can stay on,' Gopali would say to the man.

'No...if you're going out...'

'Please stay. We'll get going now, but we'll return by 11:30.'

'That's okay,' the visitor would say, getting up. He would slip into his sandals and leave.

'This is becoming like a bazar! I can't even remember some of their faces. Looks like your fame has now exceeded mine!'

'What can I do? How can I ask them to leave when they're talking? And there are some who speak so well. If I keep thinking of how to send them away, then I can't listen to them. This circle of friends has come about only through you. None of them are what you can call 'ordinary'. I don't like to discriminate. Everybody is the same to me. Each body holds a secret, a message. The man who sells dates, the coriander woman, the fruit-seller, Professor Aghoram, the Nandi of *Kali Yuga* who plays the mridangam for you...How else do I spend my time?'

'Your only problem is that you don't know how to spend your time? Is that it?'

I wasn't quite ready to say that I couldn't spend my time. From the front rooms I could watch the pools of sunlight shift and play or look at the leaves of the tree. Stare at the flat opposite. Watch the clouds change shape. Listen to the silences of noon. When the woman on the ground floor cooked, a variety of sounds could be heard, of utensils being used, water running. I heard the evening chimes of the Pillaiyar temple. There were two buffaloes tied in the ground adjacent the house opposite—not the kind from Annavasal, but the cattle of Madras. They munched dry hay and stared at the tether-peg all day long. What did the buffalo think about? The ox who mated with it just once in Saidapettai? Of its owner? Of its next life? Was it a tranquil beatitude? Or nothing at all? One could contemplate these the whole day long. At night one could hear the sounds of cockroaches, lizards and insects. The rustling of leaves on the tree. They too have thoughts. My ears have sharpened. My eyes have sharpened. I can hear any sound. I can smell any scent. I can think. I can even observe my own thoughts and my mind.

'If you're bored, there is that grandson of my aunt,' said Gopali. 'Just recently, about four days back, he's joined the Polytechnic. He comes from a poor family. A family that was once well-off but has now become poor. He can stay with you, cook for you, eat with you and study. I would be most grateful to you! My cousin, his mother, brought him to me. I don't think he can manage to study at my house. There is music there and visitors all the time. And Kunjali never seems to have enough assistants for her work. She won't spare him the time for his studies. He can come and study here. He could be your best defence against all these people who come here just to chat. The lad is a clever, discreet fellow. Can he come and stay here, in one room?'

'Sure.'

'You're saying yes without even thinking about it?'

'Why should I think about it when you already have?'

'But you haven't even met him!'

'Why do I have to meet him? The place is there, ready for him.'

Two days later, the boy turned up, with an old tin box and a bedroll.

2

Is this the boy that Gopali had spoken of? Poor, derelict, looking to Gopali for sustenance? I was expecting a spindly, emaciated body living on inadequate food, somewhat anaemic, head bent, with shy, frightened eyes that refuse to make contact. I'd also imagined a boy wearing a short-sleeved shirt that reached his waist and a dirty yellowed dhoti of four cubits around his body, walking with an uncertain gait.

'I come from Gopali Mama's house', he said, straightening up as he introduced himself. A box in his right hand, a bedroll in his left, with a 'T' square of the Polytechnic thrust under the rope of the bedroll. A bag hung from his shoulder.

'Mama asked me to go over. He'll follow me in a while.'

'Come in,' I said, lowering the top bolt. I opened the other door and said, 'Give the box to me.'

'No.'

'The staircase is narrow. You can't come up with the luggage in both your hands.'

'I can manage. Please go ahead.' Lifting the heavy box with his right hand, he swung it over his shoulders and perched it on his head.

I hurried up the stairs ahead of him. Reaching the top floor, I turned right and led him to the front room.

'This is your room.'

The boy took a look. At the pools of sunlight. The leaves and branches of the tree that brushed the balcony and leaned over it. The two windows. He looked pleased.

Then he said, 'I don't need so much space, Mami.'

'What did you say?'

'I said why should I have so much space?'

'But you also said something else in the end.'

'What?'

'Say it again, whatever you said at first.'

'I said why such a big place.'

'No. You added something else, like how one addresses a relative.'

'I said I don't need such a big place, Mami.'

'Take a good look at me.'

He lowered his eyes and looked at me. I too looked at him.

'Now tell me which one of your uncle's wives do I look like? Gopali Mama's wife or the wife of your mother's brother?'

The boy looked intently at my stern face for a few moments, and then broke into a laugh. 'Tell me how I should address you then. Shouldn't a younger brother be six feet tall if his elder sister is five?' he said with a broad smile.

'Don't you know my name?'

'But how can I address you by name? Gopali Mama has such a temper!'

'Really? So you respect his anger? Put the box down.'

He put it down. I caught his hand and shook it. 'Good. I had wondered if Gopali would send some miserable, pathetic-looking nephew. Put your bedroll down. And the shoulder bag. This is the room for you, and the right one.'

I looked at him, and remembered some of the cooks I'd seen at weddings or in a hotel. The skin stretched tight over the bone, arms and legs stiffened in a cramp by long hours of work. Large feet. Long fingers. A dusky complexion, somewhere between dark and wheatish. His ears, nose, eyes and lips—each looked somewhat disparate and not quite in harmony with each other. He had large eyes like Gopali's, perhaps a family resemblance. When he spoke, his lips and mouth twisted slightly, as if he knew a lot and was bragging. He had a thick crop of hair and eyebrows like a moustache. When I shook his hands, they felt as broad as his feet, with the same stiffness of a cramp. One had to make an effort to clasp them and shake them.

'What's your name?'

'Pattabhiraman. People call me Pattabhi. There's a song, *Mamava Pattabhirama* which Gopali Mama would sing very well. My mother heard it and insisted that I be named after it,' he said, narrating these details like a five-year-old.

'Haven't you heard the song?' I asked him.

'I don't listen to music,' he said.

'Don't like it?'

'It's not exactly a dislike. I only have a scientific interest in music, nothing beyond that.'

'Which means?'

'Why do people listen to the *jalatarangam*, but not to the sounds of a bicycle bell? They listen to the mridangam, but not to the sounds of paddy being threshed. They listen to a flute, but not to the cry of an eagle. They listen to the notes of music, but not to the tapping of a typewriter. When they can listen to the *ghatam*, why can't they listen to the whip-handle placed in the wheel of a moving horse cart? This is how my mind works. I am kind of neutral to music.'

'Oh. Is that why your uncle sent you here? What do you like then? For instance, I dance. Do you like dance?'

'That'll also be the same.'

'Same as what?'

'If there is a dance performance, people go and watch. Why don't they care to watch someone walking down to the rice mill with a sack of rice on his head, or someone walking to the vegetable market with a basket, or someone balancing pots of water on her head? They marvel at a dancer articulating an *abhinaya*, but not when someone rolls their eyes and moves their hands or smiles when they speak. This is how my thoughts run on,' he said.

'Here, give me your hand,' I said, and shook it. Apparently, I too had developed a 'scientific' perspective. I was also hungry. I went in to put some water to boil for cooking rice.

Gopali came.

'What's this? All the doors are wide open!' he said, removing his sandals.

'It was I who forgot to close them, Mama,' said Pattabhi, coming out of his room.

'Oho! So the *grihapravesam* is over?' said Gopali and walked into Pattabhi's room. 'Is it passable?' he asked.

'I never thought it would be so good, Mama.'

'Yes. The trees, the breeze and the balcony. You may even forget to study! Keep the doors closed. There'll always be visitors here who'll keep on talking. Don't get distracted by all that. Stick to your studies and keep to your room. Answer Ammani if she calls you and do whatever she asks you to do. There will be educated people among the visitors who come here. Don't mix with them and don't start talking to them on your own!'

Pattabhi stood in silent compliance to this sermon, head bowed.

It was a Sunday. Pattabhi cooked and served both of us. Then he ate and cleared the leftovers. Tidied up the kitchen. Took the utensils to the open terrace and kept them in the backyard for washing. Then he went into his room. For the next seven or eight days, I didn't see much of him. When I woke up early morning, coffee was ready. He made idli or dosai for breakfast, served me and after having his share, left the house by seven. Returned by dusk. After dinner, he gave the vessels to Pachiappa for cleaning and went into his room. Till twelve or one at night, the light would be on in his room.

On the fourth day, two young men dropped in for a chat.

'Are they going to eat here?' Pattabhi asked.

'No, no...it's getting late. We must be going,' said the two, getting up.

'But it is late. If you're eating, I can make something for you,' he said, looking at me.

'No, no,' said the two again, and went down the stairs.

Whenever Gopali sang, Pattabhi wouldn't even step out of his room. Velayya came to teach, tapped out the steps, and the floor vibrated with my dance. Gopali would come, sing, drink, eat, chat and go to sleep. There would be no trace of Pattabhi. I could see the light on in his room till one. One day Gopali felt a bit awkward. It was eleven in the night. Seeing the light on, he went over to his room and said, 'Hey Pattabhi, isn't it getting late? You haven't gone to sleep yet?'

The very next instant, the light went out. And within a minute, a faint snore could be heard.

Gopali did not come the following evening. He had gone for a concert. No sign of my talkative friends either. I called out for Pattabhi.

'Yes...?' he said, coming in.

'Last night Mama noticed that you hadn't gone to sleep. You said "All right" and switched off the light. And I heard you snoring the next minute!'

'Yes.'

'Did you fall asleep instantly?'

'Yes.'

'How can that be?'

'It's possible.'

'How can you fall sleep instantly?'

'I work when there is work. I can even work for three days without sleeping. When I stop working, I go to sleep instantly.'

'You mean you sleep when there is no work or when you stop working?'

'As soon as I stop working.'

'I can't believe it!'

Pattabhi didn't reply.

'Can you sleep now if you want to?'

'Hmm.'

'But it's not yet night.'

'So what? I can darken the room and go to sleep.'

'What if someone comes?'

'I will see.'

'So what...you just keep sleeping?'

'Let me go inside and sleep.'

'No, sleep here. I want to watch.'

'All right,' said Pattabhi, laughing.

He lay down on the floor, put a cushion under his head and closed his eyes. A minute passed. He scratched his arms a couple of times. The next minute there was a faint snore. Five, ten, fifteen minutes passed. Pattabhi was fast asleep. He had rolled up the world, flung it far away and retreated somewhere into himself. There was no snoring. Only deep slumber.

The doorbell rang.

He did not wake up. I soundlessly went down the stairs and opened the door.

It was Sundaram.

'Please come in.'

'I thought you wouldn't be in! What luck!'

'I didn't go out anywhere today. Gopali is not in town. I didn't know how to spend the time.'

'Is that so?' said Sundaram, obviously delighted. 'Are you alone then?' he asked, concealing his excitement with some effort as he climbed the stairs.

'What to do?'

He whistled as he came up.

'Oh,' he said, seeing the sleeping Pattabhi in the hall.

'That's all right. He's Gopali's nephew. He stays in the room here. Been studying through the night for four days without a break. He's sleeping out of exhaustion,' I said softly so as not to disturb Pattabhi.

'Then let's go in there and talk,' said Sundaram, indicating with his eyes the other room that had three chairs along with twin beds.

'All right.'

He sat down on a chair and asked, 'Have you read the review?'

'I read it. Even I didn't know so many things about myself. You've written a lot about me,' I said.

'I didn't write it. My wisdom did.'

'Meaning?'

Patting the left side of his chest, he said, '*This* wrote it.'

'But Ramana Maharishi says the heart is on the right side.'

'If it was, wouldn't he pull it over to this side if he happened to be sitting here like me? Would he just sit around, wavering?'

'I can be drawn only if I wish to be drawn, Sundaram.'

Sundaram was a sub-editor with a newspaper. He was close to Gopali. I did not mind his betrayal of friendship. There was a servility in the very nature of his job, but the way it was a predominant trait in him nauseated me. He went anywhere he was invited to, dragging his fair-skinned, fat body along with that double chin that hung like that of a cattle's skin. Before others could consume two, he emptied five or six glasses of whisky with the greed of a novice. He would roll his eyes and laugh at everything in a guttural voice, as if laughing was the sole purpose of his visit.

Come to think of it, even this did not strike me as servility. For giving me three rave reviews, Gopali had poured him glass after glass. Something else gnawed at me. What was the reason for his infatuation with me? My beauty, my youth, my charm or my conversation? I may have all of these, but why should Sundaram take a fancy to me? Did he ever ponder over his own unlikely appeal to a twenty-three-year-old girl? Or did he think he was in the bloom of youth? He must be around fifty-five. Regular drinking had dried up even the vitality of his mind. His wife was very beautiful, but that was no barrier. Man or woman, each person is guided by the eye. For instance, I am drawn to Pattabhi, who may not be every girl's idea of a man. Likewise, Sundaram wasn't tied down to a pretty wife. Did he think he had more vitality than Gopali? Did he think his infatuation in itself made him eligible for me? Or that he had won me over with his reviews?

I was amused. Not with Sundaram, but with myself. That I should have analysed his pat over his heart so carefully and patiently. He has shaken my hand several times, but each time my hand goes limp. How come he has never noticed it?

What did I think in my heart of hearts? That one old man was enough for me?

Sundaram was influential. He could get what he wanted. He had three fine sons. After repeated attempts, one had finally succeeded in suffixing a B.A. to his name. Two of them he'd planted as covenanted officers in a British firm monopolised by the sons of the I.C.S. The third, who obstinately refused to study beyond school, was made to undergo training in hotel management. Then Sundaram found him a placement as manager of an international hotel. He had even written a book of eighty pages on the Second World War, and lobbied around with every possible contact to bag an all-India award for it. He always occupied the front row in music conferences. Musicians fawned on him pathetically. It was only Gopali who would on occasion say something suitable to cut him down to size.

In a music festival last year, instead of his usual suit, Sundaram was seen sporting a dhoti and silk shirt, with a Mysore shawl draped over his head. He approached Gopali, who was standing outside with his students and admirers, and greeted him. I was also there. Gopali looked at him astonished, as if he did not recognise him.

'Anna, it's me, Sundaram.'

'Oh, it's you! But what's all this, why is your head covered like an upper-class widow's!'

'Heh, heh, heh,' laughed Sundaram.

What was there inside him, fire or water? Was it anger or inadequacy that he diverted like this? I began talking about the Mylapore Temple festival two years ago, in which Gopali had performed. 'Yes, yes...After all, he's a genius!' Sundaram responded distractedly, looking into my eyes all the while. I could see that my words weren't reaching his ears.

'And what about you? The way you complete a dance performance and leave the stage...it is an art. Until I'd seen you dance, I never knew it could have such an impact. Do you know how I feel? Shall I say it in Hanuman's words to Rama?' He suddenly got up and put his arms around me.

I didn't expect that. 'No. I don't like all this. Let me go!' I said softly.

'I've never felt this way about anyone.'

'Are you going to let me go or not?' I whispered urgently.

I don't know what happened next. Two hands caught Sundaram by the shoulders and lifted him up. Like a magnetic crane lifting a large flabby doll, Pattabhi carried him into the hall. Then he asked him crisply in English, 'Now, what is your problem, sir?'

I was stunned. How did Pattabhi keep holding up the man's weight like that?

'Speak up, sir? Shall I drop you down the stairs or throw you from the rear terrace?'

'Let me go!' Sundaram screamed in terror.

'Pattabhi, put him down!' I shouted incoherently.

Sundaram's feet gently grazed the floor.

'Pattabhi, apologise to him at once!'

'Forgive me, sir, I misunderstood. I was only half awake. I just got perturbed,' said Pattabhi.

It was dusk. The hall was almost dark.

'I should be going now,' Sundaram said curtly, and left.

Pattabhi went down to close the door and returned.

'I acted in haste,' he said.

'No, you acted rightly.'

'What!'

'It was absolutely right what you did.'

'Then why did you ask me to apologise? That's hypocrisy!'

'Scaring him like that was quite enough.'

'How was it enough? I would have done something he'd remember.'

'You did hoist him up like an electromagnet. Even I would remember that! When did you wake up?'

'Five minutes back. I tried to be wakeful. I thought it was daybreak. But there was no twittering of birds. I also heard the chimes of the Pillaiyar temple. Someone was talking. I sat up, still drowsy. The man was sitting. Then I saw him suddenly getting up. Who is he?'

I told him.

'A learned man behaves like this? Just because you're social, they take you for granted!'

I went in, switched on the light and looked at myself in the mirror. I laughed. The mirror laughed in return.

Pattabhi was washing his face.

'Pattabhi!'

He came running.

'How old are you?'

'Eighteen. I joined school a bit late. By the time I finished school, I was as tall as this.'

'How could you lift him up like that?'

'When I was small, I used to practise weights with dumb bells and staves.'

'What else?'

'I used to do carpentry. And cooking. Even when I was in eighth class, I used to work as a help for the big cooks at weddings. I could easily handle huge, steaming vessels.'

I stood staring at him.

'Why did Gopali Mama send you here? To guard me or to spy on me?'

'If that was the case, he wouldn't have asked me to keep to my room unless I was summoned.'

'Did I ask you to bundle out this man, the one who was here?'

Pattabhi bowed his head. After a minute he said, 'I should look out for a room elsewhere,' rubbing his toes.

'What's this suddenly?'

No answer.

'Tell me?'

'Maybe it was wrong of me to have handled him like that.'

'But I told you that you did the right thing.'

'At least in future I shouldn't do anything like that.'

'What does that mean?'

'You didn't like him. Suppose I too don't like someone...and I treat him the same way?' he said, dropping his eyes.

'If you don't like someone, then what?'

'It is generous of you to have put up with me for so long. But when I see all these people who come here, I feel uneasy. Suppose...I too misbehave with you?'

'Would Gopali Mama like you to talk like this?'

'I'm not fit to stay here. I'm unable to concentrate on my studies.'

'All right. Now go and wear a shirt. Let's go out and eat somewhere,' I said. And I got ready in five minutes.

At the restaurant on Mount Road, we chose a corner table in the family cubicle. As we were finishing our meal, I said, 'Now tell me, why did you say that you wanted to move out?'

'Gopali Mama brought me here with good intentions. But I'm a little scared now.'

'You're only scared that you may do something wrong. But you can't bring yourself to say that you like me,' I said.

No response.

'Do you want to say it?'

Still no response.

On our return, Pattabhi headed straight for his room. I had my night bath as usual. It was past eleven. I went to the front room. The door was closed. I tapped on it.

'Who is it?'

'Me.'

He opened the door.

'I came to say goodnight.'

He stood there with his head bowed.

'Have you decided to look for another room? Will you hoist me up too in anger? Let me see if you can…' I said.

And just like Sundaram, I was bodily lifted up, carried and deposited on the bed in my room. Pattabhi went back to his room. I lay there and thought of Sundaram and laughed. I thought of Gopali who would come and sleep here as if he'd been slugged. I wasn't sleepy just yet. There was no one sleeping beside me either.

Early next morning, there was no sign of Pattabhi. I had a vision of Gopali lying on the edge of the bed like a bundle of washing, like a lump of civet. I wanted to express my gratitude to that bundle, that lump.

There was a small note under my pillow: *'There is coffee in the flask and six idlis in the tiffin carrier. My Thatha did yagna. But he couldn't have done it the way I have. Truly speaking, only I can. And I will, till the day I die.'*

I kept looking at the note. The early morning glow had matured into white.

3

That night and the next. Then the third and the fourth nights, it was just the same.

There wasn't a single day when Pattabhi rushed back home from college or returned earlier than usual. He always returned at the usual time, did his work, went out to meet his friends, chatted with them as usual and came back.

Somehow I didn't expect this. I thought he would give some excuse, keep thinking of the night and return home by afternoon or evening. In fact, I was disappointed. My eyes would be riveted on his return. The whole day I would imagine that he approached his teacher and the college principal to say that he had some urgent work at home, that he found excuses even for his usual circle of friends and cut short his conversation, that he got into a bus and did not talk to anyone. That he spent money on an auto-rickshaw, did not notice anything on the street during his commute, and that his thoughts were only on this room. That he didn't even stop by at an eatery or tea shop to assuage his evening hunger.

But Pattabhi did nothing like that.

I was angry. I thought of the previous night and the night before. His virility. And his solicitude. I ran through all the forms he took on—nurse, attendant, husband, mother, makeup artist, the way he discoursed like a father, the way he was concerned like a younger brother.

Was he eighteen or forty?

He talked like anyone else. But he could not speak that one language: the language of adoring lovers. The language of those who know the elixir of women. Of those who cannot bear it and just jump in it and drown. Every now and then, I thought of Gopali. I heard his words, the beseeching tone, the softness and caress in his voice, the way it evoked the names of animals, birds and plants. I could hear all of this from Gopali's lips. But not Pattabhi's.

On the third day, he returned late in the evening and hung around outside the gate, talking to a friend for about fifteen minutes. After coming in, he washed his face and feet and went to the kitchen. Seeing there was nothing laid out for dinner, he said, 'Shall I cook?'

'No.'

'Why?'

'Let's eat out again today.'

Another restaurant, in Broadway. A family cubicle. Back home, he went into his room to study. I had a bath around midnight. Then I knocked on his door. I said I had come to say goodnight.

Silence.

'Why are you silent?'

'I wonder for whom it is a good night,' said Pattabhi.

'You tell me.'

'I haven't had a good night for the past four days.'

'What...?'

'Yes.'

'Do you really mean that?'

'Yes.'

I stared at him.

'Gopali Mama's thoughts must be hovering around here... Does my behaviour reflect any gratitude? By saying that my nights haven't been good, I'm not being grateful for this either,' said Pattabhi.

I actually had to look up in order to look at him. Despite that, it felt like I was looking down, at a child. It was not possible to lift him up in my arms. So I held his fingers. He came walking behind me like a child. Everything became all right once we reached my room.

In the morning, my body did not want to be roused from its slumber. But I couldn't tell if it was he who had stirred my mind and my sensibilities awake. I opened my eyes. He was sitting beside me, watching me.

'Not sleepy?'

'No.'

'You claimed you could sleep whenever you wanted. You even demonstrated it the other day.'

'As long as I stay here, I cannot sleep.'

'Still thinking of Gopali Mama?'

'It's you who's saying that.'

'You think you have betrayed Gopali Mami, and that it is a big deal.'

'I *have* betrayed him.'

'Whatever it is, how does it matter? I don't even concern you as a person. You only want the *punyam* of showing your gratitude to Gopali. You only wish that he should be pleased.'

'Even if I jumped into a river or a pond, I wouldn't drown. I can swim,' he said.

'Really? I didn't know you were so stupid! And I thought I couldn't find empathy or compassion in others. I now realise that I can't expect them from you either. Why should an inert stone live? You've been nagging me that you want to look for another room. Go ahead. Atone for your sins however you deem best. Express your gratitude however you wish. It'll be good for my reputation. Good for yours as well. It'll also be honourable for your Gopali Mama. And before you leave, get me a cup of coffee. I don't think I can get up and work right now.'

Before I had finished speaking, Pattabhi was up. In ten minutes, he got the coffee, made *uppuma*, had a bath and left for his college.

The gnawing fear lingered through the day. Will he come back? Or put an end to his life? Or give up his studies? Or go to some godforsaken place where he wouldn't be touched even by the shadow of Gopali? To forget his betrayal and his ingratitude, to conceal it or obliterate it, would he run away to the Himalayas, hide in a cave and sit with his eyes closed in contemplation?

I felt restless in the house. I told Pachiappan, locked the door and went out. Went to the station, bought a ticket to Tambaram and boarded the electric train. Bought another ticket at Tambaram and travelled to Beach station. A few people spotted me in the train and talked to me. After they got down, with no one to talk to, the fear gripped me again. I went to the house of one of the Ph.D. scholars who often called on me. He wasn't home. Went to a young lawyer's house. He was away at court. Finally, I went to Velayya's house. It was an untimely hour. My third visit to his house, and that too without appointment. He was in. He greeted me, 'How come? Did the breeze blow towards Egmore today?'

'You mean I'm someone who wafts in with the breeze?' I said to cover my fear as I sat down on the mat.

'You look tired. Are you coming from home or from another visit? Hello, come and see who is here, like the onset of *mamangam*!' he said to his wife who had just come in.

I did not look at him with the sympathy I had for Gopali, but I wondered how Velayya maintained his reputation without getting involved with the girls who learnt dance from him.

'Yes, she has indeed arrived like mamangam,' said his wife, welcoming me with a grimace that displayed all her teeth, including the vampire tooth that jutted out in front. The long use of betel nuts had stained the crevices of her teeth a deep red-brown. But they were teeth guaranteed to last ninety years at least.

Velayya hadn't come for the dance classes for a week. Assuming that I had come to inquire about that, he started explaining.

'I had fever, with pain shooting through the body,' he said. What made it worse was the news that a girl student of his had received a government scholarship and had, without his knowledge, sought someone else to teach her for half the money. 'This killed me more than the illness, you could say. Her parents had haggled with me for three days for a monthly fee of thirty rupees. I have groomed this girl right from the beginning. For five long years, I poured dance into her limbs. Then I presented her to the public. I roped in Pacha Iyengar, Krishnamurty Iyer, our own Swami and Ramadorai. I got them to write good reviews. They did. Once her *arangetram* was over, and Pacha Iyengar had praised her third performance in the papers, the mother started saying, "How can we give you half of her collections, Guruji?" And this right after the third concert! As if they had showered me with gold for the first two. I knew this would drag on. Now it has turned out to be the story of *Surabhasmasuran*.

'The girl joined college. Isn't college supposed to teach you some sense or maturity? She just goes by whatever her mother says! The scholarship required an advanced level of training.

They approached Mahalingam and came to an agreement with him. In his long flowing kurta reaching down to his knees, sporting a dot of javvadhu on his wrist or forehead, he towers like he were some deity. He's toured around Singapore, Saigon and Kuala Lumpur, and after his return, become a veritable Nataraja or Bharata. Here I'm just a primary school master, squatting on the pyol. They had come last week, mother and daughter. I got the news in advance. Hundred rupees cash, a dhoti from Thirunasaram, as if I was going to become a priest, and hundred grams of grapes, to wet my throat—so that the Guruji, after being hurt, may not also become hoarse!'

'You forgot the rock candy,' his wife chipped in.

'Oh, you're still here? Yes, there must've been a quarter kilo of rock candy. The only omission was black pepper fried in ghee to soothe my throat. They came here, bringing all these things on a plastic tray. "What's all this suddenly?" I asked. The mother said, "You've done a lot for her, Guruji. With your blessings, our child has earned a good name. About the scholarship, at first it looked too tough even to qualify for it. We were told that if we use Mahalingam's name, it would make a difference. It was I who told my husband, let's put his name down for now, we will later change it to Guruji's. We realised how difficult it would be only after the order came. It was like the folly of commissioning a djinn to dig a well! We were bewildered and anxious about our child's future," she said.

'I said, "Yes, you're quite right. Mahalingam will make a fine demon, both in name and appearance." My wife, she just stood there and burst out laughing! She's from Magizhankadu, you see. You don't need to tickle the women of that village to make them laugh. Just saunter onto the street in torn sandals, and that will make them giggle till they choke into the ends of their sarees and shake helplessly till tears fall from their eyes. I got nervous and told her to go inside. She glared at me and went in. Then the mother solicitously asked me, "Are you angry, Guruji?"

'"No, I'm not angry. I'm just an elementary school teacher. Mahalingam is the proper teacher for students of B.A. and M.A.

Your daughter has finished the stage of alphabets. So naturally you seek a higher teacher for her. Why should I get angry? If I do, won't the entire city laugh at me?" I said.

'She stood there silently for some time. Then she said, "It's getting late, Guruji. We have to visit Pallavaram. Please don't misunderstand us. We had thought of it one way, but it turned out to be quite another. This is so awkward. I wanted to explain everything to you in person, so I came with our child. Do *namaskaram* to your Guru, my child!" She did.

'"May you prosper. May you dance like Urvashi, Tillottama and Gyanambal. May you get an opportunity to tour all around the world and earn a name for yourself," I blessed her. They got up to leave. "But you're leaving all this behind," I said, pointing to the plastic tray.

'"We brought them for you, Guruji."

'"No. Take them back," I said. They wouldn't. "Will you take them back or not?" I said, raising my voice.

'"Please let them be here," said the mother, and they stepped out. Before they could reach the street, the tray with the dhoti, the money, the grapes and the rest flew past them and scattered on the street.

'Oh, you should've seen the look the mother gave me! There was so much anguish in that look that even I felt ashamed of myself. Granted they were foolish, but why the hell should *you* lose your senses, shouted a voice in my head. I hung my head and scurried back into the house without a word. It seems they picked up everything and left in a rickshaw that was waiting outside. The fever I had that night! My wife told me that I babbled deliriously several times. It was wrong of them to do what they did. But the way I behaved was even more unforgiveable. How awful they must have felt, with so many people looking on in the street.

'Ever since that day, my mind has been troubled. This woman must have looked at me for a split second, but her expression said: *Pah! Is this all there is to you?*'

'Uff! Always the same talk...about how she looked at him! He just doesn't stop! True, even I felt bad about what happened. But for how long can one go on lamenting about it!' said his wife.

My spine went cold. At first I'd been listless and bored. But after a while I got engrossed in Velayya's persuasive narration, and heard him out till the end. That was dangerous. Because after listening to the whole story, I had this hallucination that I was the grapes, the candy and the money, and that I lay spattered on the street. That Pattabhi was the plastic tray that flew out of the door and crashed on one side of the street, and that everyone watched the scene, vastly entertained. It was then that my spine went cold, for under Gopali's head there was Velayya's torso. I sat there, not knowing what to say.

'I will come after a couple of days,' said Velayya. 'Let all these things go out of my mind so that I am calmer and more at peace. All these troubles come only because there is this thing called ego. If I identify myself with you or him or her and think that I live in everybody, there wouldn't be so much spitefulness, you see. Still, there are moments when I agonise about how they behaved. And what does that Mahalingam know? He's an out-and-out sycophant who has pushed and jostled his way to the top. Come to think of it, there is no real knowledge in the world. That's why all these things happen. You know this Mahalingam came out of nowhere. He used to cling to his aunt like an urchin, living off alms given in a temple in Javandinagar. The aunt died of chicken pox. He said he would learn music from the man who played the nadaswaram at the temple. He ate whatever the temple gave him. Then suddenly he went out of circulation one day and, just as suddenly, materialised in front of our house. At that time, he didn't sport fancy shirts or perfumes. "I can tap out the *nattuvangam*," he said. I recommended him to two people. If any veteran criticised him, he would never retort with a what-do-you-know attitude. Instead, he would humbly say, "Yes, you're absolutely right, sir. You're a genius! How did you find out?", thus often reversing what was actually right into something wrong! Of course, why wouldn't they be pleased! That is how he sang and danced his way to so many fancy places abroad. Mahalingam was born lucky—he had the bull by the horns.'

My attention had again wandered. I couldn't hear Velayya's lament anymore. It was competing with mine. 'Please take your time. You can come after a few days,' I said.

'Is Gopali Aiyah in town?'

'He should have returned today. He's been out for nearly five days.'

'Ah, that explains it! I was wondering how you came over like this, without letting me know. You must have thought, even this Velayya hasn't turned up. Well, I too felt like unburdening my mind. One can do that only with people one likes, isn't it?' he said.

Despite my protests, Velayya got up and saw me off at the bus stand. There were a few women sitting on the front seat and on the ones opposite where I sat. I imagined how each one of them would have killed her gratitude, and what kind of gratitude it might have been.

It was nearly dusk by the time I reached home. When I opened the door and switched on the light, I could see Pachiappan through the rear window.

'Master came in the afternoon. The doorbell kept ringing. I thought it must be someone else. Then he came in through the back stairs. "Where is Amma?" he asked. I said, "She went out sometime back. She'll return anytime now." He waited for fifteen minutes, then left. Then he came again, at about four in the afternoon. "She still hasn't come," I said. Since the boy was also not there, he left.'

'And the boy?' I asked.

'He came half an hour back. "She left in the morning, and still hasn't returned?" he exclaimed. Then he dumped his books in his room and went out.'

'Did he say anything?'

'Who?'

'The boy.'

'No.'

Pattabhi returned after eight at night.

'Oh, you're back! Thank God!' he said, smiling broadly as he came in. The way he beamed, I wanted to hold his large hands in a tight clasp. Wanted to bury myself in his arms and say, save me from gratitude, will you? 'Where did you go?' he asked. His face looked like it was happy after a long time. There was a restlessness in his arms and his legs. As if he couldn't stand the pain of dragging his feet about on the floor any longer.

'I went to many places,' I said.

'Why couldn't you tell me and go? Do you know I called at every one of your friends' places!'

Pattabhi never addressed me in the singular in the presence of Pachiappan, Gopali or others. 'Why are you so agitated?' I asked him.

'He was worried because you've been out since morning,' replied Pachiappan.

'Did you search in the Mylapore pond, on the railway lines, or under the lighthouse?'

Pachiappan laughed. 'Yes, it's all a joke for you, Amma. I too went to the bus stop many times, looking for you. Since morning, quite a few people have rung the doorbell.'

'But I had locked the front door.'

'They know I'm in the rear portion of the house.'

'All right. Now go and inform your Aiyah that I have come home.'

Pachiappan left.

Pattabhi watched till Pachiappan was down in the street. Then he said, 'I was scared because I had blabbered something. That's why I came early today. At three o'clock. The door was locked. Pachiappan was also not there. I waited for half an hour. Then visited all your friends. First I looked up Gopali Mama's house. It seems he also came here. The next time you go out, it'll be good if you leave a note someplace in the backyard.'

'Whatever for?'

'I was really worried.'

'Why should you be? You don't like living here. For you the river or the pond won't do, you know swimming. You can't swallow poison if you wanted to, you have a mole on the throat like Neelakantan. You also can't jump into the fire, your body is conditioned to heat after a long apprenticeship with cooks who work near huge ovens...' I went on and on.

Pattabhi ignored me and went into the kitchen. He poured water into the cooker and lit the stove. Then he sat down quietly with a knife to cut vegetables.

Here was one who couldn't tell the cry of a kite from the sound of a flute, or the wail of a child from a violin, or the crisp notes of a ghatam from the tapping of a typewriter. But his mind shrieked like a kite. Tapped like a typewriter. Clanged like a cycle bell. He couldn't speak the language of Gopali. But ever since he came, I have rarely cooked or made coffee for myself. When I was down with fever, he wouldn't leave my bedside. When I returned exhausted from my performances, and if Gopali wasn't around, he wouldn't let me walk up the stairs. He would bolt the door and just carry me upstairs.

Not just those four nights, I have observed him for four or ten or fifteen years. Like Gopali, he too learnt one day that in his place, and in place of Gopali, there had been a third, a fourth, a twentieth or a fortieth man. But unlike Gopali, he did not sulk. Nor did he rave and rant when Pachiappan was not home.

4

I worried that Gopali may come back with a childish sulk on his face. I was expected to be home every time he came. On the days I was not in when he came, it took me hours to make him smile. Even then he wouldn't laugh with his lips or mouth. He would laugh with his hands, without looking at me. He would hum raga *Pantuvarali* in a subdued, private voice, as if he wanted me to melt in it, to dissolve my laughter and my worries in the music. I have stubbornly tried to resist melting. In vain. It is impossible not to dissolve and to lose myself in his voice. When he sang, there was no more a Gopali. Or a Pattabhi. I expected the same thing to happen today. And before dissolving, to spend a long time looking at the sulking, scowling face, and listening to the angry words that he would never see me again.

But there was really nothing to worry about.

'Don't start any new lessons with Velayya. We're going out. For about three or four weeks,' Gopali said as soon as I told him about Velayya.

'There are two concerts in Delhi. Then onward to Benares, Calcutta, Nagpur and Bombay. I'm not taking my disciple with me. I'll play the roles of a disciple, an accountant and whathaveyou. Tickets have been booked for the Grand Trunk Express. Hey, Pattabhi...!'

Pattabhi came running.

'I have a month-long concert tour. Mami is also coming with me. Don't just keep sitting and staring at the wall while we're away. Go to my house and look up my mail. If there's anything urgent, send me a telegram. Don't keep gaping at the sky just because Ammani is not around.'

'All right.'

I looked at Pattabhi's eyes which were as large as a cow's. Was there submission in them or anger? Both seemed to flash alternately. At last he smiled. There was an understated humour in his obedience.

The following morning, it was Pattabhi who took out my sarees, ironed them, folded them and put them into a box. What would have easily taken up three boxes he packed neatly into a single box as deftly as packing *javanti* flowers. If I took out a couple of things, only he could pack them again like before. Otherwise, it would require another box. How could I express my appreciation? I rummaged among the things again. Like the horn of plenty, blouses, books, lotions, face powder, sandalwood paste, perfumes, notebook, comb, cash, brush, medicines—everything tumbled out. 'I want this diary to be outside,' I pleaded humbly, like it was an apology.

'Oh, that's alright,' he said. Within fifteen minutes, he had picked up all the things like they were flowers strewn all over and strung them neatly into a garland again. He locked the box, put the key in my hands and then rushed off to see his Gopali Mama, probably for the same task.

Gopali was upset that we could not get a coupe for two on the train. It was a compartment for six. I looked at the reservation chart. The names of our co-passengers didn't sound Indian.

'Can't sing aloud. Can't even hum! Ask for a coupe, I had said, even if you have to cough up five or ten rupees. Now he's planted us in the middle of a market place! You're just angry that I'm not taking you with us, that's what!' Gopali glowered at the poor disciple who had come to help us board the train.

I read out the names on the chart for Gopali.

Mr. L. Bennet
Mrs. Bennet
Miss Bennet
Mr. Gopali
Mrs. Ammani
Mr. Mathur

Twenty minutes before the train started, the chart took shape in human forms. Three of them were white-skinned: the man, his wife and their seven-year-old daughter who wore glasses. Mr. Mathur was a bit short. Gopali, still annoyed over the coupe, was staring at the palms and coconuts visible at a distance. Mr. Mathur had opened his suitcase and was rifling through some files. Mr. Bennet's family was looking at the knotted tuft of Gopali's hair, his *kadukkan* set with blue jager diamonds sparkling on his earlobes, his snuff-coloured short-sleeved shirt, the gold bracelet on his wrist and the gold lace on his dhoti. Every now and then, Miss Bennet leaned over to her mother to whisper something in her ears. From her looks I guessed that it must have been to do with Gopali's jewels. Gopali untied his hair a couple of times and knotted it up again. The girl saw that and edged towards her mother's ears.

Tired of looking out, Gopali turned to look at Mrs. Bennet. He devoured her with his eyes. Devoured her legs, her arms.

'Why is she so white?

'How to become this white?

'Would we too become white like this if we stayed in their country for four or five years?

'Is it because they only eat butter, buns and bread?

'Don't get angry that I look at her so often. She isn't fit to polish your shoes. I was only thinking of the *apsara* described in our books and wondering if she would be like you, or like her. Your looks remind me of rice mixed with lentils. She looks like a piece of broken bread.'

Gopali went on like this for some time, asking questions, and answering them himself. I was quiet.

After we crossed Gudur, he said, 'What's the matter? Why are you sitting here so silently? Take out the container from the bag. Kunjali made some Mysore *pak*. Start by distributing a piece to each one here. Who can stand this funereal silence for another two days!'

I took out the container, opened it and offered a piece of Mysore pak to the child. The others also took a piece each. In two minutes there was some life in the compartment. 'Thank you! Thank you!' some twenty times. The white man took a bite, sucked at it with a jupp-jupp sound, appraised it gingerly with his tongue and said, 'Wonderful!' Five more minutes of Wonderful and Delightful.

'How do you make this?' asked the white lady.

I explained and said, 'It's his favourite sweet,' pointing to Gopali. 'If he were to be denied this, then lakhs of people will miss out on some of the most precious moments in their life.'

The lady gave me a questioning look.

'The last hundred years haven't produced a musician like him in South India. And there's no prospect either of finding another classical vocalist like him for the next hundred. He wraps up thousands of people in an audience and casts a spell over them as he sings. Meet Mr. Gopali,' I said.

'Ah!' And the introductions began with handshakes.

Mr. Bennet worked with an export and import set-up in England. He visited India every four or five years. To pay homage to Ramana Maharishi, Sri Aurobindo, the Ramakrishna Mutt, Ma Anandamayi, Gyanananda...he mentioned seven more names. This was the first time he had come with his wife and daughter.

'Sri Ramana and Sri Aurobindo have both attained *nirvana*, and this time I didn't wish to come to India at all. Still, I felt like soaking in the memories,' he said. 'Mrs. Gopali, have you met Sri Aurobindo?' he asked.

'No, I haven't met Aurobindo or Ramana. That aside, I haven't seen my mister either,' I replied.

Mr. Bennet gave me a questioning look.

'It's a mistake that my name figures on the reservation chart as "Mrs. Ammani".'

'Oh! But how could they?'

'Perhaps they knew I was Gopali's mistress.'

There was an awkward silence.

'Perhaps someone was irked that this woman lives like a wife without being wed. So they just prefixed a Mrs. without specifying just whose Mrs. I might be.'

Mr. Bennet must have felt the strands of his hair that were floating in the breeze now stick to his scalp. He looked at me once as if to say, 'Why would anyone be bothered?' His wife was looking on merrily. The girl didn't seem to understand anything.

'I hope you're not pulling my leg?'

'Not at all. Do I look like Mrs. Gopali to you?'

'I don't know how to answer that, but...' he stopped, as if at a loss for words.

'But what?' I prompted him.

Spreading both his hands, he shrugged in a gesture typical of Westerners. I've also seen my Ph.D. friend and some people in Madras who read English novels shrug like that. I said, 'It wouldn't do to shrug it off like that! Mrs. Bennet, perhaps you could answer my question?'

'I don't know...but then I have never heard a conversation of this kind before!' she said.

'What is it, Ammani? All of you are laughing amongst yourselves. Do share it with me,' interrupted Gopali.

'He addressed me as Mrs. Gopali! It all started with that. I'm not going to let that go. So I told him the truth. For a second he looked as if he was hit on the head! Then he said I was being funny and trying to pull his leg.'

'And what truth did you tell him, pray?'

'That I'm like your wife, but not married to you.'

'Now look here, don't quarrel with me. It's true that I didn't marry you. To a point, you're right to have your way. But do I get furious about it? Why do you get upset over nothing?' said Gopali.

'Who is your spy? Pachiappan or Pattabhi?'

'How is that even relevant? You can continue talking to them. It's enough if you tell me a bit now and then. That's all I ask. I don't understand the language. What should I do if all of you keep laughing? Now tell him, he's also an old man like me, maybe just a few years older...No, let it be. Tell him that our country is not like theirs. That even with a living wedded wife, one can take another woman. Let's see what he says.'

Mr. Bennet was waiting expectantly with a smile. I didn't know how to proceed. Just how much did Gopali know? In trying to discern that, my mind split into two. I told him, 'You can tell them yourself. I'll translate it into English for them.'

'Really?'

'Yes.'

Gopali cleared his throat as if he was going to sing. 'You see,' he began in English, and continued in Tamil, 'In our country, one can have two wives. We can even marry three or four times. The maharajas had the custom of marrying forty or fifty times. It all depended on their wherewithal. King Dasaratha had three hundred and thirty-three wives, but only one queen.'

'I know that story,' said Mr. Bennet.

'The story is well-known,' said Gopali. 'What I'm talking about are the internal courtly intrigues. One queen to sit on the throne. But King Dasaratha married Kaikeyi for love. This love or desire eventually drained him of his own life. To think that his beloved wife could say something like that angered and hurt him grievously. But we don't know if it made him hate her. Outraged and grieving, he brushed her off in contempt. Suppose the lady had declared, "Beloved husband, I just blabbered something by mistake. Rama need not go to the forest, and Bharata need not be crowned king," the man would have replied, "Really? Here you are...I'll grant you two more boons!" Just because he burnt his fingers once, would he discard her? Every woman has something to offer.'

'I know. I've read the entire *Ramayana*, in translation. But your...okay, please continue,' said Mr. Bennet.

Gopali said, 'Your wife is pretty, so you don't have a chance to speak like me. Ammani, tell them that I think this lady is very pretty.'

'Oh! Oh! Oh!' said Mrs. Bennet, smiling archly.

'Saw that?' said Mr. Bennet, looking at Ammani. Then he turned to his wife and said, 'You should've met him ten years back, my dear.'

Even Mr. Mathur, who'd been rather aloof and standoffish till then, smiled slightly, as if despite himself. So far he seemed to have taken a vow not to smile.

'An uncouth couple divert themselves by thinking of some beautiful stranger. Likewise, when I eat my dinner, I take pride in my wife's cooking and relish it immensely,' said Gopali.

'She introduced you as a musician, but she forgot to say that you're also a humorous actor,' said Mr. Bennet.

'This isn't humour, it is the truth. Ammani here is an amazing person. She has renounced everyone and come to me.'

'That will do,' I told Gopali firmly.

'You will have to say that in English for me. You started it all by asking me to talk. All right now. Ammani is a wonderful person. Ramana was like all old men, had flat feet, a grey beard and flesh hanging loose. But for that reason can one regard him as an ordinary man, a common man? The same way, she looks like any other girl—she's pretty, fair, drapes her saree primly, she can sing, she can dance. But beyond all this, Ammani has something unique in her.'

'I am not going to translate you into English anymore,' I told Gopali.

'She says she won't translate me anymore. Look, you aren't saying any of this. *I* am. I will say what I have to say. And you must translate what I have to say. So...She has something in her. For one so young, she left everything and came to me. She may have a fascination for me or for my music. But beyond all that there is a stubborn wilful streak in her that makes her live life on her own terms. Can you do that? Can I? I'm always afraid of something or somebody. You may be afraid too. Your wife may also have some fears. Your country has a court for these things and you may have to be accountable to it. But *she*, she does not fear any of these things. If she doesn't like me, she'll just brush me off one fine day and walk out. The fact that she hasn't yet done so suggests that there may yet be something in me that still appeals to her. The day it goes, she'll certainly drive me out. But even that she will do gracefully. And she won't consider any obligations thereafter. She also won't change her original ideas for your sake or mine. She'll change them only for herself, and only if she is convinced that it is right for her to change them.'

'Ah! He loves you with all his heart!' said Mr. Bennet with a smile, glancing fondly at his wife.

5

Gopali talked about me for ten more minutes. I couldn't make out whether he was talking in earnest or in jest. I was translating all that into English without adding any colour to it, without a smile or a frown, impersonally, as if I wasn't the subject of the talk at all.

'I don't know English,' said Gopali. 'She keeps using this word love. I thought love is about a man loving a woman, or a woman loving a man. I had a cousin called Apparaja. He was a professional cook who set up his own sweet shop near Sarangapani temple, selling *pakodas* and *bajjis*. After closing his shop for the night, and having his meal, he would sit and write a novel. He wrote sheets after sheets, stacking bundles of them on the shelf where we keep the *vibhuthi*, or over the stand where the pot of water is kept for washing feet, or in the crevices of the box for utensils, he would keep them just anywhere. Whenever he met me, he would narrate the story of his latest novel. Each story was about a woman going alone to a temple, or a river bank, or travelling in a train. Then suddenly two men will come and grab her and make love to her. In every blessed story it was the same—she went someplace, men intercepted her, grabbed her and made love to her. It was then that I realised that 'love' here had another meaning. And going by what Ammani says, I now realise there are many more shades to it. Ammani wants to love everyone born in this world. She shakes hands with everyone. She wants to hug men, women, children, the old, relations, strangers, everyone. There should be no such thing as a husband or a wife, she says. She not only tells me all this, she also tells everyone that she comes across. But how is this possible, I ask her? It should be possible, she asserts. Only I didn't understand how. One day, I understood.

'In a dream, I was going somewhere in a crowded city. Perhaps it was for an election meeting or a shopping centre, it wasn't clear. There was a sea of faces. Even if you dropped a til seed, it wouldn't touch the ground, so dense was the crowd. She was also there with me. She kept shaking people's hands, hugging them and moving on. There was a veritable orgy of hugging. In a far corner sat an old man on a pyol. He had a grey moustache and beard, a good physique. Watching her shaking hands and hugging everyone he said, "So it has come!...It has finally come!" and he kept laughing loudly. "What has come?" I asked him. "Love! Love has come to earth at last. All of you are animals—only *she* is human. In a few hours, everyone will become human once again, just watch. I'm hanging on to life just for this day...even after my hundred years. You just wait and watch..." said the old man, all the while loudly cheering Ammani and laughing. She immediately turned to me and said, "Look at this old man, so ripe in wisdom! And look at you, standing here so silent and aloof. Why don't you too shake hands with everyone and hug everyone?" I said okay, and I shook hands with a woman who was sitting beside that ripe wisdom. Oh! You should've seen how the man instantly leapt at me! "Hey you! If I ask you to love everyone, does it mean that you should grab my wife's hand!" he shouted, grabbing my throat. The ripe wisdom's head had transformed into the head of a wolf who was strangling me. What's more, every head in the crowd had turned into a dog's head or a wolf's head. "You sinner!" shrieked the wolf-head, "You have turned everyone into dogs and wolves!" I too shrieked back in fear. Then all the wolves and dogs came at me together, snarling, baring their fangs.

'Finally I woke up, and heard my wife asking, "Why are you shouting?" She was massaging my chest. I sat up breathing hard, drenched in sweat, and stared around in fear. "What was the dream about?" she asked. I didn't tell her the whole thing. How could I? I only told her about the dogs and wolves falling over me and tearing me up. Even a wolf thinks that a wife is his property or that a husband is her property. Like I consider my voice, my music as my property. Like a stray dog that appropriates the whole street when it barks.'

Gopali stopped. I too stopped translating. For some time, only the noise of the speeding train could be heard.

'Why don't you say something?' Gopali asked Mr. Bennet.

'A dream is always funny. Can't make head or tail of it. I was trying to locate the end and the beginning of yours,' said Mr. Bennet.

'But that was a very clean dream, with the head and the tail all in their proper places.'

'You have never mentioned this dream to me all these days?' I said to Gopali in Tamil.

'And if I had, what would you have said? That it must be the result of indigestion. That all dreams are false and nonsensical, just like God. You would have said...and translate this as well in English for them.'

I did.

'Don't you believe in God?' Mr. Bennet asked me.

'No.'

'Really? Why is that? I need something to hold on to. I need an anchor, a protection. How can one live without a path, without a haven? Ultimately, we all do need some security.'

'So what if there is no security? Life is always without guarantees. That's normal life. Why should we fear? What should we fear?'

'Then, you only believe in yourself?'

'Yes.'

'But, if you believe in yourself, it means you also believe in God.'

'No, no. I don't believe that I am god or that god is within me. Please don't get me wrong.'

'Then you don't believe in yourself?'

'I said that I do. I also said that it's not how you put it...I wish to embrace everyone, to touch everyone with love. And that is enough for me.'

'Alright. Tell me honestly, would you do the same for a man with a festering, diseased body?'

I was silent in thought. I wished such a situation should never come about. But Mr. Bennet was waiting for a reply.

'Why do you harass her like this?' said Mrs. Bennet with a reproving look.

'You must forgive me. Ever since we started talking, I thought we could each let down our hair and speak frankly. I thought we mutually understood one another. If, as my wife says, my question is distressing to you, then please let's talk of something else.'

'I didn't think of it that way,' I said. 'You are quite justified in asking what you did. Sometimes we speak without thinking. Whatever I told you I have told others as well. But unlike you, no one has ever asked me anything in return. Perhaps they thought if they agreed with me without demur, I may do them a favour later. Or perhaps they thought there's a point in what I said. Anyhow. I could just keep responding to you equivocally and say, for instance, that I'll work towards conducting medical research to eradicate disease and to eradicate even the possibility of any man having a putrefying body. But that would not be an answer to your question...which you were right to ask. I think if one moves closely with a man who has a festering body, one wouldn't be disgusted to touch him. I think that in due course of time, it would be alright.'

'Hmm...' said Mr. Bennet. I felt like someone had trod all over my five-foot-six-inch body and reduced it to the size of a peanut. One could keep responding to this man's questions. What if I believed in god or didn't? How does it concern him? How does it matter to him whether I touched a sick man full of sores or didn't? Essentially, I was annoyed that I had run out of talking points.

'What are you all talking about?' asked Gopali.

I told him.

'Didn't you initiate the talk? Now you're cornered. If you ask me, it would be sensible to just keep quiet,' said Gopali.

'It wasn't I who wanted to break the ice by distributing Mysore pak.'

'I merely asked you to talk to them. I didn't ask you to get cornered. Now you tell them in English for me: You see, my only love is singing. After I harmonise the shruti and sing for some time, I keep on singing. When I sing I'm not aware of anything else. Even of myself. For that time, *that* music alone is my one great love. And when I finish, I wonder why I was born into this world. Sometimes I even feel sick.'

'True. The human body cannot endure that kind of *samadhi.* The system breaks down. That is why people like you should toughen your body,' said Mr. Bennet.

'In that case, if the body must stay fit, then one shouldn't contemplate on God all the time,' said Gopali. 'I believe you just said that I should make my body tough.'

'I said so because you mentioned that you felt sick and lost sometimes. If you do not wish to dissolve, to disintegrate, to melt in that great all-consuming love, then you must certainly toughen yourself. How many can really be like that? If everyone could be like that, then what is there to talk about?'

I thought that the conversation had jumped the rails and was now drifting. Why were they vexing themselves like this? Why this idle talk about love and god? It was unbearable.

'Mr. Bennet, from your conversation, it seems like you have met god,' I said with a laugh.

'I haven't. Like you, I too get angry when people talk about God. I wander about in search of what God could be like. You said one should move with people, love people, not discriminate against anyone. That is how I too have disciplined myself. When you said in the beginning that you felt like touching everyone, hugging everyone, I felt that a gateway had been opened. But when you issued a proviso explaining that only healthy bodies qualified, I felt that the gateway had been shut again.'

'What gateway?'

'The gateway for the building within which God is seated.'

'If one could eradicate all hunger and disease, one needn't even open the gateway.'

'We don't have to. He will himself open it and look at everything in wonder. "But this is great! Man has truly advanced," He will say, amazed. But somehow I doubt if He would look at it that way. See how the old man's head metamorphosed into a wolf's head when someone tried to shake hands with his wife—I mean the old man in the dream. The rotting body is only a physical manifestation of a rotting mind...So long as you think this is mine and that is yours, the body will rot, and the old man's head will certainly transform into a wolf's,' said Mr. Bennet.

As he kept talking and as his words kept falling on my ears, I remembered something. When I was ten, a neighbour's child came down with small pox. The affliction reached a peak and then surfaced virulently as eruptions on the body, which festered like cow dung. It choked the eyes, ears and throat of the child and burst out in a furious rash all over his small body. But the mother laid him on her lap and tried to soothe him as best as she could. Her mother-in-law, sister-in-law, neighbours and friends—no one came near her. There was no medical treatment. No doctor either. The child was moaning. Nothing would go down his throat, neither milk nor water. Finally, the mother wailed and said, "Take him, oh Lord, please take him! Take him or take me. No...no! Don't take me. Take him instead...If he survives with this disfigured body, only You will be blamed," she cried. In the end, death claimed the child. No one came near. No one took the child on their lap to relieve the distraught, hungry, sleepless mother. Only Death volunteered.

Mr. Bennet had stopped talking. As if I'd woken up from sleep, I said, 'What you said is true,' and I narrated to him the story of the child's agony and the mother's anguish.

'Why didn't your god save this child?' I asked him finally.

'But He did,' said Mr. Bennet.

'By asking him to die?'

'Yes. How do we know that by relieving him of his misery, God has not saved the child? But more than the child's agony, I can only think of the mother. Laying her child on her lap, oblivious of herself, praying for him with all her soul—these are the signs of her vision of God. God does not show Himself as a flame over the crucifix. He does not appear with a trident or with a conch in hand. He will be found in that state of oblivion and selflessness, with a baby on His lap,' said Mr. Bennet.

'What a god!' I said, laughing loudly.

'Your smile is very pretty. Ever since I started talking to you, you've been smiling at almost everything, so I thought perhaps you were born with a smile. And I've been wondering why I am unable to smile like this. But the way you laughed just now, saying "What a god!"...that is something I didn't like.'

'Why?'

'It is the chuckle of a Marxist.'

'Correct. You said that I don't have a god. If I were to believe in a god, I would say it is Marx,' I said, still laughing.

'Marx is an agent of Satan. He thought he would bring prosperity to the world without God's help and that he could eradicate poverty. Poverty can be eradicated and prosperity can be brought. But one cannot bring about happiness. Envy cannot be banished. Instead of fighting on an empty stomach, people will eat well, belch and then fight. If people don't fight for food, they will fight for money or fame or power or for what you term as love,' said Mr. Bennet.

'Isn't it better to fight on a full stomach rather than hungry?'

'People will fight at any rate. Do you at least accept that?'

'No, I don't. You talk as if men are knaves. I don't think so. Even if they were, isn't it better to fight on a full stomach?' I asked with a smile.

'But that's even more dangerous,' said Bennet.

'Who knows!'

'I say this after having witnessed how well-fed, prosperous people fight.'

'You allude to a country in which only a few are prosperous. What I mean is a country like the Ramarajya of Marx,' I said, and laughed again.

Mr. Bennet threw up his hands. His wife laughed. I too laughed.

'What...? What happened?' asked Gopali, excited.

'He surrendered, admitting defeat.'

'How did he lose?' asked Gopali.

I told him.

'Ask him this: Does raising your hands mean you admit defeat? Or do you mean to say, "Oh God, save her!"?'

I did. And just like my Ph.D. friends, Mr. Bennet shrugged his shoulders.

Delhi. Calcutta. Nagpur. Bombay. I wasn't feeling too good even as we reached Nagpur. On reaching Bombay, however, it turned to fear.

'What's wrong? Why are you so off-colour?' Gopali asked me, still high at the end of a brilliant concert. He had forgotten himself in his ecstasy. It was an oceanic ecstasy, heaving at the sight of such a huge audience, a feeling that he transmitted to everyone.

'Gopali, was it truly you who sang!' gushed a brahmin widow draped in a coarse silk saree that was drawn over her head. She must have been seventy. Then quite unexpectedly, she bent down and touched Gopali's feet, placing her brow upon them.

'Oh ho! How sinful! How terribly sinful!' said Gopali, springing back as if he'd been stabbed. 'What is your age, Amma, and what is mine? Aren't you like a mother to me?'

'To have a son like you and to prostrate before him is a blessing for a mother!'

'But I'm a *pashandan*, Amma, a depraved man,' said Gopali, not looking at me.

'How does it matter? Didn't the Devi drink toddy? Didn't she call out to her faithful ones, "Hold on, I am coming!" and then drink and rout the demons? Didn't Krishna wed a thousand times? In what way are you depraved? And if you are, you have a right to be. So many *apaswara*, discordant singers sporting gold-laced dhotis and javvadhu drink themselves silly and fancy themselves as great music *vidwan*s. As if these caterwaulers can do anything without brandy! These things are appropriate only for you. I have been initiated by the Devi. I do not prostrate before anyone except the Devi,' said the widow proudly.

The old woman was laying it on thick. Her son, daughter-in-law, grandson and granddaughter were all watching, speechless. Gopali shrank back from her flattery as if a prickly caterpillar had crawled all over him. There was an awkward silence when she momentarily seemed at a loss for words. Then she turned to her son Natarajan and said, 'Nataraju! You throw all these parties for this boss and that of your upstart company, where liquor flows like water. Honestly, if you had learnt music like I did from my grandfather, you would've given your glass, bottle and everything to Gopali and admitted that, "I deserve nothing. This is all for you. Who else can sing like you!" He is an avatar. And he calls himself a drunkard! What a thing to say!'

We were put up on the first floor of her son's house. After dinner, Gopali sat down with Natarajan and opened the bottle. I was sitting on the floor in a corner, writing a letter to Pattabhi.

'...I think perhaps it would be better if, like all of you, I too believed in God. I long for a God who would instantly respond to my call. It's been over thirty-five days now. Do you understand? When I think of it, fear grips me. Yes, even me. I always thought I was brave. You, Gopali and the whole world think that I am very brave. But in a situation like this, I don't think even the most reckless person can help trembling like a sparrow. That is why I long for the humility and the strength of trusting in a God, my own private and personal God...'

6

I couldn't hear what Gopali and Natarajan were saying. I was going through my letter over and over again. The entire letter seemed to appear in the shape of Pattabhi's back, his brow, his chest, his stomach. As if I had inscribed with my fingers every word on the parts of his body...as if I was observing Pattabhi inside out. Only he could show me a way out in a moment like this. He never backed out of anything or hesitated or said 'No' to me, ever. He always got me whatever I asked him for, even at midnight or in the afternoon. One by one, the brute naked energy of each one of his gestures rose up in my mind and filled it...I remembered his lifting me up. Hoisting me over his head like a doll of pith, laughing. I too had laughed with him. I knew he wouldn't drop me.

One by one, all these memories were being relived in the letter. His grotesque height, his uncouth awkward gait. His feet, ankles, thighs, arms, torso, nothing looked in harmony with each other. And yet I saw them as one unified whole. Nothing about his body struck a false note. I could trust his legs, his arms, his feet, his eyes, his speech, his desire, his toughness, his audacity, his affection with my eyes closed—none of them were deceitful. What has he ever refused me? Pattabhi, why aren't you here right now, beside me, and not eight hundred miles away in Madras?

'Can't you hear me? I'm calling you, Ammani!' Gopali said, almost shouting now.

I got startled.

'How many times should I call you?'

'I think she is contemplating something deeply,' said Natarajan.

'What are you contemplating? Are you building castles? What are you writing?' asked Gopali.

'A letter.'

'To whom?'

'Pattabhi.'

'What made you suddenly think of Pattabhi now? Why don't you come and sit here? I brought you along so that you can speak in English, but here you are, brooding about Pattabhi.'

I stared at the bottle. Three-fourths of it was empty. I thought it better to go and sit near him. It would also help me forget myself for a time.

'Ha Amma...Ma Parashakti!' I heard someone muttering.

The old lady, exhausted by her climb up the stairs, now stood there panting, holding her hips.

'What is it, Amma?' asked Natarajan.

'What's this, Nataraju? You've both settled down again with the bottle? There was a session before dinner. Now why again?'

'Is there any ordained time for worship?' said Gopali, looking at Natarajan.

'Some worship!' said the old lady, plonking down on a sofa.

'But it was you who said that brandy, whisky and all that have been made only for me. That's why I'm drinking, Amma!' said Gopali with mock humility.

'True, but you have turned the tables on me!'

'What have I turned?'

'I said that all these were made for you. Should you now reverse it by saying that you are made only for them?' said the lady. Then she adjusted her glasses and looked at me. 'What's the use of your accompanying him, Ammani? Did you come along just to hear your Guru sing? And to watch while he drinks—before dinner, after dinner, at bedtime and on waking up! You should snatch the bottle and put it away in the almirah. It is you who must draw the line. Kittappa used to be like this. Finally his liver became hard like stone and he died. If one is moderate, one lives to drink. But if you jump in head on, you'll choke and drown!'

'But that is the very thing to do, Amma! That is the right thing,' said Gopali.

'What?'

'I cannot sing when I grow old. The voice will not obey my dictates. Neither will my body. But even so, no one will leave us alone. Nor will the desire of youth leave us. Why sing and chafe everyone's ears and ruin our reputation? An old man of ninety remembers the flame of his youth when he sees a prostitute of eighty. It'll be such an offensive sight for the young. Why court such a risk? The right time to die is when one is still able to sing well.'

'That is quite enough! You talk smartly. The two of you, now just get up and go to bed. I say Natarajan, get up! It's twelve-thirty.'

'Just half a round more, Amma, with your blessings,' said Gopali. 'Please serve us with your own hands.'

The old lady laughed. 'All right,' she said. Taking the bottle, she poured them half a spoon each. Then she stood there with her hands on her hips and said commandingly, 'Natarajan, now gulp that down and get up.'

I took the bottle from her and kept it inside the almirah. Not seeing a way out, Natarajan downed his glass in one gulp and got up. The lady rinsed the glasses under a tap outside and put them inside the almirah. 'The Devi drank to wage a war. You men drink to stay in peace. What can one say to that! Why do you need all this nonsense when music itself is so intoxicating? The Devi who wrote music in your destiny, why couldn't she write this too? O Devi Ma Parashakti, what kind of divine frolic and play is this…!' she muttered aloud as she doddered down the stairs.

As she was going down, Gopali looked at me and softly murmured, 'The fact that I had two children by Kunjali is because I drank this and forgot myself. But if I tell this old woman, she'll again start talking endlessly!' He unrolled the mattress on the bed and lay down. And in a few minutes he was fast asleep. He didn't even think of calling me.

I thought of the old lady's mutterings and wanted to laugh. But what I actually felt was pity. I sat at his feet and pressed his legs. As she said, it's not just brandy and whisky that are made for you. I, Ammani, and many others like me, are also made for you, I ruminated as I massaged his calf, the soles of his feet, his toes. Gopali slept on, oblivious. I thought of Pattabhi.

Again, that fear. I got up, opened the box and took out the letter I had written to Pattabhi.

'Pattabhi, do you recall the white family on the train that I mentioned, the Bennets? Like everyone else, Bennet commented on my smile. He said that I smile beautifully, and that he was unable to smile like that. But he didn't like the way I laughed at god. In Delhi, I laughed at the trees standing in thousands of rows. Laughed at the berries of the neem tree. Laughed at the birds. When the Maharaja ruled Mysore, whenever an ox cart or horse cart passed through the street, leaving dung in its wake, a man would instantly materialise from somewhere, sweep up the dung in a basket, and disappear. But after we attained independence, people just looked on pitifully on the dung and left it on the road. I had the same apprehension about the trees in Delhi, that they may cut them to the ground and lay the city

bare. I felt like laughing at the people ruling Delhi. It was as if they looked upon trees and birds as rustic, backward things.

'A top government official in Delhi once invited Gopali and me for dinner. There was a large garden around the bungalow. The host and Gopali were having drinks in the veranda. The host's wife was also there. The man was telling Gopali about the superior vintage of the drink. That it was stored in a wooden barrel and fermented for a long time. Then they talked about music. He asked Gopali about the frequency of pratimadhyama. *Gopali blinked. The host's expression said:* Do you venture to sing without knowing even this? *Then he explained the number of notes for each swaram and demonstrated each note by tapping on everything—the whisky bottle, the table, the glass, the ash tray, the cigarette carton. Gopali could make nothing of it. Still, he turned to me and said, "Ammani, did you note how he researches into music? This is genius. It's not surprising that he administers such an important department," and he kept looking at the hostess. She was very lovely, and had no understanding of music. But she invited every musician to her house for dinner. It seems the first dinner any visiting musician, dancer, singer or newspaper editor had in Delhi was at their house. "Chowdiah visited our house, also Madurai Mani. Ariakkudi was here, Rajaratnam, and Vasan," she was telling me. As we talked, a minister turned up. Elucidating what the* Silappadikaram *says about music, he also sang a little.*

'That's when I laughed aloud. Surprised, they all turned around. "You sing exactly like that!" I said, turning my laughter into a note of wonder. "Like what?" he asked. "I felt as if it was Eswaramma singing!" I said. "Good! You've put it so crisply," he said. "After all, she is Gopali's disciple. Do you see how attentively she follows a conversation?" said the hostess in English. Then she said to me, "Why aren't you saying anything, Ammani?"

'"You have such lovely trees in the house. Who planted them? I feel like climbing all of them," I said. Everyone gave me a strange look. The hosts' married daughter joined us after a while. Her mother said her son-in-law was studying abroad. I said, "You're all such learned people. Yet you haven't taught your

daughter free love. You've treated her like a backward rustic and married her off," I said, smiling my usual smile. Did they think I was impertinent or an upstart or just plain insane, someone who reads a lot of rubbish? Or perhaps they thought I was an uncouth person who speaks anyhow she pleases in the company of educated people? Perhaps all this.

'We were invited to two other houses. The boy in the house repeated what Bennet had said, "Your husband sings very well." "He is not my husband," I said. "Oh, do excuse me! I thought you were married." "No," I said. "You are...to him?" he persisted. "I'm Gopali's sister-in-law, but I can also be called his wife," I said softly, but made sure that his parents heard me. None of them knew what to say. The lady took the boy inside on an excuse.

'That night Gopali asked me why I kept giggling like that and telling lies. I said, "All of them want to impress upon you that they know more than you about music. So I have to shock them with something. That's why I blabber like this. So that they get a little perturbed and wonder why they invited a madwoman like me, given their status and importance. I'm having some fun at their cost. But no one will misunderstand you. They'll take you for a true musician and leave you alone. They'll just assume that you're running around with a pretty nut and perhaps feel sorry for you. Their displeasure will be directed at me, but that's okay," I laughed.

'While in Calcutta, at the house of a pious company officer, I scared the hostess and the other women in the family by declaring that I had many lovers. The host showed us around town in his car. We were all on the back seat, he, his wife, I and Gopali. The host had his left arm stretched out behind. A couple of times he touched the flowers in my hair. Abruptly, I asked him with feigned annoyance, "Mama, why are you disturbing the flowers in my hair?" This was one of the many laughs.

'Now I want to compensate for all that and have a good cry. Thirty days were already over when we were at Nagpur. I remember we had a Sanskrit master when we were studying for the Intermediate. One day, while teaching the Shakuntalam *in prose, he remarked that pregnancy was the entertainment tax*

on love, and laughed like he laughed at all his own jokes. We used to join in his naïve laughter. Now this memory makes me cry. I keep rubbing my midriff. It feels just as usual. It should be. If it were you, you would say, "O God, let it be." I cannot bring myself to say that. I wish you were with me.

'Perhaps there is such a thing as God. Perhaps he is like a devil or just an ordinary rogue. Will he mock me because I mock everyone all the time? On whom is the joke now? I want to come away right now. I know you'll show me a way, you'll give me courage...I'm laid up in a hospital, shrieking that something is turning in my stomach, that someone is gagging me with a cloth to stifle my shrieks...

'Gopali doesn't seem keen to leave. There's a concert this evening. He is still exhilarated with yesterday's concert. He is fast asleep, drunk on everyone's encomiums. I feel like doing away with myself at such moments...I only feel that way, but I won't do it...Who is there to bother about me?

'In the beginning did girls get married only to become mothers? What difference has it made a million years later? Though I go on like this, a thick fear is percolating down like a hot calcium injection into my heart and stomach. What am I scared of? Of disgrace? Of dying? At times I wish that I'd been born in another country. But where is that country? After meeting the Bennets, I think that the white people are even more cowardly and obscurantist than us. I'll have to create my own kind of country within me. I only have to smile disdainfully and say, "Of what concern is it to you?" and that country will be born. But will I be able to? It is said that in sleep or in dream, you cannot run. Like that, I have a terrible doubt: will I be able to laugh disdainfully? If you are with me, I can. But not when I'm with Gopali. My mind is restless...I don't know why I'm so scared...There's a big stone in my stomach...'

All this wasn't just a dialogue in my mind. I was writing it all down, but didn't know how to proceed. I kept the two sheets back in the box and closed it. Looked at Gopali. Opened his box. Took out the bottle wrapped in a silk cloth and opened it. Taking a glass from the almirah, I poured some, mixed it with water from the tap outside. I drank it in the balcony. Mixed some more. Drank that too. My stomach was on fire. I switched off the light and lay down.

7

When I woke up, the street noises, the honking of cars and the rattle of automobiles assailed my ears. For a few moments I was completely disoriented. There was an indistinct dreamy feeling that this was the house in Madras. But there was no sapodilla plum tree or mango tree outside. No coconut palm fronds. I couldn't see Pachiappan's face outside the window. There was no rice-paper lantern hanging above. No, this was not the Madras house. It took me two minutes to realise that it was Natarajan's house in Bombay.

I looked around. There was no sign of Gopali. I felt a heaviness and slight headache as I got up and rolled the mattress. I could smell a certain odour in my blouse and my arms. A nocturnal odour of liquor and perspiration. I brushed my teeth, washed my face and wiped my body with a damp cloth. I powdered my face and neck, back, chest, arms and legs, rubbed it into my skin. I thought of the old lady, standing hands on her hips, bearing her weight on her spindly legs. She seemed to chuckle: 'So you too joined the worship of the Devi after I went down? From where did you get it? Did Gopali have another bottle inside the box?'

It was well worth going down, if only to see that laugh. It was a pleasant smile that exuded the spirit of a live-and-let-live forgiveness. Suppose I spoke to her, while she was still pleasant, about 'this' as well?

The thought resurfaced. A stone in the stomach. Who were these people? I didn't know them. Who was I? They may be solicitous to me, but once I leave this place, they may laugh at me behind my back. Or they may strike their foreheads in shame and put it all down to fate. Then I also have this headache. I powdered my whole body again to obliterate the smell. Combed my hair. But the odour still seemed to persist. I rinsed my hair under the tap, dried it, applied a little hair oil and combed my hair again.

When I went down, Natarajan's wife brought coffee for me.

'You were studying till late it seems,' smiled the old lady, hands on her hips.

Ah! I got that smile!

'Natarajan and Gopali went out on a visit while you were asleep. They may return any time now. It was eight when they left,' she said.

'What's the time now?' I asked.

'Quarter to eleven.'

'Oh dear! To think that I slept so long!'

'What "Oh dear". You've been continuously travelling by train for a month now. So what if you slept a little longer? Gopali wanted to wake you up, in fact, but I would have none of it. Have a bath and get ready. When the two of them return, we'll eat,' said the old lady.

Even as I was changing my saree, I could hear Gopali and Natarajan shuffling in.

'You're back? You've taken a long time,' said the old lady.

'Yes. We looked up a couple of people, and also booked tickets at the Victoria Terminus. He has to leave tonight,' said Natarajan.

'Who?'

'This Gopali of yours, who else.'

'What's this, Gopali? Do you have time to finish the concert and then board the train?' asked the lady.

'I'll finish the concert at eight-thirty. Then have supper and head straight for the station.'

'Didn't you say that you were going to stay on for two or three days and go around the city?'

'No Amma. I'm in a hurry. I'll have to go.' To all her probing, Gopali merely repeated that he had some work to do. What had happened so suddenly?

I went to the concert in the evening. Predictably, he sang the *mangalam*, the concluding song, at eight-thirty. But there was no life in his singing. He kept glancing at his watch as he sang listlessly.

When the train moved, Gopali rolled his eyes and asked me, 'Satisfied?'

'What about?'

'You can see Pattabhi as soon as you get off the train, that's what! Thank god, you didn't lock the suitcase before you slept. Otherwise, I would still be scuttling around the Gateway of India, the Marine Drive and other places. What madness! I know that I don't work with Pattabhi's solicitude. But for that reason, you don't even consider me a person!' said Gopali, with a hard stare.

I listened to him like a wedded wife.

Opening the suitcase, he took out a bottle, poured some into a silver tumbler and offered it to me. 'Drink this up,' he said. 'What on earth is there to worry about now?'

Have I ever broken down in Gopali's presence before this? After Periappa's visit, yes. But that's an old story. Today I sobbed in much the same way.

Suddenly, he was like a father, his hands gently stroking my hair.

8

What did I want?

Why didn't I ask myself this question all these days? Was it Pattabhi who gave shape and substance to that amorphous and wordless thing that was swirling within me?

I didn't give an immediate reply to Pattabhi. Even if I had, what would he understand? For that matter, what would I understand?

Suddenly, Pattabhi stood before me like a guru. I must have asked a hundred others the same question that he asked me.

But not the way he did, straight and blunt. I have been asking them without recourse to words. With my eyes. With my body. With my anger. With my laughter. When I brought about a rift between a couple, I put out a hand between the estranged couple, pushing them far away from each other and widening the gap between them till they could not even see each other. I asked them the very same question, without their knowledge.

Is there anyone that Gopali hasn't touched with his voice? Anyone who is not caught in the whirlpool of his music? Even government officers who had grown numb, gambling away their eyes and lives on dog-eared papers stuffed between brown folders, even they woke up to look around in wonder and stirred with life when they heard Gopali singing.

With his influence, I have travelled by air, mingling with troupes of performers in culture festivals. I have danced in China, Japan, London, Paris, Russia and its neighbouring countries. The impresario ushered me onto the stage with a wave of his arms and introduced me with the same flourish. At the end of my dance, the audience stood up in a standing ovation. And applauded each time I came forward to acknowledge it with a bow. Even after retreating backstage, I would respond to curtain calls by coming back on stage four or five times. When I re-entered the stage for the fifth time, I felt like laughing. Laughter exploded from within the quiet smile that I outwardly wore. What had they discovered? Why did they call for me again and again? What had they understood? What had they seen in my performance? But under all of this arrogance, a little unease fluttered within me—had they perhaps seen and understood something that had eluded me? Why did I dance? Why do I dance? Even I didn't know. So what had they discovered?

An old man came into the green room and, with a *namaskar*, said, 'That was great! Great!' I caught his hands in mine and shook them. Mr. Aggarwal, our manager, must have felt like an army of black ants was crawling all over him. He had been firmly upholding the Indian custom of just folding our hands together in a namaskar by way of greeting. What greatness had this old man discovered in my dance? What had he understood? I recalled what my friend, an ageing danseuse, had shared after a performance. 'Only now am I truly beginning to understand what dance is. But I'm unable to dance anymore,' she said regretfully, referring to her ageing body. That is why when the old man said 'Great!' I silently told him, come now, don't blabber! Here, shake my hand. It is a twenty-eight-year old hand, that's just what you want. I remembered Pattabhi who had asked with his huge eyes and height, 'What do you want? What do *you* really want?' In a corner of my heart, his question glowed like the pearly pool of light from the bedroom lamp in the dark. I had become tired of it all. Except for the first time, or perhaps the second, third or fourth time, I have been dancing mechanically like pedalling a bicycle. What could they possibly discover in my dance when even I felt so jaded? How can one keep repeating the same thing time after time? Is all this applause only for a parrot-like repetition!

Back home after the third tour, I got irritated with Gopali. Since I had only toured South Asia then, I didn't have much fatigue. Gopali had listened eagerly to all my anecdotes about Tokyo, Singapore, Bangkok and Jakarta.

'Now all that's left for you is Africa and America,' he said.

'I won't go anywhere now wearing these anklets,' I said.

'Why? Why are you so angry suddenly? With whom?'

'With myself! With you! You can learn a hundred *kritis*, study thirty ragas and keep minting money for thirty-five years, repeating the same songs. *I* cannot. My legs ache.'

'Your legs ache?'

'The legs in my head ache. The legs in my heart ache. Why keep on doing the same thing endlessly? What for?'

'Sometime back you got furious that something had got into your stomach. You were hissing at me that all children should be dumped into a garbage bin. Today you're tired of repeating yourself. What do you want anyway?'

That hit me on the head. What was the difference between this question and Pattabhi's? I felt angry. But I also felt like laughing at the truth of it all. When you dance publicly for the first time, it is fear. Dancing the second time is courage. Dancing the third time is habit. If there is anything new the fourth time, it is entirely in one's imagination. The fifth time, it is boring. From then on it is just like an ox going round and round at an oil press. I hate it. Everyone clapped and praised me. It was pathetic to see so much praise bestowed on a pancake machine that keeps on turning on its grooves. So I felt at least they could have a touch of my hands. It was incredible. By shaking a hand, one can also guess its profession. Sometimes on a bus in this city, on certain routes you see fishermen board it. Each one has stubby fingers, with nails as wide as one rupee coins. I guessed this was due to the casting of nets and the rowing they did. Yes, one can guess a person's work by shaking hands. But no, even that is not always true. In Belgrade, two newsmen shook my hands. One man's hand was like cast iron, the other's felt like a kitten's skin. I tried to find out why when I held each hand the last time I went out.

'Is this all you got out of that big trip?'

'That's what I also ask myself. But everyone was happy I shook hands with them. More than understanding dance, the handshake seemed to be a great satisfaction.'

'Does it satisfy you?'

'What is it to people if they watch my dance or listen to your music? Are they going to sing or dance on their own?'

'I don't understand anything that you're saying.'

I didn't understand what it was that Gopali didn't understand. When I returned from my first international trip, Gopali asked me boldly but conversationally, 'You had no fear this time, like you had in Bombay?'

'Now I have learnt to be careful,' I retorted.

Would he understand if I were to say that I wish to live with all the men in the world like a wife, if only for a moment? He might just smirk. People smirk when they don't understand. Floren, Ludwig, Ivan, Pinet, Giovanni, Parvene...if I listed the names of these young men, he might get annoyed. Or he might liken me to a grinding stone and pity me or scoff at me. He had given me an indication of it once. There was one Narayanaswami in his village who lived a stone's throw from his house. He was closeted with his wife night and day. Narayanaswami's old hunchbacked, one-eyed aunt rebuked her nephew's wife, saying, 'Don't you have any sensitivity? If you make him realise that your body is not a grinding stone, he would go out and work in the fields like other men.' Gopali had narrated this to me. If I told him about all that happened on my tours, he would start talking about the body and its disease. I tried to put an end to the day's chatter by saying, 'Hereafter, I'm not going anywhere to dance.'

'You don't want any more tours?'

'I didn't say that. I said I won't go out *to dance* anymore. I'll go out just for my pleasure. I'll roam around, talk, look at people, stand on a hill, face the sea, wander about in market places.'

'If someone asks what have you come for and what do you want?'

'I'll say it's none of your business, and move on.' Even as I said this, Pattabhi had walked into a corner of my heart to ask: What do you want, Ammani?

9

Pattabhi wasn't there even when I returned from my first foreign tour of dance concerts. Gopali had turned him out of the house within three days. On the fourth day, Pattabhi brought an auto-rickshaw, loaded his boxes into it. Then came upstairs for his remaining things: a bedding, a water jug and a wooden box.

'Where are you going?' I asked.

'I've fixed up another room.'

'Where?'

'In Saidapet.'

'Did I ask you to look for another room?'

'No.'

'Then with whose permission are you moving out?'

'Gopali Mama's.'

'Is he your boss?'

'In this house, he is.'

'Am I not your boss then?'

Pattabhi smiled.

'Aren't you ashamed to leave like this?'

'I am more ashamed to stay on.'

'For that reason, should you leave so abruptly...without even telling me?'

'Why all this propriety now? Does respect have to be declared?'

'I'm not talking about respect.'

'Respect is about observing limits, in drawing a line somewhere. It cannot be measured in words.'

'Now look here, will you bring your boxes back here and dismiss the auto?'

'I must get going now.'

'I didn't know you were so hopeless!'

He smiled again.

'Do you find this lowly?'

He shook his head in a 'No.'

'Just stay on then.'

'Ammani, I asked you the other day: what do you want? You didn't answer. If you'd given me the slightest hint, I would've even rented a house. My mother adores me. And she is far braver than you are. Just one word from me, and she will summon a priest, fix a *muhurtham* and bring us together.'

My ire and vexation evaporated on hearing this, and I started laughing loudly, helplessly. I wanted to hold my stomach and control my laughter, but couldn't. In the grip of that laughter, I didn't think of stopping him. It took me minutes to realise that he was gone. I rushed to the balcony and looked down. Pattabhi was getting into the auto-rickshaw. I ran down the stairs, but before I could reach the front yard, the auto-rickshaw had left. Running out of the compound wall,

I stopped near the gate. The auto-rickshaw had just turned into another street. I stood there, looking blank.

New Mambalam suddenly looked desolate, like a dark and gloomy forest. Everything looked and felt dark. Was it fear, anger or humiliation? But who had humiliated me? Pattabhi or Gopali? I felt very restless. There was a key ring in my hand, my thumb was fiddling with it but I'd no clue from where or when I'd got it.

It was an effort to walk back home. The housewife on the first floor was staring at me. With the usual expression that everyone in that house wore—the man, the woman, the daughter and the son: 'So, you are *that* kind of a woman,' said their poker faces. As usual I ignored it, closed the door and went up.

I called out to Pachiappan. No reply. I looked out of the window and saw that his room was locked.

I felt a mad wild frenzy grip my hands. I walked up to the pictures that Gopali had put up on the wall and ripped them out savagely. Tyagaraja tumbled out with a nail. Rama and Krishna dangled from snapped strings. Some lay face down on the floor, some lay face up, inert, helpless.

I went to my room and lay down on the bed. Closed my eyes. I felt fearful again. What was Pattabhi's new address in Saidapet? I didn't know. He hadn't disclosed.

'Bring us together'? Whatever for? In *marriage*? If I was the marrying kind, why on earth would I come and live here like this, Pattabhi!

But if it's not marriage, then what *do you want?*

'To slap you hard!' I said aloud, giving Pattabhi a tight slap in my head. He rubbed his cheek.

I heard the sound of a lock clicking open. Someone coughed and cleared their throat.

When I woke up, it was evening. There was light in Pachiappan's room. He peered through the window. Then he came in and looked at me.

'Shall I switch on the light, Amma?'

'No. Let it be. Did you see Pattabhi?'

'Only in the morning.'

'Where are you coming from?'

'From Aiyah's house.'

'Pattabhi has moved out to Saidapet,' I said and, opening the door, stepped into the rear verandah.

'Moved out?'

'Yes. To Saidapet.'

'Why?'

'You should ask your Aiyah that.'

'The Master?'

'Yes.'

Pachiappan bowed his head, silent. Then he saw the pictures lying scattered on the floor and said, 'For that reason, is this the way to react?' He picked up the pictures and patted them as if they were children who had fallen and bruised themselves. Wiping them lovingly with his cloth, he leaned them against the wall.

'Go tell your Aiyah that I want him to come.'

'Right now?'

'Yes.'

'Amma, please listen to me, and please don't think I'm being impertinent. I'm saying this only out of my loyalty for you.'

'What is it?'

'I'm getting married next month. I was thinking of building a hut here, in the backyard. Till then, please don't do anything. If you have a row with Aiyah over something and if you get angry and go away somewhere, it is I who will suffer.'

I didn't understand anything. 'You are getting married?' I repeated mechanically.

'Yes Amma. Next month. You should stay here, please. That would be a big favour for me. You should attend my wedding. Perhaps the senior Aiyah doesn't like the junior Aiyah. But please don't say anything to senior Aiyah right now and please don't quarrel. He need not come here right now. Please sit down for a moment, Amma, and please listen to me calmly.'

Was there a command in his tone? No, just an affectionate request. Was my body still trembling in anger? Has he noticed it, and is that why he is taking advantage of me? I spread the mat on the floor and sat down on it.

'Tell me, when did you fix up your marriage?'

'A year ago. She is related to me.'

'But you never told me.'

'I didn't want to, even today. Thought I would tell you when I give you the invitation card. But today it just spilled out on the spur of the moment.'

Why was he telling me all this? Of all the people, why do I have to hear about marriage? My first and only impulse was to warn him.

'Pachiappa, don't think I'm talking crazy. But tell me, why should one get married?'

Silence.

'Do you really think everyone is happy in marriage? For a month or two, there may be some love. Then it begins to turn sour. The man may look at another woman. The woman may long for another man. That's where it starts. If they fear the neighbours or don't have the courage to fight, they'll keep snarling at each other like wild cats. If they're clever, they'll camouflage their feelings. And if they're naïve, they may fight openly. But don't think that I've gone mad and that I'm rambling on like this just when you've told me you're getting married.'

'No Amma, no. What you say is funny. You say the love lasts only a month or two. Is that all? You think it won't work beyond that?' he asked with a shy smile.

Pachiappan stood at the mouth of a cave called marriage. I stopped for a moment to ponder what that cave might hold. An aroma of incense sticks wafted from within. Perhaps a sadhu was doing a pujai. When you entered the cave, he ceremoniously offered you sweets. And when you reverentially prostrated before him, he raised his sword and brought it down on your neck to make his human sacrifice.

'Pachiappa, shall I tell you something?'

'Yes, Amma.'

'You must have heard the saying that a young calf knows no fear?'

'Yes.'

'For a child, it is all the same, whether it is a scorpion, a baby snake, a lump of jaggery or a *laddu*. The child will tug at the baby snake by its tail. All of us are also like children...that is, until we marry. Or else, why would we pick up a scorpion in our hands, mistaking it to be a butterfly? Only when we marry do we realise our mistake. That very moment, the child in us grows up.'

'And grows wiser?'

'Not just wiser, but really old!'

'You mean all those married people out there are doddering around on crutches?'

'Yes, except that the crutches are invisible. Even those with old bodies are loath to use crutches. How else can they convince others that they're not yet old? Only when they trip someday and get their brow or nose bruised do they realise the necessity of a crutch.'

Pachiappan laughed till his whole body shook and tears ran down his cheeks. He laughed with his mouth open, revealing betel-stained teeth. There could be only one meaning to his laughter: 'You mad woman! You talk as if you know all there is to know in all the three worlds!'

Was it only Pachiappan and Pattabhi that I argued with? I must have argued with hundreds of people. Countless men and women who passionately and ignorantly claimed that marriage was a civilised relationship—their scheming wiles, their blunders, their pathetic blinkers, their instability, their infatuation, their flagellant masochism, their self-love, their gods, their fears, their cowardice—I had descried them all.

There was this renowned *sarod* player, a man who was ecstasy personified, who listened to me intently, pausing only to express his devotion to his guru. Having heard me out, he looked as if he'd had an epiphany and excitedly said, 'This is completely new for me. I've met thousands of people in America and Europe, but no one who spoke like you. Now, wherever I go, I'll share what you said.' He married thrice. His last wife died before he could divorce her. Three months later, his English disciple who visited Madras reported that the sarod maestro had married again a week back.

Remember the Ph.D. friend I had mentioned? He would nod in agreement to everything I said, like the *ambili* ox paraded in the street by his owner for giving oracular nods. This went on for four years. Then he went to Ernakulam and got married. A year later he wrote me an apologetic letter:

'Ammani, this may come as a shock to you, or even seem contemptible. But all I can say is that life is like a flow of blood. In everyone's circulation, there is a clot. It may be tinier than a mustard seed. But a clot is a clot. Depending on where it forms, it can cause a constriction. Today, tomorrow, next month, next year, in ten years or thirty, it'll reach the heart and block an impenetrably slender vessel. Just like that, in the flow of our sensibility too, there is a clot. Someday, some place, it comes and blocks. Naturally, our mind gets defeated; there's a danger to life or a danger of paralysis of limbs. I don't really understand what happens. When I got acquainted with Rita, I didn't think of this. One day she said, "Why shouldn't we get married?" I laughed and said, "Why not?" and thrilled, I took her in my arms and hugged her. This wasn't the first time we'd hugged. Probably the hundredth or the three-hundredth. We'd gone far beyond hugging. Yet, when she asked me this question, it felt like we were hugging for the very first time. I was oblivious of our bodies or our surroundings. The next week, we announced our intention to the marriage registrar and, after waiting out the mandatory one month, we got married. What I said about my novel feeling when we hugged, the sense of a blissful oblivion, the way a flow of blood is arrested by a blood clot...I wondered why I got such a feeling.'

I wanted to stop reading the letter and shout: You idiot! You *wondered* why you got this grand new feeling when she asked you that question! When all she really asked you was, 'Why shouldn't I appropriate you as my sole, exclusive property?'

And when all you really said in reply was, 'Yes! Why shouldn't I do the same?' Do you need to do a Ph.D. to know this?

The letter continued. Rita is a sweet girl...the two of them are very happy and so on. He wrote as if he had received some kind of initiation from me, which he was now betraying.

Then, a year and a half later, I got a stream of letters from him, about seven or eight in a month: *'Rita is a very coarse creature. A jealous woman. There's no limit to her suspicions. Sometimes I feel like killing her. She's hysterical. Her throat swells up like a pillar whenever she screams—such terrifying shrieks! And invariably she plants herself at the window closest to the window of the next house, as if it were a platform with an amplifier, to tell the whole world about me.'*

Dear Ph.D., and what are you doing with yourself now? The doctorate has retreated into the cell of silence and suffering. Like Mahatma Gandhi who, with his tolerance, had saved his truth. The truth of cowardice. The truth of keeping up with the Joneses. The truth of not letting your fellow Ph.Ds and the world know that your marriage was a failure. You don't want their pity.

Let's leave Ph.D. aside. Among my other friends, there was Nat (Natarajan), Kamakshi, and Lenin—a brahmin boy whose father went to Moscow once and vowed to christen his first child Lenin. Then there was Rayappa, Tirumalachari, Sriramulu...we were twenty-two in all, including myself. People congregate to hold discourses and sing litanies on their gurus, on Vedanta and Bhakti. Likewise, these twenty-two got together day in, day out, to sing praises of Marx. In this group of Marxists, there were schisms: rightists, leftists, centrists and others. But all these people agreed that marriage was a graveyard. Now all of them, barring only two, are living in that same graveyard. Lenin got married to a girl from a village on the banks of the undivided Kaveri, the daughter of an orthodox, religious, roughneck landowner. Rayappa, Tirumalachari, Verghese and Rajapathar, they all married within their clans—Catholic, Vadakalai, Syrian Christian and Madras Mudaliar. And they are all carrying on bravely.

The amazing thing was Bangaru's 'blood coagulation thesis'. Bangaru was neither Marxist nor capitalist and didn't follow any 'ism' in particular. He was an independent angry young man of thirty-four. His hair was half the length of mine, worn in a style that looked like something out of the classical Sangam period. He teamed bright multi-coloured floral T-shirts with shiny blue trousers that hugged his crotch so tight that one had to avert one's eyes. He wrote short stories and free verse, waged a struggle on behalf of cubism in art and was member of a film society. He once dragged me to a movie called 'Life is Crimson', insisting that it was for someone like me. It was blood-curdling; they broke heads and trampled over children; tufts of knotted hair floated in pools of blood. After enduring seventy minutes of slashing, cutting and ghastly electronic wails (Bangaru called it electronic music), I wanted to throw up and told him so. 'Two women who saw it in Hamburg had miscarriages,' he said with a proud smirk, as if he'd made the film. Then he said, 'The reason I asked you to see it was because I think it should've instead been called "Marriage is Crimson." Because that's what marriage is, wouldn't you agree?' Controlling my nausea with difficulty, I asked him, 'Is this your idea of paying my tuition fee?' Bangaru said, 'The film depicts the basics, the roots of life, visually.' I still didn't get it.

Bangaru, a beautiful Telugu word which means gold, was my pet name for Kumaraswamy. His brusque manner of speech, the way he would abruptly ask you something like one possessed, and the way his eyes dripped with gratitude for me, as if I was the cause of it all, made me name him Bangaru. He was conscious and proud of being classified a 'minority', and held exclusive opinions. Eating *halwa* in Coimbatore in Krishna Iyer's restaurant, he would grimace and say, 'Ugh! This stuff is too rich in calories!' He shunned weddings. 'Tirumalachari is getting married, Ammani. Won't you offer your condolences?' he would say. Then all of a sudden, this Bangaru vanished. He went to Pudu Vayal in Chettinad and got married to a brahmin's daughter.

A fortnight later, I got a call. 'Ammani, will you bake my funeral cake?' asked a bright and chirpy voice.

'What? Who's this?'

'Bangaru, your old gold. Bangaru is dead. He's become base metal.'

'What!'

'I will explain. In person.'

A couple of weeks later, the doorbell rang. When I opened the door, Bangaru stood there, grinning. 'I should've said *We* will explain in person. Machumi, come, this is my Guru. And it is because of you that I've betrayed my Guru. So it is you who will touch her feet and seek her pardon.' I smiled. Encircling the girl's waist with his arm, he led her up the stairs.

'She is my *Athai*'s daughter. She has studied up to Pre-University, works with the Railways, supports her family, and has also saved up money for her marriage. My *Athimber* proposed this match. I agreed. Where is my funeral cake?' he demanded, laughing fondly at the girl.

'You said marriage is crimson. Is that why you got her a blood-red wedding saree?' I said. What else could I say?

All these various sad disasters happened. Some during the early years and some later.

Pachiappan is so much better off than them! He is way beyond all this. The way he had laughed and laughed at what I'd said before his wedding was quite appropriate, I thought.

I went to Vadapazhani to attend his wedding. Gopali also accompanied me.

10

To my memory, there have been few things more shocking than this wedding. The bride was simply stunning! I was struck speechless and gaped at her like a man. She was dusky, but her darkness dazzled. How to put it? To say that she was dark as kohl would be inadequate. I have seen black people, but this darkness seemed to have been created just for my eyes to marvel at.

Then I realised it wasn't just her lustrous dark skin that amazed me. Ninety-nine faces out of a hundred on earth are asymmetrical. That's nothing new. I traced on her face an imaginary line that I draw on all the faces that I see, from the forehead to the bridge of the nose, on to the centre of the lips, down to the chin and neck. It was startling—like placing an invisible mirror on that line! The right side of the nose and the left, the right eye and the left, each was a lateral reflection of the other. Her hair was plaited and coiled into a bun. I wanted to undo the bun and see the hair hang loose on the back. I examined every part of her with the same wonder—the ear lobes, the finger tips. It was astounding.

There was a baby softness to her whole body. And a breathtaking charm on her exquisite face. How could anyone be born so perfect? Was I jealous? I didn't think so. I had no time to be. I was too busy measuring and examining her. How could anyone be so ravishing? Hers was a beauty that hit you like a slap on the cheek. Her elegance and symmetry of form, her suppleness of body were overwhelming.

Was she at all conscious of her beauty? Had she ever looked at herself in a life-sized mirror? I wanted to rave like a lunatic about her figure. I wished I were a man. I had no sexual thoughts, though. Still, I wanted to be a man.

Pachiappan was looking at me. Gopali was also looking at me.

I was looking at her nose. Having drawn a line through the middle of the face, I was verifying if the left side was a cast of the right. Usually, the nose is always just slightly displaced, either to the right or to the left. A naked eye can miss it, but a mirror throws back this irregularity. If by chance I've spotted a single straight nose out of a hundred, I've dismissed it as unnatural, like a machine-made doll. I would tell myself that it is this small defect that saves a face from looking like a doll.

But this girl was astonishing. Her right half was the exact cast of her left. It was the same with her lips, eyes, nose, chin, fingers, toes...all of her. She was beautiful. Her large eyes had a glow. Like a shell washed out of the sea, the whites of her eyes had the palest hint of blue.

Gopali had bought a saree, a blouse piece and a dhoti. He presented them on a tray. What should I give? I removed the two gold bangles from my wrists and said, 'Come here'. She came. I took her hands and slid one bangle over each wrist. I didn't turn to look at Gopali—the bangles were his gift to me. Having slid them over her wrists, I stood there holding her hands. She kept looking at mine. She was taller than me.

'What's your name?'

'Maragadham.'

'How old are you?'

'Twenty-two.'

'Do you know that you are very beautiful?'

She was shy.

'Do you know that no one can equal your beauty?'

A shy smile.

'Tell me honestly, do you know how incredibly beautiful you are?'

Another shy, breathtaking smile.

'I won't let you go till you tell me.'

'Please let go of my hands, Amma. Or even yours will become black like mine,' she said at last, her eyes lowered.

'*Chhee*! What rubbish!' I said and hugged her. 'Let me see if my body also turns black now!'

'Did you hear what she said, Pachiappa?' I asked.

'What, Amma?'

I told him.

'What else can she say?' said Pachiappan, mischievously rolling his tongue into the corner of his mouth.

Pachiappan accompanied us as we walked out of the lane to the car, his new dhoti rustling as he walked. He wore a ring on his finger, a terylene shirt and a chain on his arm.

'Amma, how is the girl?' he asked me.

'Only now I realise how clever you are,' I said.

'You are an extraordinarily lucky man, you know!' said Gopali. 'Thank god she is dark. If she wasn't, anyone would just whisk her away!'

Pachiappan bowed his head, brimming with pride.

'Didn't you say she was related to you?' I asked.

'Yes, Amma. Four others vied for her. But she said "No" to them all.'

'You never let me guess that she would be anything like this.' Just then I remembered the way he'd said to me the other day, 'Will love last just two months? You mean to say that marriage won't work beyond that?' and had burst out laughing. When the car moved, I murmured, 'What a girl!'

Gopali was silent.

As soon as we reached home, Gopali said, 'When I think of the boy, I get worried.'

'Worried about whom?'

'The one who should protect her, Pachiappan.'

'Why? So what if he is unable to protect her? She has something to be proud of.'

'Should she be like you then? As if her beauty will be proven only when everyone falls all over her and paws her!'

'Why are *you* so anxious? And for whose sake? For Pachiappan? Or for yourself?

'What!'

'Are you worried that you shouldn't be the first hawk to snatch her away?'

Gopali stared at me for a few seconds, then he smiled. 'As far as I am concerned, there's nothing to fear. What's there in so much beauty? It will soon cloy. There must be some defect, a little masculinity perhaps, a thickness in the voice or some eccentricity,' he said, looking at me carefully.

'Thanks,' I said. 'What's all this supposed to be? Or are you perhaps trying to give me some kind of an assurance?'

'Why? Do you need any? You don't have any of these problems. Why are you talking so strangely today, Ammani?'

I too felt as if I was blabbering.

Then he said, 'Those who are beautiful must also be a little foolish, or it is of no use. If theirs is a chiselled perfection, it feels insipid, like looking at one's sister.' Wagging a thumb at me fondly, he shook his head and said, 'That's how little you have understood this man.' In other words, he was mocking me. 'Rama got all his glory from Sita, who was a paragon of beauty and virtue,' he continued. 'If Ravana was enamoured of her and lusted for her, it only shows that he was lowly. Considerably lowlier than me!'

There was neither Ravana nor Keevana. Gopali had nicely dug a pit for me to fall into, and was now boasting that he was a Ravana. Ever since he'd driven out Pattabhi, he had been teasing me like this. I had carefully avoided all fights related to that. Pachiappan had quietly replaced all the fallen pictures of Tyagaraja, Rama and Krishna. And I went about as if nothing had happened. Today Gopali was rejoicing over the fact that he could insult me. The way he smugly said, 'You have a lot to learn,' and slid his feet into his sandals as he went out, it did look like he was laughing up his sleeve at me.

But I ignored it all. I wanted to think about Maragadham. I thought of her all the time. Even at midnight. Like ten nights pressed together, her luminous darkness rose before my eyes. I wanted to gaze at her like one possessed. I grew arrogant in my belief that only I could truly appreciate her unique, distinctly individual beauty. Would Pachiappan ever understand this kind of beauty? He had built a hut for himself in the backyard. But it wouldn't occur to him to look at Maragadham in the nude, at her glorious body. Was he even aware of her beauty? Did it bother him that she was beautiful? He was fully preoccupied with his work in Gopali's house and his services to me. If granted a week off, he wasn't one to spend it inside his hut talking to her, admiring her, watching her as she moved about. Did he have any such thoughts?

Then again I was vexed by thoughts of Marx. Was it only the middle class and the leisured upper class that had the aesthetic instinct and the eye for beauty, and not the working classes who toiled through the day and night? Are those who write poems in praise of beauty or those who sing of beauty as a gift of god all idlers? Do only those who eat the fruits of others' labour have the time for admiring beauty?

During the first year, Maragadham would come to the house once or twice a day. She would drop in at dusk. As a new bride, she did not go out much. Occasionally I would tease her, wanting to ferret out information. 'Does Pachiappan know you are so beautiful?' I would ask her point blank. And she would bashfully reply, 'Oh, go on Amma!' and change the topic or go down to the ground floor. It was as if she floated on the shyness that permeated her entire dark lustrous body.

It took Maragadham nearly two years to start moving about freely in the house and to run the household. When I asked her the same question for the fifth or the sixth time, she stood there looking at me for some time.

'What are you looking at?'

She wasn't so shy like before. For the past few months she had been cooking for me occasionally. She brushed my hair, washed my sarees and hung them out to dry. She washed the vessels, and learnt to make first-grade coffee. When the doorbell rang, she went down to open the door. She brought *kanakambaram* flowers and strung them up for me.

Maragadham stood there, looking on.

'Won't you tell me?'

'Tell you what?' she finally said, lowering her eyes.

'If Pachiappan knows that you are beautiful. Don't you understand if I ask you once?'

'But Amma, you have asked me this seven or eight times.'

'It doesn't look like you'll answer even if I asked you seventy times!'

'What should I say? Wouldn't a man know even this much?'

'What do you mean by "even this much"?'

'A man should certainly know when a woman is pretty.'

'Should he, or does he?'

'Amma, you are naughty! One must be careful not to get caught when talking to you!'

During the second year, in November, along with the rains, a cyclone came down in fury one day, snapping off the tops of coconut trees. Pachiappan's hut swayed and fell to the ground like a dead crow. He brought his two tin trunks, two plates, a pot and other things upstairs.

Then the storm stopped and the sky cleared. 'Pachiappa, the two of you can stay here. There is a room at the rear. You can take that. Both of you can join me in cooking,' I said.

'How can that be, Amma?'

It wasn't as if he was particularly surprised by my offer. The expression on his face was more like: What new craziness is this?

'You mean to say, we'll all cook and then share the food?' he asked.

'Yes.'

'You don't discriminate, Amma. But would Aiyah agree?'

'Is this my house or Aiyah's?'

'That's not what I meant, Amma. Why should you trouble yourself?'

'Where's the trouble? After all, I stay alone.'

'That is why I asked, Amma.'

'Meaning?'

'You are alone because you want to be alone. Then why should we come in?'

'Don't worry about that. I can keep to myself when I want to.'

Pachiappan was silent.

'You have seen this and you know. At least seven or eight people call on me every other day. Even then, I am lonely.'

He remained silent.

'Back home, there would have been brothers, sisters, a husband, a sister-in-law or a brother-in-law staying with me. So, the two of you can also stay with me the same way.'

Pachiappan smiled. Then Maragadham came in with coffee for me. It must have been three in the afternoon. When she went inside, he said, 'The other day you told me that in a couple of months we would start quarrelling. Since we haven't yet, you think we certainly will in two years' time, and you want to stop that from happening perhaps?' he said and winked mischievously. Pachiappan couldn't wink with one eye. He always winked with both eyes. And his wink always lasted a full second before his eyes reopened, as if to say, look at me—I'm being funny!

'Hah! You will never quarrel with her! You're curled up at her feet like a slave. As if her beauty may wither and crumble if you so much as raise your voice at her!'

'So then you admit that even I know she is pretty,' he said, winking again.

I gave him a hard look. 'Aha. So Maragadham reports every little thing that she and I talk about, is it?'

'I also tell her. Otherwise, like you said, how can it run beyond two months?'

'Pachiappa, what is your objection to moving into the house?' I asked him seriously.

'I am ready to stay here, Amma. But she has to agree, you see. So many people come here,' he said, now looking down.

Maragadham brought out the coffee utensils and told Pachiappan, 'I've kept coffee for you inside.' Then she went to the back of the terrace to wash up.

'Are you suspicious?' I asked him.

'About what?'

'Because I live a different kind of life?'

Pachiappan shook his head as if to say, 'No.'

'Just say whatever you have to say.'

'What does that have to do with it, Amma?'

'Then why do you wait for her consent?'

'I know you well. But I don't know how she will respond,' he said.

'Call her.'

Pachiappan brought her over. Maragadham had got up in the middle of her washing. Rinsing her hands, she wiped her hand on her saree as she came in. The devil! How she walked, her toe-rings making a soft nick-nick sound on the floor. She wore a pastel blue saree. Two years of marriage had spread a proportionate layer of flesh on her shoulders, arms, belly and hips. An excitement rippled through my body as I watched her walk in. Oh, if only I was a man! I wanted to hug her tightly that very moment, wrap my saree pallav around her and protect her from all harm.

Why have I collected this shelf-load of books? Why do I keep reading books in order to encounter new experiences? Why do I keep collecting new friends, students, long-haired musicians, artists, actors, writers, weavers, architects...? Why do I roam all over the place in search of people? And why doesn't she? Why is she like this, washing vessels, sweeping the floor, washing my sarees, tidying up my house...?

'What is it, Amma?' she asked, wiping her hands.

'I wanted to ask you something, Maragadham. Your hut was destroyed in the cyclone. Why don't you stay here? See that room there, at the rear? It is enough for two. You can keep your trunks and belongings there. The two of you can eat here. When you cook for Pachiappan, you can also cook for me. And on the days I cook, I'll cook for all of us. What do you say?'

Maragadham laughed. My heart skipped a beat.

'Why do you laugh?'

'What does he say?'

'He has agreed, but he wonders if you will. I think he's worried about you having to live with someone like me, given that I am a curious sort of woman. Possibly, he thinks of me as an unmarried woman who carries on with so many as if she was married. And would it be proper to bring you into this marketplace? But he leaves it to you. You know about me, of course. He would have also told you. But how does my way of living matter? I would like the two of you to stay here. I say it because I don't have anyone else.' I said all this in a clear, matter-of-fact tone.

Maragadham neither raised her head nor met my gaze.

'What do you say?'

No response.

'If you don't like the idea, just tell me so to my face. If you agree, good. If you don't, it doesn't matter. Either way, there's nothing to fear or regret. So, what do you think?'

Maragadham looked up. I was surprised. Her face was wet with tears.

'Now what?'

She nodded as if she agreed.

'What?'

'We will stay here, Amma,' she finally said, wiping her eyes with the end of her saree.

Pachiappan was looking at her fondly. 'Do you want to stay here? Or do you want to build a hut again?' he asked her.

'We will stay here,' she replied.

'Did you hear, Pachiappa?'

'I heard. But what's there to weep for?'

Maragadham turned and, for a brief second, gave him a severe look out of her brimming eyes, before lowering them again. Her wet eyelashes glistened and her quivering lips were parted. God! Such a knockout beauty!

Seeing that look, Pachiappan walked away to the rear room.

'Why did you sob like that?'

'It's nothing, Amma. Let me go finish the washing,' she said, and went back to the terrace.

Later that evening, when Pachiappan was out, I cornered her again. 'Now tell me, why did you break down like that?'

'It's nothing.'

'Maragadham, you know very well that I won't leave you till you tell me.'

'What else could I do when you spoke like that, Amma? It was distressing,' she said quietly.

I wasn't satisfied. I wanted more. So I rehearsed that I would say: Does it upset you that I have discarded my family to live like this, and then I long for company? But before I could fully rehearse it, Maragadham said, 'Who can really do what and to whom? And what is there for anyone else to say? Ultimately, everyone lives their life as they please. There is a man among our relations, a building contractor. He undertakes contracts and builds houses. He came to my parents and pleaded for my hand for a whole year, said that he'd give me a four-strand gold chain, gold bangles, this, that and the other. I said "No". My mother was furious. "You prefer a menial servant to this well-to-do man?" she taunted and rebuked me. I told her, "If you like him so much, invite him over and cook him a nice, *masala* supper. But don't you ever invite him as a son-in-law!" Was that a matter of my wish alone, or my mother's? That's just how it is for everyone, Amma.'

'You love Pachiappan so much! No wonder then that he refused to say yes until you had agreed.'

She was silent.

'I hope you won't get the wrong vibes by staying here?'

'Amma, why do you keep saying such things? Do we look like we are scared?'

'Come here.'

She came.

I held her hand and said, 'All right. You stay here. If you want to say something, feel free to tell me anything you want, boldly, without hesitation, without fear.'

Maragadham neither hesitated nor feared. She answered the doorbell for everyone—for Gopali, for Velayya, for those who came for conversation, for food and drink, and for those who were in the 'inner circle'. She served them coffee, brought them betel leaves and cigarettes, made uppuma for them. Gave clever replies to clever talk. If someone reached out a hand for whatever she was serving, she handed it to them without setting down the plates, and if her hand was touched by chance, she ignored it. She even ignored bodily brushes which were deliberate. If a touch lingered, she flashed an angry look at the person and moved away. On the three occasions that I toured abroad, it was she who looked after the house in my absence, and Pachiappan. I always came home to a house that was sparkling clean and tidy.

When I returned from the second trip, I learnt that two of my friends, Tirumalachari and Hakim, had visited several times knowing fully well that I wasn't in town. 'I told you for the third time last week that Amma will return only after fifteen days. Why do you keep coming here repeatedly?' she told them off. When they again turned up, exasperated, it seems she also said, 'It is *Amma* that you really wish to meet, isn't it?'

Maragadham reported this when both of them again called to see me. The very next day I wrote to them that hereafter I would prefer to see them in their own dens, and that Maragadham didn't quite approve of them, so we should meet elsewhere.

When I called on him, Hakim said, 'Ammani, are you mad?'

'Yes.'

'What yes?'

'Yes means yes.'

'Some grand joke this is! This whole business of guarding your maid's virtue, even if one assumes that what she said was true.'

'All right, call it a joke if you will. But my friend doesn't lie.'

'Your *friend*?'

'Yes. She is both a friend and a maid.'

'Oh I see! So your "friend" doesn't lie. That's a joke piled on a joke! Is this the result of your latest overseas tour? A fermented Marxism? Or perhaps a distillation of comradely feminist compassion?'

'Whatever it is, from now on, don't come anywhere near my house. She doesn't like you or Tirumalachari.'

I don't really know why I flew into such a rage. I just couldn't tolerate that anyone should seduce Maragadham even in their thoughts. It was to me, as Hakim said, a monstrous joke.

I held fast to Maragadham's purity even as I consorted with Giovanni and Pinet, the two young men I met in France and Rome. On my fourth trip, I wandered from one country to another without any sponsorship or dance concerts. In London, Subala and I were doing an experiment at Piccadilly Square. We masqueraded as whores, and took two young men back to our rooms. The man, a rough-looking American soldier, was walking along with me, taking long strides. Even at that moment, I was thinking about Maragadham. I had this obstinate desire that more than Pachiappan, or anyone else, it is I, only I, Ammani, who will protect her, her body, her mind.

11

After we had walked some distance, he asked, 'Is there anything to eat at home? Or shall we eat out?'

'I'll cook dinner,' I said.

'What is there to eat?'

'Uppuma and mango pickle.'

'What?'

'Indian supper, instant supper.'

'Are you both Indians?'

'Yes.'

'That explains why you're so beautiful!'

'Really?'

'I haven't been to India, but I've seen Indians at Saigon. That wheat complexion alone is enough. I'd be glad to stand in the sun for a whole year just to get that tan.'

Then he asked, 'Do you have anything to drink?'

'No.'

He bought some whisky.

After we reached our rooms, he seemed to have forgotten the purpose of his visit. He just kept drinking and talking. He had a good physique and looked like a seasoned drinker, but he spoke like a child. He was on his way back after three years in the Vietnam War. Said he was twenty-three.

Subala made uppuma and prepared a soup with whatever vegetables we had. After consuming half a bottle, his tongue had apparently loosened itself completely.

'You won't call me chicken, will you, if I spoke frankly?' he asked.

'I don't get it,' I said.

'Please don't think this is tipsy talk. I can wash down two such bottles, just like that. And keep sitting here without stirring.'

'In that case, we should've bought two more bottles.'

He laughed and said, 'Don't make me laugh. I'm in no mood to laugh.'

'Want to cry, then?'

'How did you guess? Yes. That's how I feel. I want to have a proper good cry. Do you know why?'

Subala switched off the homogeniser in the kitchen and looked at him.

'Because this looks and feels like home,' he said.

I didn't reply.

'Somehow, it just feels like being in my own house. Your smile, your laughter, the way you talk, your empathy and your attentiveness. And your friend there, cooking for us with such care—all this adds up to a home for me.'

I nearly said, watch out, lest you end up marrying us! But didn't. Something in his tone held my tongue. His voice had turned husky and it trembled. He really did want to cry. He bit his lips and remained quiet.

Subala looked at me, the corners of her lips curling, as if to say, now what do we have here?

'I haven't killed many people,' he said. 'I've kept an actual count. Twelve people died by my gun. Some of my fellows have taken fifty, even sixty lives. I've killed just twelve. I've seen women running the minute they saw us, terror on their faces. Some wives stayed petrified on the spot, like a squirrel or a frog would on sighting a snake. Hand on mouth, terror in their eyes. If they were pregnant, the foetus would've slipped down or the mother would've just curled up in a swoon and dropped down. I went into one such house. There was a mother and her son, a small boy. She pushed her boy behind her, hiding him, and stood staring at me. She said something. It sounded like: Don't come near me. I couldn't understand her language. I stood there, looking at her. She was working up her lips.

Spittle, the size of a berry, suddenly flew and fell on my shirt. I drew out my handkerchief and wiped it. I came out. I want to forget it all completely, wipe it off in a total amnesia. But her spittle is still sticking on to me. Whenever I take out girls like you, the spittle falls on me. So I sit down to drink and keep talking. I doze off. Get up in the morning and go away.'

He did the same here. He kept drinking. And kept talking. 'How desperately she had spat at me! What audacity! What was it that she feared to lose so much that she emptied in that desperate act? I could've assaulted her. There was no one to stop me. No one to rescue her. If I'd told my men, they would've torn her apart and worse. They would've burnt her house down with her and her son. No one saw her spitting at me. But when I came out I felt as if the whole world had seen it. The things we do when we think no one is looking... the good, the evil, the humiliating—*everything* is seen. I felt that the incident had not escaped the eyes of a single soul in the world.' Then he abruptly asked, 'Why have you both come away from India? Are you students?'

'My friend here, she's a student. I came just to see around the places.'

'Are you hard up for cash?'

'No, not at all.'

'Then why were you soliciting in Piccadilly Square?'

The other young man, who hadn't spoken a word till now, opened his mouth and said, 'Even I wondered...they don't look like that kind.'

'Are you bored with my talk?' said the soldier, to no one in particular.

'Maybe *he* is,' said Subala, pointing to the other man.

'I'm not bored. I have to get going soon,' said the man.

Subala took him to her room.

'He is a lucky one. He can focus on what he came for. I feel sleepy,' said the soldier. He consumed the soup and the uppuma and asked for coffee. After coffee, he lit a cigarette. While he was eating his uppuma, the other man came out of

Subala's room and said, for the sake of etiquette, 'I do wish I could stay, but I'll have to go.' And he left.

'Will you also spit on me?' the soldier asked.

'What a question!' said Subala. I couldn't make out if she was bored or angry. Her eyes looked sleepy and tired and seemed to say: what's all this now...it's well past midnight. But she couldn't say anything to me. She yawned a couple of times, then got up and went into her room.

'Your friend is annoyed,' said the boy. I can only call him a boy. 'Can I sleep here tonight?' he asked.

'Haven't you come for that?'

'Good. I do feel like sleeping here. I feel like talking to you. Not to your friend, just you. You've been listening quite patiently. You won't spit on me while I'm asleep, will you?'

I laughed.

'You shouldn't spit. And you shouldn't laugh either. Please don't scoff at me that I'm no good. Okay?'

'Okay.'

'Whenever I see a new girl, the spittle rises before me and it scares me. It chases me like the bubble of a balloon. A bubble that won't burst.'

After a while, he grew quieter, calmer. He fell asleep as soon as he lay down. He got up in the morning and left. 'See you again,' he said, waving. Under an empty cigarette box over the fireplace I later found thirty guinea notes spread out.

He also turned up the next day. And the next. He listened to my stories. I went gallivanting around with him for fifteen days. Birmingham, Oxford, Manchester, Wales. We stayed at Stratford for two days and saw a few plays of Shakespeare. Wherever we went, we stayed in the same room. He would lie down on the edge of the bed. No amount of coquetry worked with him.

Then out of the blue, he would say, 'I'm in my house.'

'With whom?'

'With everyone, of course. My kid brother, my mother, my elder brother, everyone'.

'You left out your wife.'

'But I'm not married.'

'You talk of a house and a home as if you knew a lot about family.'

'And what about you?' he asked, laughing.

There was nothing I could do. Teasing didn't work. He just laughed. Whenever I heard that laugh, the way he would remember the spittle, his voice dipping low and soft, and the way he longed for a home, I seemed to become transformed into Maragadham. The same darkness, her dark blue or green saree, her alertness and sensitivity, her tendency to take on the entire load of work—my body would undergo a subtle change. I was anxious to suppress her, and emerge again as Ammani.

After seeing a play at Stratford, we were eating at restaurant called *Dirty Pig*. A fire crackled brightly in the fireplace. Huddled together on the bench in the warmth of the fire, a few small families were sipping grape wine. Bruce started all over again. That was his name, Bruce. 'This entire world teems with brigands,' he began. 'Without exception. The brigands are everywhere. In America, Russia, Europe, Asia, just everywhere. The capitalist, the communist, the socialist, all of them shelter and patronise them. It's a world that hurls rocks on seeing a dog. But do you know who the real exploiters are? It is the educated and the intellectuals. One who isn't educated is like a street dog in the eyes of the highly educated. It's not the wealthy alone who prey on others. The rich are assisted in their plunder by the highly educated. The intellectual does not hanker after money. His need is simply to dominate over everyone else, but escape being called a "brigand". Someone else must accept and bear that label. It's the intellectual who has made the rich man rich. I don't accept that the rich have enslaved all those with brains. There are only two categories of people in this world: those who know and those who don't. Those who know grab everything and let the ignorant go adrift or enslave them.'

Bruce's voice kept rising steadily. He didn't look like he was drunk. It was more like a fervour stimulated by alcohol. The chatter around us had ceased, and people were now turning their heads to stare at him. They looked again and smiled. It was an effort to make him get up and come out. He realised it only after I told him, 'Our talk is disturbing them.'

'Excuse me,' he apologised to them, and we came out.

'You were embarrassed because I was talking loudly, weren't you? Why should I be ashamed or apologise for my loudness? Do war bombs apologise? Do books in shop windows apologise, I mean those with lurid covers that cry out to be bought? Do politicians apologise? Is the male bird that dances and fusses around the female embarrassed? What about hoardings? Do professors and experts and those who accumulate knowledge apologise? The platform speaker? The singer? The dancer? The ranting preacher? No...? Then why should I apologise for my loudness? All I wish to say is that it is the intellectuals who plunder. Intelligence is the tool of a house-breaker. It is what aids in plundering, raping, stealing and duplicity. With intelligence comes malice, deceit, avarice and annihilation!'

Bruce continued talking loudly as we walked along the street. He didn't stop even after we reached our hotel room. For a minute I wondered if I was going around with a mad man. When he quietened down a bit, I wondered if he was mad or just cranky.

Using his arms as a pillow, he lay in a corner of the bed and said, 'I am haunted by the girl's spittle, and you by your intelligence.'

'Oh! So all this time, was it *me* that you were really angry with?'

'With you too, yes. But not angry. More like pity, and curiosity. See, *I* am different. *I* have killed twelve people. *I* have been spat at, and it haunts me and it drives me around the world. But what about *you*? Why do *you* roam like a homeless, rootless nomad? What are you going to do after meeting all these many different people? Seeing all these new places? When someone talks discordantly, you rave about "Fantastic Man". When common, illiterate people show warmth and affection, you call them fantastic. If they speak gracefully or knit some colourful patterns in wool, they're again "fantastic" and "beautiful". What makes you keep hopping from place to place? Why did you leave your country and come here?'

Our friendship of a fortnight had brought us this close—close enough to quarrel, to challenge each other's beliefs and assumptions.

'Tell me honestly, what's new for you in this country?'

'I am also searching for something.'

'Isn't it just to brag that you've seen this and that, to exhibit to people your bag of memories and experiences? You claim to have kissed over five or six hundred men. Slept with at least half of them. What is yet another man going to give you that the previous three hundred couldn't?'

'Only time will tell.'

'A wild wish—could I be the one?'

'But you're a castrated ox.'

'I'm not going to jump at that and disprove it.'

'Well, this is an instructive surprise for me.'

'Instructive? My impotence in the face of your beauty, and this privacy and this freedom...instructive?'

'Yes.'

'You will collect all these *instructive* experiences and then one day when your hair goes grey, your skin wrinkles, your teeth fall out, your digestion forsakes you, your joints ache and the flesh of your buttocks starts thinning so that your bones hurt even over a bed—will you then piece together all your *instructive* experiences into a warm and colourful quilt to lie on? Will they serve for the lost teeth, as a balm for the joints, or as a digestive? Your cheekbones are overlaid with flesh because of your indulgence in alcohol. Will that increase even more and will it comfort you, in that it will also be instructive?'

'Is that what scares you...growing old?'

'No. It doesn't. Not one bit. You really are an amazing girl. You're dying to hug everybody. Coming from the field of carnage and death, this is something new to me. It still is. But you say that you're going to hug everyone and discover something through that. Now that's what I don't understand. I started going out with you in that confusion...'

Bruce had moved closer to me. He stroked my cheeks with his hands. Brushed my eyelashes gently with his thumbs for a long time. Caressed my arms, my thighs, the back of my neck. He had really got close.

The crickets chattered shrilly outside. The same crickets that were in Prague, Budapest, Mambalam and Annavasal—they called here too, at Stratford. Even from somewhere inside the room, they called shrill and harsh like a damp, murky night call shrieking of the terrible, unendurable night.

True, Bruce was a soldier. Even now he seemed to be warring with someone or with something. He was my hero, coming after the three hundred. I used to defy Giovanni and Pattabhi and say, 'I'll exhaust your sap.' I have screamed this challenge at the puny and the tough young men who've dropped in for a chat. This spittle-haunted battle hero was taking revenge on me for all that defiance of mine. As dawn approached, I lay like spittle myself, like jellyfish washed ashore by the tide on the sands of Madras beach.

A terrifying night.

The crickets were subdued and now a rooster crowed from a rooftop somewhere. It crowed over everything, including my pain and my fear. I thought of Maragadham and I trembled in fear. I lay back like Maragadham.

12

Not only Maragadham. There were countless other girls too who lived within me. Girls who were dark, fair, yellow, brown or white. Girls who were ugly, pretty or commonplace. From Annavasal, from Madras, from Stratford, from Tokyo... girls from all over the world were inside me. I experienced the orgasm and the pain on behalf of all of them.

Bruce was sleeping beside me. He was breathing so softly it was almost inaudible. I was amazed to see him. I couldn't believe it was the same Bruce of last night.

If this weren't Stratford and if we were in London, the two of us, Subala and I, could have easily put our hands on his neck and ensured that he slept for the last time. Why, I could very well do it alone. It is said that a sleeping man is defenceless. His slumber gives his foe a weapon. I felt like clasping my hands around his neck and pressing hard.

But only mentally. This is an inability I have brought upon myself. The inability of Maragadham. Of all women collectively. The mud we heap on our heads. I stood there looking at him inertly.

Bruce opened his eyes. He looked at me and then closed his eyes. Perhaps he heard the rooster crowing in his house. When he opened his eyes again, he looked at me intently without blinking. 'Morning,' he said. I returned his greeting.

'I thought I was sleeping in my own home.'

'A home is where there is a woman.'

'True. Sorry.'

'Why do you instantly hoist a white flag and say sorry?'

'Because I could understand what you said.'

'Could you? You aren't yet fully awake, looks like.'

'I am. I counted the stroke of eight just now.'

'Do you remember the date, the day, the year and all that?'

'I do. The night was timeless. Now a sense of time has returned. Even in the vigil of the night, I had no sense of time whatsoever.'

'You were so blissfully oblivious!'

'Yes, I could forget myself. Briefly.'

'How? How could you forget yourself when you were all set to demonstrate your virility?'

'I don't recall having such a thought. It was actually you who kept taunting me, even though I wasn't eager to prove my manhood or my brawn. I only gained the assurance that the spittle won't chase me from now on. I even took your taunting to be out of affection.'

Was he speaking the truth? I hadn't expected this response.

'Now I am content and at peace. Even happy. But you seem angry, and disappointed.'

'Yes. I thought you insulted me. As if you avenged yourself for some of the things I had said.'

'Good heavens! What do we have here?' he said, getting up. He cupped my cheeks in his hands. 'Why are you talking like this?'

I couldn't stand my own indignation. I smiled my usual smile.

'Ah! Good. You're back to your old self. Get up and wash your face. I'll order for coffee,' he said.

I got up, went to the washroom, brushed my teeth, washed my face and patted it dry. Coming out, I said, 'Guess what I'm thinking?'

'What?'

'I imagined we were in the year twelve thousand B.C.'

'What!'

'Twelve thousand B.C. or twenty thousand or thirty thousand B.C. At that time, all the women were on top. They made love being on top. You men accepted it. You were supine and laid out helpless. You acknowledged that we were one up on you. Then some few lazy women traded their positions and said, let the men who go out to chop wood and hunt for food do this work too. And so the contagion spread! Who wouldn't like to relax and live on another person's labour?'

'Ha ha ha!' Bruce guffawed loudly.

'Why do you laugh?'

'You said you knew music and dance and so on. You didn't tell me that you edited a woman's weekly as well!'

'Thank god I didn't try my hand at that! They carry on with such pathetic things just so they don't lose their kingdom of laziness. Why on earth would I follow suit?'

Bruce phoned for coffee. Keeping the receiver down, he said, 'Okay. What happened next?'

'That's it. All was lost.'

'There's no hope of survival then?' he asked, laughing.

'There is. We should be like what we were before Christ,' I laughed.

'Up there?' he said, grinning and pointing upwards.

'Yes. Then everything will be fine. You won't have to go to Vietnam. Bombs won't fall. No spittle will fall on you. All of this springs from human weakness.'

'Who is weak?'

'Ten thousand years ago in our country, woman was personified as Shakti. She rode a lion. All men were laid down prostrate in the form of buffaloes. Now that self-same Shakti has become enfeebled. She often reminisces about the good old B.C. days. So, just once a year, for nine days, she is represented as sitting astride a lion. On the tenth day, it is taken off. If it is an image in clay, it is immersed in a river or pond to ensure that she remains silent for another year.'

Bruce was excited like a child. I had to narrate to him the entire mythology of the buffalo demon.

Then he suddenly said, 'I am sorry.'

'Now why are you sorry?' I asked, puzzled.

He wouldn't reply. I probed him again.

'I do think now that I've humiliated you,' he finally said.

The spittle must have loomed again in front of him. There was the same pensiveness on his face. The same remote look in his eyes.

'Are you going to regress into B.C. and morph into a lion?' he asked.

'You can't bear it, can you?' I said.

'Why do you talk like this? All this spiel about being up, being down...Why can't you just say side by side instead?'

'Not side by side. If that was the case, I wouldn't be wandering around like this. Remember how you taunted me that I was just running around, seeking this or that. It's not really like that at all. I roam around just for the sake of roaming. I don't seek anything.'

'Will anyone roam around for no reason at all?'

I did not answer. What I said wasn't entirely true. But it was true for that moment. My body felt exhausted. And contrary to my usual state, so did my mind.

We saw a play again that night. *The Merchant of Venice.* I felt like laughing at Portia. Jessica was equally amusing. You know nothing about the year of thirty thousand B.C., nor do you know how to ride a lion, I lamented for them both.

Back in London, Bruce spent a few more days with me. 'What should I do?' he asked me at least twice a day. I didn't answer. Not once. He didn't have the courage to ask me why I never replied. On the fifth day he again asked, 'What shall I do?'

'See me off.'

'Where to?'

'The airport.'

'What?'

'I'm leaving tomorrow.'

'Leaving? For where?'

'My place, Madras, India.'

'Really...?'

'Yes. They confirmed my seat this afternoon.'

'Honestly?'

'Yes. I had to throw away some things.'

'What!'

'Yes. Twenty kilos.'

'But you never told me?'

'I'm telling you now.'

'Only after I asked you. Suppose I hadn't asked?'

'You would have come and seen for yourself. Subala would have told you that I left.'

'How can you speak like this?'

'I can, Bruce, as you can see.'

'*How*...? I've been with you for three weeks. It could've been three births. I was convinced that I got to know a rare human being. You may have slept with three hundred people and kissed a few thousand. But you are a very pure woman.'

'Because nothing and no one sticks to me?'

'You may well mock me. But I think you are a person without any dirt, without any stain. It was you who gave me the assurance that the spittle won't haunt me anymore. You have listened to me. You have made fun of me. I am the greenhorn, the suckling infant. But I've learnt much from you. How to look at people. Men. Things. Clouds, garbage cans, dead cats, the Thames, films, trains, a loaf of bread—I have learnt to look at everything there is. Clothes, chairs, doors, dogs, insects, girls, their bodies. In future, I won't look at any of these as I did before I met you.'

'What's this, a farewell speech or something?'

'Come now, you know I'm not lying. While eating, walking or talking to people, I will not be who I was before. I seem to have been released from something. I hesitate to confess, but I want to live with you forever. I'm prepared to give up everything and come with you. I'm even prepared to marry you—why didn't you laugh? I'm prepared to live in the ten thousand B.C. that you described.'

'Are you asking me to cancel the ticket?'

'Do you always have an automatic impulse to mock?'

'Where do you see the mockery? I am asking you if I should cancel the ticket.'

'I'll buy a ticket for myself too. If it's not available for tomorrow, then for the next day or the next.'

'Why?'

'To be with you.'

'Nobody can *be* with me. In my country there is a saying: You cannot leap over a snake or a twisted straw. I am like that. I have no relations or friends. I cannot. Because I drop each friend in their place and move on. Like that I have thousands of friends. I can't even recall their names.'

Bruce held my hands. 'Will you forget me too?'

'I won't forget. I'll write. I'll reply to your letters. I'll remember all that you did when I go to the movies. Cinema moves on cloth.'

'What a woman you are!'

'Are you angry?'

'How can anyone be angry with you, Ammani?'

'Derision? Hatred? Surprise?'

'Not even those. Nothing surprises me after I got to know you. You did surprise me in the beginning, though. But that reaction has worn off. It's perilous to get so close to anyone. The subtlety and marvel of wondering at you, at each moment, is also gone. But I'll have to keep reviving this wonder again and again.'

'It really does look like I've got on the back of a lion and gone back to the B.C.!' I had to keep changing the topic to pull him away from this melting mood. He was quiet for some time, all the while smiling at me without taking his eyes off me. Suddenly he said, 'Are there rich people in your country?'

I took his query seriously and answered, 'Yes, there are millionaires, industrialists, landowners, the traditionally rich, the new rich, contractors who maintain three-fourths of the politicians in luxury, there are all kinds of people.'

Then he said, 'Didn't anyone want to maintain you that way?'

'They would've done that too. But I'm like a temple, you see. If you were to make an endowment for a church, you can't keep it exclusively for your visits. Bruce may come there. So will Pattabhi. So will Giovanni or a Marxist.'

Bruce suddenly got up and hugged me tightly. Then he sat respectfully away from me.

'I'm a public girl. At the same time I'm also not public. I can be bought. But I'm also not for sale. It's possible to stick to me, but it won't last. Why are you looking at me as if I was an exhibit?'

'What should I do?'

'There you are, back to where we started. Go back to your country. Get married. They'll give special privileges to a Vietnam War hero. They'll give you a good job. Be happy. Be content.'

'*You* are advising me to marry? You of all people!'

'I am. But I've told thousands of people the contrary. It didn't work. Please do one thing, though. Make a deal with your wife. The day she begins to dislike you, ask her to take your bedroll and throw it out on the street. Pick it up without a fight and move into another apartment. Carry your bedroll to another woman's flat if you like. Otherwise throw it away and sleep on the floor.'

Bruce seemed to be laughing. 'The three hundredth and first mattress,' he grinned.

'There is one who needs mention. He is not a millionaire. He is a musician,' I said.

'Ah. *That* one?'

'Yes, the very same. Like the Japanese, he has fastened his mattress onto the floor. So it may take some time and effort to tear it out.'

Bruce spent that night with me. Lying on the edge of the bed, he said, 'The other day, even when I was so intimate with you, my respect for you did not diminish, even slightly. It's incredible.'

'That's the glory of Stratford for you. Just because someone wears Ophelia's costume, she can't very well die in reality, can she?'

'Teasing has become your second nature,' he said. He kept talking, with a gratitude mixed with joy and sadness. I almost felt as if he had become me. Looking at him, I felt like telling him, be like a child. A child looks at a rattle, but forgets it the moment he sees his mother. He blinks at people he hasn't seen for three days. Be like that, Bruce!

Bruce came to the airport. Subala came too. It was time to go for the customs check.

'I am going to make it to Madras one day,' he said.

'Don't go with spittle on your shirt. Go with a mattress,' said Subala.

I boarded the aircraft, took my seat and looked out of the window. I could see Bruce still waving. He couldn't see me.

The plane taxied to the end of the runway, then turned around and ran up the same way again. The belt was fastened. The plane gathered speed. I could see from the window how fast it ran. I imagined that Bruce was still waving. Only when we went up did I feel the shame consuming me. Why, oh why did I brag about myself like an upstart, as though he was my meek disciple? Memories oppressed me. My waywardness, my hurry to shake off people then and there leered at me.

Passing Rome, I could see Mount Vesuvius in the midst of the sea. Then Cyprus. Then Crete. But they all fell off the horizon one by one. Only the Stratford movie kept on running in my head.

Arrived in Madras. Reached Mambalam, with Gopali. Pachiappan was not around to open the door. No sign of Maragadham either. It seems Pachiappan had quit the job and moved out.

13

The house looked like it had been newly washed, not like it had been locked up for six months. One had to look close for signs of dust. The walls were freshly painted, white with a bluish tint. The three mats spread out in the hall had been washed. The huge brass temple lamp that hung suspended in a corner of the hall had fresh hibiscus flowers, their tongues shooting from the tips for wicks. There were fresh garlands of jasmine on Tyagaraja, Rama and Krishna. Even the kitchen was gleaming and spruce. Coffee in the thermos, sweets, uppuma, rice and curds in the tiffin carrier, and fresh fruits in the basket. Even the silence in the house seemed to have been freshly bathed.

Everything was in its place. Only Maragadham was missing.

'Didn't Maragadham know the time of my arrival?' I asked.

'Aren't you hungry? Have some coffee first,' said Gopali.

'I thought Maragadham would serve me as soon as I got home.'

'Can't I have that privilege?' said Gopali and, without allowing me to talk, he went into the kitchen, brought out the coffee vessels and the thermos. He put out the food, laid the plates, then sat down beside me and served me.

As I ate, I again asked, 'Why hasn't she come?'

'Why don't you eat? I'll tell you.'

'I am eating.'

'Finish eating then. Must we fight as soon as you arrive?'

'Why fight at all?'

'I told you that Pachiappan left his job...Come on, you first eat.'

I finished eating. I had the coffee. Gopali opened the betel-leaf box, prepared a betel leaf and offered it to me. As I chewed, he said, 'Pachiappan threw away this job. Maragadham was here only for his sake, so she too stopped coming.'

'And why did Pachiappan quit?'

'Must you know everything right away? We can talk at leisure tonight. Get some good sleep, then put on our boxing gloves tomorrow morning! What did you do with yourself these six months? Why don't you tell me about it?'

'I was thinking of roaming around for another six months. A week ago, I had a sudden strong longing to see Maragadham. So I decided to return. I had so looked forward to her welcoming me home at the doorstep. I even thought she would come to the airport with Pachiappan to meet me. Somehow I just had an overwhelming desire to see her.'

'Perhaps Pachiappan thought I too had the same desire!' said Gopali, avoiding my eyes. He was struggling to close the betel-leaf box.

I was looking at him steadily.

Gopali looked at me through the corner of his eyes. Was there a hint of fear in them, or guilt? He couldn't close the betel-leaf box. Turning around to face me, he rubbed his hand over his chest, as though he had pulled a muscle.

'What is it?'

'A slight pain here,' he said. I massaged his chest.

'You know my age!' he smiled ruefully.

Last year, around May-June, Gopali had turned sixty.

And I? I suddenly remembered my own age. It hurt. Thirty-five? No...thirty-seven. No. In fact it is three months since I turned thirty-eight.

'Please get me some water,' he said.

I did.

He drank it. 'Oh Lord!' he sighed.

Unconsciously, as it were, my legs drew me to the room on the left. I stood in front of the mirror. Thirty-nine. What liberties do mirrors take! What proprietary rights they assume! I looked at my cheeks, my cheek bones. And I distinctly heard Bruce say, 'Your excesses with alcohol have made your cheeks plump.' What did he say next? But his words faded. Just like thoughts that jump the tracks on half-wakeful mornings. Perhaps I don't really wish to hear them.

I chuckled. Bruce had only noticed the flesh on my cheeks. Not my hair. No one has carefully observed my hair for the past seven or eight years. No one knows that almost three-fourths of it has turned white. Not Gopali. Not Maragadham. Whenever I heard the doorbell, I used to quickly touch up my hair with a brush dipped in dye from the cane box, and only then go down the stairs. But this mirror of mine—which I hadn't looked into for the past six months—accentuated my present. It returned a dubious look that asked me: thirty-eight or forty-eight? I felt a small knot of fear in the pit of my stomach.

What are you going to do after recounting all your myriad amazing experiences? After describing all your fantastic and wonderful friends? After describing all the incredible sights you have seen and the brilliant conversations you have heard? This was how Bruce talked. Not in the same words perhaps. Or was it I, putting these subconscious thoughts of a half-awake mind into his mouth?

What's this sudden peculiar feeling around my pelvis?

Did Bruce get intimate with me the other night only to say that I should stop roaming around? That it was time to call it a day? Was it Bruce, or was it All Men combined? Or was it Time itself in the form of Bruce? After that night, why didn't I ever feel like teasing Bruce? Why did he lapse again to his earlier position, sleeping on the edge of the bed? As if he was content that I realised there could be no greater climax than that?

After having stayed for months in cold countries, and weaning myself off tamarind extract and chillies, my face glowed noticeably. Yet, behind the mask, the question dangled: 'Thirty-eight or forty-eight?' My hair shone black. Not even Maragadham knew.

But where was Maragadham? Gopali had diverted me. I went back to the hall.

'Are you feeling better now?' I asked him.

'Yes.'

'Where did it pain?'

Gopali pointed to the left of his back, the left of his chest and ribs.

'Shall we go see a doctor?'

'Oh no, that's not necessary. It's just a sprain for having taken a wrong turn while sleeping, that's all.'

In a deliberately casual tone, I asked, 'Will Maragadham never come here again?'

'He has probably told her not to.'

'What happened?'

'I came here last month. I was sitting here. I felt warm, a little feverish. I also had a cold. I asked her to make coffee for me. Then I asked her to see if I had fever and I put her palm on my cheek. She abruptly pulled back her hand. "Do I have a temperature?" I asked. She felt my cheek with her hand. "It feels a little warm," she said. Pachiappan came in just then. That was all. The next morning he announced that they would stop working here. I asked him why. He said he'd got a government job, with government quarters. He also said that his mother-in-law was ill and that she needed Maragadham to help her out for a few days. He said they would be with her for a few days, and then shift to the government quarters. What could I say to that? The same evening, they vacated the room and left.'

'Hmm...'

'The fellow misunderstood me. What government job, quarters and all that...'

'Did he misunderstand, or did he understand the situation correctly?'

'What situation?'

'That you had neither fever nor cold.'

'So you also take it out on me!'

'Kunjali, Ammani—is it just the two of us that you have? I know very well that there are several others. But I don't get angry. Then why should you hide it from me?'

'Come on now. Did *you* discover it? It was I who told you what happened.'

'But you didn't tell me what made it happen. There's a thermometer in the desk drawer for measuring temperature.'

'I wanted her to feel it with her palm and tell me. So...?'

I too agreed with that. But now anger was welling up within me. It was difficult to talk to him face to face. I was silent. Gopali was eager and curious to know all about the places I had been to and the things I had seen.

'But I wrote about all that in my letters. I wrote to you from Iran, Rome, Prague, Paris, Nice and London.'

'Didn't you give any concerts?'

'Whenever I needed pin money, I danced. I even danced for the television. But my primary desire was to travel. When I didn't get booked for concerts, you can guess very well how I would have made money, can't you?'

'Sure I can. What else did you do with yourself? Why don't you tell me yourself?' he said.

'You wouldn't understand. You have no idea what I do and why I do it. You assumed that just because I am made this way, my friend would also be the same, didn't you?'

'Which friend?'

'Maragadham.'

'Oh! Now when did she become a friend?'

'How does it matter? All that you know and understand, or *can* understand, is so piteously little.'

'All right. Fine. I am a rascal and a rake. But for that reason, can't I be eager to know about what all you did and what all you saw abroad?'

I laughed aloud. I got my spirits back only after I heard my self-same usual laughter. How oppressive it felt when one didn't laugh!

'Why are you suddenly so jealous of me?' asked Gopali. He lost his poise when he heard me laughing. He was not in the habit of asking such questions.

'Jealous? Of you? For what? Certainly it is a deficiency that one can't sing like you. That apart, what is there for a woman to feel jealous about here?' It was coming on to me like hysteria, the wish to hurt him somehow. I couldn't control it.

I got up and opened my box. The four shirts that I'd bought for Gopali, the bottle of whisky, the wrist watch, two bottles of perfume, a *shruti kuzhal*, a red saree for his wife, pens and sarees for his son and daughter—I spread them all out and said, 'Here, all these are for you'. I'd also bought a saree for Maragadham, a shirt for Pachiappan, and some things for the kitchen.

'Didn't you buy anything for yourself?' asked Gopali.

In response, I opened my hand bag, spilled out the twelve tubes of permanent hair dye, and told him what they were for.

'What's this? When women travel abroad, they bring back solid gold or sets of jewellery. Prasad's wife brought back some twenty gold biscuits and diamonds too, all cleverly hidden,' said Gopali.

'I've also brought some,' I said, flourishing the crisp thirty guinea notes in front of him.

'What's this? Looks like currency.'

'It is currency. Thirty guineas. Worth nearly six hundred rupees. A single night's earning when Subala and I stood at the Piccadilly for some fun.'

'Who is Subala?'

'I'd written to you about her. She's a rough communist who is in London for her studies. I told you that she was always instigating the coloured people to do something. Well, both of us were standing there, craving to do something bad, something naughty, like pretend to be whores, street-walkers for a day. Two men approached us...'

I told him the entire story of Bruce, omitting nothing. His drinking, his hallucination about the spittle, his failed manliness at crucial moments, the thirty guinea notes that he left behind in the morning, Stratford, *that* night, the conversation we had the following day, the legend about women being on top of men in bed twelve thousand years ago...I told him everything.

Then I showed him the thirty guinea notes and said, 'I will never get these changed—everything is contained in them. And, even if I got thirty thousand guineas to do so, I will never occupy that room again. Not even for *this*,' I said, patting Gopali's chest. And I laughed, perhaps more to cover up his shock.

Gopali was looking at me like I'd gone mad. He also looked like he was struggling, making an effort to understand what was beyond his ken—Bruce's ecstasy, his fears, his relief, his dismay. While I kept on laughing.

'Guinea! The Pelf and the Self! Pelf-Self! Isn't that a pretty chant? Pelf and Self...nice on the ears, isn't it? The Pelf...and by Oneself! You've turned sixty-one. And I am thirty-eight. At no time in my life have I felt any jealousy. And hereafter I will feel none at all. Pelf and the Self—see how well they rhyme, just like an old poem.'

Gopali continued to stare at me with his large, popping eyes. All his virility seemed to have gathered together to settle in those eyes, as always. Then he looked away for a moment and said, 'I used to feel scared of flying to Delhi, for concerts. Before leaving the house, I would drink at least half a bottle to ensure that I stayed tipsy when I landed. Like that, did you too have any fear, like the time when you had returned from Budapest?'

'If that was the case, you would have smelt it beyond the uppuma. I was cooling my heels at the customs check for two hours till my legs got cramps.'

'Your speech is steady.'

I ruffled the thirty guinea notes with my fingers and waved them at him again.

'That means I'll have to leave at dusk,' he said.

'As you please.'

'Please what?'

'This house is Gopali's.'

'Only the house?'

'I am tired. I want to get some good sleep,' I said.

'I have a concert at Tiruchirapalli tomorrow. I had a mind to go tonight. When I got your cable, I wired them my cancellation.'

'You can wire them again to say that you'll come.'

'I have to think about it.'

'I really do feel like being alone. Please go ahead with your concert. We can talk later. And...don't let anyone know that I have returned. At least for the next two or three days. Or they'll throng here to chatter. I don't want to meet anyone as yet.'

'Should I too keep away?'

'Just for four or five days.'

Gopali stared vacantly into space. Drummed on the mat with his fingers. Then supporting himself with one hand, he got up, sighing, 'Oh God!' Went and stood in the veranda and stared at the road through the grill. Looked at the sky. Then he said, 'I'm going.'

I drew the latch on the door upstairs and went to bed.

'There are no friends. You cannot leap over a snake or a twisted straw. There are no relations. I shake them all off, each one of them, and move on...' Everything that I said to Bruce came back to me in bits and pieces. His memory hurt me in the throat. I picked up the guinea notes again. I lay there looking at them and dozed off.

When I woke up, it was dark. I switched on the light and noted the time. It was past ten at night. I went to the washroom and doused my head. Shampooed my hair, scrubbed and rinsed several times till the dye had washed off. Bathed. Dried myself and stood in front of the mirror. The dye was superior stuff. Didn't wash off completely. But it was clear that nearly all my hair had turned white. As I ran my fingers through them, one or two strands stood up.

Shampooing for three more days restored total whiteness. Such a pleasant whiteness! My records registered thirty-eight, my face registered forty-eight and my hair registered seventy-eight! A beautiful whiteness. How effortlessly this face of thirty-eight supported this ancient head of seventy-eight!

I have tried lifting Maragadham. She's tall, with a proportionate weight. She could not be lifted. She had broken into convulsions of laughter, burying her face into the end of her saree.

I did not stir out anywhere for the next three days. I called out to the boy who lived on the ground floor and asked him to inform the milkman about my return. He was a little confused when he saw my hair, but said he would. I kept a container out for the milk near the stairs.

I sat looking at the coconut trees in the backyard, the wisps of clouds above, the leaves on the tree outside through the blue, red and green glass panes on the window.

I swept the house, cooked, washed the vessels.

The mirror reflected the ancient head with a lucid face, clearly registering its changing moods and emotions.

In the nights, I lay alone on this bed. I alternated between the bed in this room and the one in the room on the left. How many times have I slept alone? Maybe only four or five times in a year. Even then, the thought that I would have company the next day would reassure me.

But now? The next day, and the next day, and the next day followed seamlessly…

The nocturnal insects chirped and whirred, tattooing the silence in the dark. The cricket knit a golden waist-band. The stars embossed sequins. The clouds daubed white on my hair.

Someone is sharpening my senses on a whetstone. The sounds are so clear. Everything looks crystal clear and sharp. I can smell everything sharply in my nose, like a dog.

Bruce nudged into my thoughts. His words flowed into my mind without impediments. I had lied to him that I was not wandering in search of anything. That I roamed without a purpose. I now realise that one doesn't need to search for anything. Just look at whatever comes your way. And look at it closely. Look at it keenly.

How the vessels made music while cooking!

Bruce, even if you hadn't put me on so high a pedestal, even if you hadn't hurt me so much, the solitude of these three days would have told me all that you once did.

On the fourth day, after my bath I applied the dye, allowing a few grey strands to show. I must see Maragadham, but I shouldn't startle her. She may get scared that something has happened to me.

I took a bus to Vadapazhani.

'Amma!' she said as soon as she saw me. She hugged me in the middle of the road and looked me up and down. She looked at my hair. 'When did you come, Amma?'

'It's been four days. I expected you to open the door for me...Is this the way?'

'I know all that you're going to say. Come in, Amma.'

'Where is Pachiappan?'

'He has gone to the temple.'

'Why? Isn't he working?'

'How can he go for work without asking you?'

'What!'

'Yes. He's been sitting at home these days. Says he must ask you after you return, and then take up some work...Come in, please.'

'I believe you came away because your mother was ill. Is this your mother?' I asked, looking at an old woman seeding a basket full of tamarind on a sickle-stand.

Maragadham laughed.

Pachiappan came after a while, and began asking me for news, just like Gopali had.

'If you come home with me right away, I'll talk to you. Otherwise, I won't even have a sip of tea here,' I said.

The three of them glanced at one another.

'No, Amma...Please.'

'Nothing doing. Just keep quiet and come along with me. Aiyah is not in town. And I have no one to talk to.'

It took me half an hour to make them come with me.

When we reached home and went up the stairs, Pachiappan said, 'You tell me Amma, what is there for us to say?'

14

'What was your great hurry to quit work and leave before my return? Was it necessary to spin a yarn about a government job, getting quarters and all that?' I asked Pachiappa sternly.

'What is false and what is true, Amma? Why do you keep needling us? Let bygones be bygones.'

'Which one of you decided to quit first? I must know that.'

'It was I,' said Maragadham.

'I too,' said Pachiappan.

'Pachiappa, can I make use of your services at least for a few hours today?' I asked.

Pachiappan laughed. 'Who can refuse you, Amma? For me, you are the Government!'

'All right. Then first of all, go to the market. I must talk to Maragadham.'

After he left, Maragadham said, 'Amma must be angry that we went away.'

'Of course I am angry.'

'What else could one do, Amma?'

'Tell me everything.'

'Whenever there was no one around, you should've seen Aiyah as I went about doing my work. He would fumble awkwardly like a twenty-year-old. He would stutter and stammer, not knowing what to say. He would ask me for water. While drinking it, his hands would shake and tremble. He wouldn't notice if it went down his throat or dribbled down his chin. Initially, for a few years, I was unsuspecting. But since the past couple of years, I began to understand.'

'A couple of years...?'

'Yes. Please don't be angry with me for having kept it from you for so long.'

'So, you do realise then that it was wrong of you to have kept it from me?'

'Yes. But if I had told you, Amma, you would have ripped him apart. I felt sorry for Aiyah. Felt sorry for you too. When you went out this time, I gradually tried to disengage myself. But it wouldn't work. I knew Aiyah would do me no harm. I had no fears on that count. But I felt miserable to see him suffer like that. I used to turn it over frequently in my mind. I thought what if one day I was moved a little too much? Felt a little too sorry? That could be dangerous, isn't it? So I decided it would be better for Aiyah not to see me at all.

'It is only after much thought that I told my man we ought to vacate this place. And it was I who also asked him to stop working here. More than anything else, Amma, leaving you was so painful to me. But I knew it would do Aiyah no good to keep seeing me. I am a married woman. I have a family. Suppose I did something like giving food to a beggar...then what would happen to my man? And what would happen to me? Where would I go? So we stopped working here. Please don't ask me anything more, Amma...I implore you.'

I didn't ask. In what other way could she have articulated her inexpressible distress, her tenderness and generosity towards Gopali, the pathos of the situation, and her steadfast love and loyalty to Pachiappan! It was the way she looked away from me, the way she pinched her nails that spoke eloquently and communicated all that she wanted to tell me.

I envied her. And I felt ashamed of myself. The intimacy that I had developed with twenty or two hundred people—did it spring from independence or audacity, insensitivity or impudence, or was it just a refusal or inability to enter into the minds of others because of my own hardened nature? Could I boast of such refinement, such delicacy? Was I even capable of such tenderness and compassion? The way Maragadham saw everything through Pachiappan's eyes and through his world of values may seem like an ordinary woman's discipline and restraint. But when I think of her sensitivity with regard to the situation and her feelings, my spine tingles.

We brought the vegetables. We cooked together. We ate together. And washed the vessels together.

Then I went to sleep.

When I opened my eyes, I found Maragadham fast asleep in a corner of the hall. Pachiappan was sleeping outside, beneath the grill. Maragadham was sleeping on her side, using her arm as a pillow. Crazy as he was, Gopali would certainly settle his property on her! Of what he had earned in the name of god, he spent three-fourths of it on Tyagaraja and me. Whatever remains, he will without fail give to this girl, forgetting Kunjali, his son and his daughter. That is how exquisite she was, Maragadham.

I looked at her again as she slept. And at Pachiappan.

I saw Bruce the day we returned from Stratford. He had said, 'If you go on like this, what'll happen when you grow old? When your youth fades and the body becomes a second-hand, third-hand thing, something no longer pleasant to behold in the mirror, something you don't want to look at anymore, what'll happen then? Who'll take care of you?' he had asked, his blue eyes melting.

I was surprised. A body as a second-hand, third-hand thing, something to shy away from the mirror...how could this boy visualise all that? I'd looked at him intently. I felt like an eighty-year old when he looked at me like that. He must have seen me as someone so lonely that she could not endure a youthful friendship. He had such a remote look in his eyes. I wore his eyes on myself for a while and looked through them.

There is a certain street. A cow lies on the edge of the street. Pedestrians passing by invariably look at it and move on. Some stand around for a while, look at it, say '*Tchu, Tchu*' and try to make it get up. 'It is dead,' they mutter and walk on. So what if it gave buckets and buckets of milk when alive. Not one of them bothers to find out who its owner is. It is lying abandoned. 'It will lie there till its owner comes searching for his missing cow. He has to identify it and lift it,' said a man in the crowd, before walking away. Not that he went in search of the owner. His words were mechanical, like sounds produced by a machine.

The dead cow starts thinking—Why am I not a wooden cow? I needn't have given milk and died in this manner then, in the middle of a street. There wouldn't have been any flies swarming over me. Or the need to hire men I don't recognise to drag my carcass away.

I laughed. Softly, of course.

'Do I sound funny?' asked Bruce.

'How can you joke about it? For one so young, you don't talk like an adolescent. Your leaders have despatched you soldiers by the thousands to root out communism in a godforsaken spot on the globe. Having killed a lakh people, you have now begun to wonder how these decadent old men of the country are going to stem the spread of communism. How can you bring yourself to joke about that?'

'What you say is hundred percent true. What right do these old men have to stall communism? Even that isn't the pertinent question. They aren't bothered about any 'ism'. Their consuming anxiety is about the dumping of all the things they manufacture—their guns, cannons, bombs, planes and tanks, lest they all turn to scrap. They may tolerate a cabbage rotting, but not a rotting plane. I can think of only one therapy for all this: to enforce a law that says only those past forty can enlist in the forces. Then there will be no guns or gunpowder—only rice and tomatoes.'

'And the eighteen and twenty-year olds wouldn't be lying rotting and dead in some godforsaken place. And I too wouldn't regret why I'm not a wooden cow.'

'What did you say, a *wooden cow*?'

'Yes, a wooden cow doesn't give milk. So no one can milk it and butcher it later when it goes dry. It doesn't have to lie dead in the middle of a road. The wooden cow would be admired as a table-top attraction. No ageing, no grey hair, and no insecurity of losing a master.'

Bruce laughed. The next moment he bit his tongue and the smile vanished. 'Did I say something that hurt you?' he asked.

'Nothing hurts. You asked me if anyone would bother about me when I grow old. I was thinking about that,' I said, describing my hallucination about the dead cow lying on the street.

Bruce laughed again. 'Oh! So even you've started thinking about an owner for the cow to ensure a decent burial!'

'What's a decent burial and what's not? There could be two ways. Either tearfully attend to the burial yourself. Or hire men to arrange for it, and be content for having spared people the stench of the rotting carcass. There's a heartless complacency to it.'

Bruce did not respond. He must have concluded that my claims were fake.

'Don't worry about me. Even if alive, I'll be a wooden cow. Even when I grow old and my hair turns white, there'll be plenty of admirers who would be happy to keep me. Of a hundred or three hundred, at least two or three would qualify for that. Those two or three will have the faith that I gave myself to them in the belief that it was intended for everyone born on this earth, and with the desire to give unto one and all, but that in the actuality of things, it had to stop with three hundred. There will be one or two who think they are equal to the three hundred.' This is what I wanted to tell Bruce, but I didn't.

Maragadham and Pachiappan woke up. After coffee, I dropped them off at Vadapazhani in a taxi. I chatted with them for a while, then came out of the house. Above the horizon where the sun had set there was a redness spread out like a vermilion sea. A little higher hung a crescent, perhaps in the third or the fourth phase. Above the crescent, a bluish white star could be seen. This place was quiet, without the din and the traffic noises of the city. I couldn't take my eyes off the horizon. It was so…what should I say…One can only merge with it wordlessly. Sometimes one feels like asking, what is the significance of this ravishing sight? The answer is that perhaps there is no significance. Just standing and absorbing the scene is momentous in itself.

'When was *amavasya*, the day before yesterday or the day before that?' asked Pachiappan, looking at the sky.

'Ssh!' Maragadham silenced him.

As we watched, the redness of the sky darkened.

'You tell us, Amma.'

'What?'

'Tell us when you want us to come back for work. What is there for us to say?'

'Work or no work, I'll stay only with the two of you. Pachiappa, look for a small house in Saligramam or beyond for rent,' I said.

'For whom?'

'For all of us, of course.'

'Why?'

'For all of us to live in. From now on, I'm not going to stay with Aiyah.'

There was silence.

'Yes,' I said.

'Because we said something?'

'Stop your chatter. Just do what I say.'

ω

When I went home, there was mail lying under the stairs. A blue envelope. I went up and hurriedly opened it. It was from

Bruce. The same lament as that of the two or three hundred others. The same adulation. I was an amazing woman. A rare individual. *'Just let me come. Say yes, and I'll start right away. If you refuse, I won't take it as heartlessness. You will always be with me wherever I go. When I go home and get married, like you said, and acquire a family, even then you'll be with me. Which is why I don't insist that you let me come over. But the experiences and sensibilities that I got from you I will never get them again. That is why I long to be near you again. If I cannot, I'll have no regrets. The memories of my days spent with you are enough for me.'* He was repeating himself.

After I finished reading the letter, I too sat down to write. Not to Bruce. Let Bruce be where he is. To Pattabhi.

'Pattabhi,

'I have come back home. Remember, I last wrote to you that I planned to take six or eight months more? But I thought of Pachiappan and Maragadham, and I returned. I met a boy just like you—Bruce. For a fortnight, we were close. After that, nothing seemed to matter.

'It has snowed and my head is now white, like an eighty-year old's. But only you can see it and endure it.

'Pattabhi, the city of Calcutta may be a vast paradise for you. You had written that I won't believe you're a Chief Designer now, earning three thousand rupees a month, you who have gone hungry for days on end. What made you write like that? Why did you mention money when you wrote about yourself? I can believe anything that concerns you. If I were to ask you to quit your job and come down here to live with me, I know you will. I have that implicit trust in you.

'Pattabhi, I've now become a super communist. That is to say, I now believe in belonging, in owning. I have no faith in marriage still. I'm governed though by an obstinacy and certitude that I belong to you. And that you too belong to me. Only you can look at my ageing face and my white hair without looking away.

'What emerges like a monster is the certainty that I don't have even a nominal admiration for Gopali Mama anymore. The

jewels he gave me, the sarees, the furniture—I will return all to him. He is welcome, if he chooses, to nurse the thought that I once belonged to him.

'I've asked Pachiappan to look for a small house west of Saligramam, comfortable enough for three people. Only a moment ago, it occurred to me that it should be for four.

'Many have come into my life and gone out of it. All the while I would speculate, what would Pattabhi be doing at this time? I've got used to boasting that I leave people behind and move on. I've said so and scared so many who embraced me, who went to bed with me in the hope that the relationship would continue, with or without marriage. My words may have struck them as an empty boast at first. But later they realised I wasn't lying. In a way, it also confirmed my own conviction.

'Only with you I've never bragged like that. Not even in a moment of forgetfulness. You are not handsome. Nor are you company for intellectual banter. But you wouldn't call for whisky to redeem the poor. Nor do you need a house of your own, a car, an estate or a pedigree. You don't need to sing of Tyagaraja and Rama and go around philandering and chasing women.

'After I stayed alone for three days, I was overcome with fear. That Gopali was waiting to crawl over Maragadham like a small snake crawls over a sleeping person.

'No one yet knows about my return. They will in a couple of days. I fear that the old story may get repeated. I don't want to listen to a Tyagaraja kriti with a whisky belch. To Marxism reeking of rum. Don't want to listen to a man who flies to a khadi meeting in Delhi and talks with his eyes glued to my bosom.

'I'll be content to look at you. At your round eyes. Your silences. Your arms which hoist me up at the mere mention of an ache in my legs. Returning home from work, I'll be content to talk to Maragadham. Pachiappan would do equally. But what work can I take up? What shall I do till you come? I have an ocean to cross.

'When I lock up the sarees and jewels, lock up the house and hand over everything to Gopali, I cannot imagine what his incoherent rage will be like. He is so attached to me. But his style

is that of a widow shrieking on the street and beating her chest as her husband's corpse is borne away on the shoulders of four men. Ah, I have an idea! I'll make an inventory of the sarees, jewels and furniture, send him the key by post, and leave the house in just the saree I'm wearing that day.'

I couldn't wait for the day to dawn to post the letter. I hailed a taxi hurriedly, to the Post Office on Mount Road, and dropped it into the mail box.

After eating the leftovers of lunch, I opened every almirah, folded the silk sarees, secured the jewels carefully, listed the silver glasses separately, and then…Everything stuck out a tongue at me.

How will you talk about Marxism without me?

How will you weep for the poor without me?

How will you bring about a revolution without me?

How will you become a human being without me?

How will you spite the rich without me?

What can I say by way of reply? I will have to ask Pattabhi.

'*Everything seems funny to you.*'

Glossary

abhayam: Protection.

abhinaya: Ideas and emotions communicated through facial expressions and hand gestures, it is a central feature of classical Indian dance forms like the Bharatanatyam.

Adi: The fourth month in the Tamil calendar, corresponding with mid-July to mid-August.

Advaita: The Vedantic philosophy of non-dualism which denies the separateness of any reality from the impersonal oneness of Brahma.

agrahara: The area in a village or town where brahmins traditionally live.

aiyah: Master; respectful address for a man.

akka: Elder sister; respectful address for a woman.

alapana: In Carnatic classical music, a form of improvisation that introduces and develops a *raga*, setting the mood for the composition that follows.

Amavasya: The day of the dark moon or new moon when the dark side of the moon is visible.

anda: A large vessel with a wide mouth used for storing water in the wash room.

angavastram: A long pleated piece of ornamental cloth draped by men over their shoulder.

anna: Elder brother; respectful address for a man.

anna: A currency unit used in British India equal to one-sixteenth of a rupee, or equivalent to 6.25 paise.

anupallavi: In Carnatic music, anupallavi comes after the *pallavi* and is usually the second section of any composition.

apsara: In Indian mythology, a beautiful celestial singer or dancer who inhabits the heavenly court of Indra, the king of gods; apsaras provide sensual pleasure for both gods and men.

apaswara: Singing or playing on a discordant note; in context, one who sings or plays discordantly.

arangetram: A classical dancer's first public performance or debut.

arasilai: A silver plate or pendant shaped like a peepul leaf attached to the chain around the waist of a small girl child.

athai: Father's sister.

athimber: Father's sister's husband; also an elder sister's husband.

atma: Soul.

auto-rickshaw: A versatile three-wheeler public transport popular throughout India and across the subcontinent, it is less expensive than a taxi.

avartana: In Carnatic music, *tala* is the rhythmic framework which provides a broad structure for rendition, comprising fixed length time cycles called *avartanas*; each avartana is divided into units of time called *aksaras*.

avataram (or *avatar*): A new form or incarnation.

bhajanai (or *bhajans*): A choral rendering of devotional songs.

bhakta: A devotee.

Brindavan: A holy town in Uttar Pradesh where Lord Krishna is said to have spent his childhood.

burfi: A sweet made of condensed and desiccated milk.

Chithirai: The first month in the Tamil calendar, corresponding with mid-April to mid-May.

chittira kullan: In Tamil folklore, a dwarf believed to bring about miracles.

dasi: This alludes to the *devadasi* tradition in southern India wherein a woman dedicated herself to the worship and service of a deity or temple for the rest of her life; devadasis also danced in temples.

Dandakaranya: A densely forested region of the Dhanda Kingdom and a stronghold of the Rakshasa tribes, it was a turning point in the epic *Ramayana*.

deeksha: Initiation by a guru to take a vow and follow a spiritual path.

dharbai: Long dry grass, also called *kaus* and considered sacred.

dharma: Virtues and right conduct as specified in the scriptures.

dhavani: Upper garment worn by young girls around their *pavadai*, also called a half-saree.

dhoti: An unstitched garment variously worn by men around their waist.

Dhritarashtra: In the *Mahabharata*, king of the Kuru kingdom and father of the Kauravas who was born blind.

Draupadi: In the *Mahabharata*, daughter of King Drupada of Panchal and wife of the five Pandavas.

furlong: Approximately two hundred metres.

Garuda: The mount of Lord Vishnu in Hindu, Buddhist and Jain mythology, he is half-human, half-eagle.

ghatam: A large clay pot with a narrow mouth played as a percussion instrument in Carnatic music. Made specifically for music, care is taken that the tone of the pot is good and the walls are of an even thickness to produce the tone.

grihapravesam: A ceremony usually performed prior to occupying a new house or soon after.

Guru: The planet Jupiter; also teacher, mentor.

halwa: A sweet dish made of semolina, sugar and ghee, or cashew nuts or almonds in place of semolina.

jalatarangam: A unique and soothing kind of music based on the idea of water waves, it is played by striking China or ceramic bowls containing water with a beater to produce sound.

japam: A recitation of mantras or slokas, chanted aloud or silently.

javvadhu: A strong perfume extracted from the gland of the civet cat.

kaasu maalai: A necklace of flat gold coin-like pieces.

kacheri: A musical concert or gathering for a cultural event.

kadukkan: Ear studs, usually set with diamonds or other precious stones, traditionally worn by men of a certain generation.

Kali Yuga: In Hinduism, the last of the four stages that the world goes through as part of a cycle of *yugas* or ages described in the scriptures. The others are *Satya* (or *Krita*), *Treta* and *Dvapara Yuga*.

kanakambaram: Vivid orange or deep yellow flowers, also called the firecracker flower, native to southern India and Sri Lanka.

kollu thatha: Great grandfather; *thatha* is grandfather.

Kanchi hymns: Hymns recited for Devi Kamakshi in Kanchi.

kriti: A musical composition.

Kunti: In the *Mahabharata*, foster daughter of King Kuntibhoj, wife of King Pandu of Hastinapur, and mother of the Pandavas.

kuzhambu: A thickened broth prepared with vegetables.

laddu: A ball-shaped sweet variously made of different kinds of flour, clarified butter, sugar, raisins and nuts.

mangalam: The word means 'auspicious' in Hinduism; traditionally, it is the conclusion of a Carnatic classical music or dance recital for the invocation and welcoming of God.

mamangam: A period of twelve years, the term implies a long lapse of time.

mami: Maternal aunt, wife of one's *mama* or mother's brother; also a respectful address for an older woman.

maruda: Another name for the *arjuna* tree, its bark has a reddish tint.

mridangam: A cylindrical two-sided drum played with both hands, it is an important percussion instrument in Carnatic music.

muhurtham: The auspicious time of day for a marriage ceremony or any important Hindu ritual.

mutt: A Hindu religious institution similar to a monastery.

Mysore *pak*: A delicious sweet made of *besan* or gram flour, sugar and ghee.

nadaswaram: A wind instrument with a long pipe, usually played at Tamil weddings and southern Indian festivals.

namaskaram (or *namaskar*): A traditional respectful Indian greeting with folded palms.

Narada job: In context, the act of manipulating or instigating one person against another. The reference is to Narada (or Narada *Muni*) in Hindu mythology, a sage-god who is variously represented, and associated with both wisdom and mischief.

nattuvangam: It is performed by the *nattuvanar* in a Bharatanatyam performance using cymbals for measuring temporal co-ordination between him/her and the dancer.

Nayanars: A group of 63 saints living in Tamil Nadu during the sixth to fourth centuries A.D. who were devoted to Lord Shiva.

Neelakantan: Another name for Lord Shiva, *Neela-kantha* means 'blue-throated'. In Hindu mythology, during *samudra manthan*, the churning of the ocean by the gods and demons in quest of the elixir of immortality, a terrible poison was unleashed upon them. To save the world, Lord Shiva gulped this poison, which turned his throat blue.

naivedyam: An offering to God; food offered to the family deity as part of Hindu worship rituals before it is eaten by the family.

nirvana (also *moksha*): In Hinduism, Buddhism and Jainism, the final goal of attaining a transcendent state in which there is neither suffering nor desire, and the person is released from the effects of *karma* and the cycle of birth and death.

padhigam: A poem of ten verses on the presiding deity of the place.

pakoda (or *bhajji*): Savoury fried snacks prepared with vegetables and chickpea flour batter.

pallavi: In Carnatic music, the thematic line of a song that is usually one cycle long and is repeated twice in order to give the percussionist the idea of a chosen *talam* (*taal*) or beat.

pandal: A temporary structure of bamboo poles and colourful cloth erected for holding marriage ceremonies, and cultural and religious events.

Pantuvarali: A Carnatic raga.

pavadai: A traditional long skirt worn by young girls that reaches up to the ankles.

periamma: Father's elder brother's wife; also mother's elder sister, or maternal aunt.

periappa: Father's elder brother.

Pillaiyar: Another name for Lord Ganapathy.

prasadam (or *prasad*): A sacred offering to the deity.

pratimadhyama: The sharpened fourth note or *madhyam*; it also refers to those ragas of the *melakarta* system that contain this note.

pujai (or *puja*) room: In a traditional Tamil Hindu household, the room enshrining all the deities worshipped by the family.

punyam (or *punya*): The favourable effect of blessings earned through virtuous deeds and good *karma* that brings benefits in this birth and the next.

Purandaradasa: A renowned composer of Carnatic music and a *Haridasa*, or great devotee of Lord Krishna, he was born in 1484 in Shimoga district, Karnataka.

pyol (or *pial*): A raised platform for resting at the entrance of a traditional Tamil house.

raga: In Indian classical music, the series or network of ascending and descending notes on which a melody is based and which expresses different moods for different times of the day as well as the season.

Ramana Maharishi: A revered Hindu sage born in Tiruchuli, Tamil Nadu.

rosewater tree: Called *panneer* tree in Tamil, it has broad leaves and in season, blooms with long, white flowers.

samadhi: Attaining salvation or nirvana; it also means experiencing a sublime moment.

sambandhi: Related by marriage; parents of a son-in-law or a daughter-in-law.

sanyasi: An ascetic, a Hindu religious mendicant.

sapota (or *chiku* in Hindi): Sapodilla plum, a soft sweet fruit with a thin brown skin.

saptapadi: Literally, seven steps, it is a central rite in a Hindu wedding in which after tying the *mangal sutra*, the newly married couple circles the sacred fire seven times.

sarod: A stringed instrument used mainly in Hindustani classical music.

Shakuntalam: A classical Sanskrit play by the poet Kalidasa, said to be dated around the fourth century A.D.

shradham: Death anniversary of a person and Hindu rituals associated with it.

shruti: In Indian classical music, the smallest interval of pitch that a singer or musical instrument can produce.

shruti kuzhal: A pitch pipe.

Shukra: The planet Venus, said to bring fortune.

silambam: A southern Indian martial art practised with a staff.

Silappadikaram: One of the greatest epics of Tamil literature written by Ilango Adigal, probably composed in the fifth or sixth century A.D.

slokas: Couplets in Sanskrit verse, usually devotional in nature.

Soundarya Lahiri: A Sanskrit work believed to have been written by Adi Shankara, dedicated to the goddess Parvati, it means 'waves of beauty'.

Surabhasmasuran: Bhasmasura was an *asura* or demon who was granted the boon to burn and turn into ashes (*bhasma*) anyone whose head he touched with his hand. He was tricked by the enchantress Mohini, Lord Vishnu's only female avatar, to turn himself into ashes by touching his own head.

tala (or *talam*): In Indian classical music, the beat or musical metre that measures musical time; however, in context of the passage on p. 10, it means 'suffering a lot'.

tambura (or *tanpura*): A four-stringed instrument that supports and sustains the melody of a singer in an Indian classical vocal music performance.

til seeds: Sesame.

Tiruppavai: A Tamil devotional hymn attributed to the poet-saint Andal.

Tyagaraja: A renowned composer of Carnatic music, highly influential in the development of India's classical music tradition. He was born in 1767 in Thiruvarur, Madras Presidency.

uppuma: A savoury breakfast dish prepared with semolina, cashew nuts, oil and vegetables.

vadu manga: A pickle of small mangoes in a thin gravy.

vatral kuzhambu: A spicy preparation made with tamarind and dried vegetables.

vibhuthi: In Hinduism, the sacred ash made of burnt dried wood that is applied on the forehead by devotees to honour Lord Shiva.

vidwan: A scholar; in context, an expert in Indian classical music.

yagna: A ritual sacrifice made for a specific purpose.

yantram: A copper plate with a mystical diagram drawn on it and kept for worship to drive away evil spirits and bring luck and prosperity.

yellow thread: The *mangal sutra*, traditionally worn by married Hindu women.